GEORGIANNA

MISS WOLFRASTON'S LADIES BOOK 3

JENNY HAMBLY

DEDICATION

To Annie
Thank you for all your encouragement and being part of my
world. My life is richer for it.

CHAPTER 1

Georgianna left Cranbourne with mixed feelings. Although Marianne's aunt, Lady Brancaster, had taken very good care of her, she had held her on a light rein. She had enjoyed more freedom and been afforded more amusement in the last few weeks than she had at any other time in her life. She had also developed a close bond of affection with Marianne; it had been quite a wrench to part from her. Lively, kind, and friendly to a fault, Marianne had the knack of making friends easily, something Georgianna found very difficult.

Georgianna's mother, if she had known Marianne's history, would have called her a hoyden, she was sure. She would certainly not have encouraged their friendship, but Georgianna did not despair; Miss Montagu of Harwich Court may have been beneath Lady Westbury's notice, but much might be forgiven a countess. If Marianne did not become Lady Cranbourne within a very few weeks, Georgianna would be most surprised.

She was, of course, pleased that her brother had recovered from his illness, but she returned home to Avondale uncertain of her reception. She had told Marianne that Lord Wedmore's letter to her father absolving her of all blame for failing to attach him, and Lady Strickland's missive to her mother singing her praises, could leave her parents with very little to say. But she was not nearly so confident of this as she had intimated to her friend.

She was even less so when almost as soon as she entered the carriage, her sour-faced maid said, "So this is what happens when you're left to your own devices. Seems your manners have become a little easy, ma'am. I could hardly believe my eyes when I saw you *hugging* that young lady. Your mama will be quite shocked to hear of it; you know she don't approve of shows of emotion. As if she isn't worn down enough by Master Rupert's illness. Not that she complains. She bears all her trials with such dignity."

Georgianna had been craning her neck to catch the last glimpse of Marianne before the carriage turned a bend in the drive, but at this she turned and raised her brows, her eyes glacial. "And I see that *your* manners are what they have always been, Stokes. Insolent."

Her maid gasped. When Lady Westbury had taken her on, she had made it clear that it was no part of her duties to befriend Lady Georgianna. She had informed her that she had been forced to turn the previous maid off for just such a breach of her trust. She had also made it clear that she was expected to give her regular reports on Lady Georgianna's behaviour and activities, and if she found that she had been keeping anything from her, she would suffer the same fate. Lady Georgianna had always treated her with cool indifference, but she had never before spoken to her in such a manner.

"As for Mama," Georgianna continued, "if she has spent as much as five minutes by Rupert's bedside, I will own myself astonished."

Stokes' bosom swelled. "Lady Westbury will hear of this, my lady."

Georgianna gave a harsh little laugh. "Of that, I am in no doubt. You have ever been her informer. But think on this, Stokes; I am no longer a child, and once I either marry or find some other occupation, you will be superfluous to her requirements for you cannot expect me to take you with me. You may be my mother's loyal spy, but do not expect to find that loyalty returned when she has no further use for you."

It was nine long hours spent in icy silence before they reached Avondale, which lay in a fertile valley not many miles distant from Bristol. Georgianna had plenty of time to contemplate the wisdom of alienating her maid in such a rash manner. But it was only now that she had witnessed the relationship of Nancy, Marianne's maid, with her mistress, that she fully understood the perfidy and disrespect of her own.

She felt her stomach tighten as they at last passed through the gates of her home. A large square edifice built from a warm honey-coloured stone, Avondale was a fine example of Elizabethan architecture. It was a shame Georgianna reflected, that very little warmth permeated its walls. Only when Rupert escaped the nursery was the austere, formal atmosphere that lay within the house disturbed.

As the carriage pulled up in front of the impressive entrance, Georgianna was relieved to note that the flicker of a candle brightened none of the numerous large mullioned windows on the ground floor. It seemed she might escape an interview with her mama this evening, at least.

A footman opened the carriage door and held out his hand to help her alight. She accepted it with promptitude, eager to at last escape the constant rocking of the coach and step onto firm ground once more. As she walked towards the house, it felt as if she was still swaying. Even when she paused in front of the grand pillars of the portico, the gravel seemed to be moving beneath her feet. She took a slow, deep breath, willing the sudden nausea that gripped her to subside.

"Welcome home, Lady Georgianna."

She glanced up quickly at these softly spoken words, a genuine smile curving her lips. Adams had been butler at Avondale for twenty years. Although he performed his duties with all the cool haughtiness his master could desire, he and his wife, who was house-keeper at Avondale, had always had a soft spot for her. Adams had once taken the blame when she had accidentally broken one of her mother's favourite vases. She had felt terribly guilty when Lady Westbury had berated him for his clumsiness and assured him the cost of the item would be deducted from his wages. Georgianna would have admitted the fault was hers if she had not known that the butler's attempt to shield her would have been considered a far more serious misdemeanour. Mrs Adams had been just as kind, often managing to smuggle a slice of cake or pie to her on the many occasions she had been confined to her room when she had displeased Mama in some way or other.

"Thank you, Adams," she said, her smile sliding from her face as Stokes came up beside her.

The butler's dignified mask descended once more and he handed them both a candle.

"Lady Westbury would like you to step up to her room," he said to the maid in a frigid tone.

He waited until the long shadows cast by Stokes' candle had disappeared around the first turn in the grand staircase before saying softly, "You look tired; I suggest you go and lie down. Mrs Adams will send some supper up to your room."

"Thank you. I will go to bed, but I am not at all hungry. I feel a little queasy if the truth be told."

Adams frowned. "She asked cook to make your favourite plum cake, ma'am, and will be most put out if you do not try a little."

"That would never do," Georgianna said. "Have her send some up by all means."

Mrs Adams brought the cake herself. She found Georgianna slumped in a chair by the empty fire, her drooping head supported by her hand.

"You look fit to drop," she said, shaking her head. "I will not pretend to understand why Stokes was granted the luxury of staying at an inn to break her journey when she travelled into Wiltshire, yet you were not afforded the same courtesy. I expect you have a headache."

Georgianna straightened and smiled. "Yes, but I'm sure a slice of plum cake will soon set me to rights."

"I hope so, ma'am. I have brought you a small

glass of wine to wash it down with. It will help you sleep, and that's what you need most I suspect."

"You are very kind, Mrs Adams."

"Nonsense. I'm not doing anything any decent Christian wouldn't. Did you enjoy your time with your friend, my lady?"

"Oh yes," Georgianna said softly. "I have never enjoyed anything more."

"Well, that's not saying much," Mrs Adams said dryly. "But I can see you've put a *little* flesh on your bones, at last. I don't know whether to be pleased or insulted. You don't know how disheartening it is to try to tempt you with your favourite dishes only for Adams to inform me that you ate barely a mouthful of your dinner."

Georgianna sighed wearily. "You know how morbidly afraid of becoming fat Mama is. Having a fat daughter would mortify her nearly as much."

"There's no chance of that in your case. You take after your father and it makes not a ha'p'orth of difference how much he eats; he still stays as thin as a reed."

Georgianna raised the cake to her lips and bit into it appreciatively. "Delicious," she said. "I assure you, Mrs Adams, I shall eat every last morsel."

"Just make sure you do, Lady Georgianna, and then into bed with you."

When Stokes did not come to her, Georgianna made herself ready for bed. As she brushed out her long, ebony locks, she gave herself a critical glance in the mirror. Mrs Adams was quite right, she realised. Although she knew the combination of her dark hair and deep blue eyes to be striking, her face was too thin. Her glance dropped to her shoulders and she thought the delicate bones there jutted out a little too much. They became even more pronounced as she shrugged.

What did it matter if her figure did not benefit from the softly rounded curves gentlemen seemed to so much admire? If her mother had her way, she would be married off to the next gentleman who showed an interest in her. Respectability and fortune would be all that would be considered on both sides. She stood and crossed to her bed. As she slipped between the covers she sighed, and her heavy eyelids clamped shut. Her thoughts scattered and within moments a deep sleep had claimed her.

Georgianna awoke early. Feeling rather drowsy and lethargic, she made no attempt to rise. Her eyes wandered rather aimlessly about her chamber eventually coming to rest on a small chair tucked in a corner. Upon it lay a small wooden doll propped up on a cushion. It had once boasted bright red cheeks and lips, but they had faded to a pink smudge now. Her black painted hair had also lost its gloss, but most of it was hidden under a small lace bonnet. She was very finely dressed; Georgianna frequently replenished her wardrobe, sewing many small gowns from scraps of velvet or silk. The doll had been her companion and confidante for years. She had very much wished to take her to the seminary but had thought the other girls would laugh at her attachment to such a childish thing.

"Good morning, Peggy," she said softly. "I am very pleased to see you."

She pushed herself upright as she heard rapid footsteps on the landing. They came to an abrupt halt, and her door was suddenly thrown open. A small boy of about six years charged into the room, skidding to a stop beside the bed. Golden curls clustered around his head, a soft pink glow warmed his smooth, pale cheeks, and the eyes that rested on Georgianna were as blue as her own. He looked quite angelic, but he was already on his second nurse. Mrs Flannel had left in high dudgeon soon after his fifth birthday. She had stoically weathered his tantrums and disobedience but had drawn the line at frogs in her bed and spiders in her shoes.

"Good morning, little devil," Georgianna said, a small smile playing about her lips. "I am pleased to see you looking so well."

Her brother frowned and puffed out his narrow chest. "You should not call me devil," he said, his nose in the air. "I shall be an earl one day and will walk in the footsteps of a long line of earls, unbroken for hundreds of years."

"Indeed you will," Georgianna acknowledged, reaching out a hand and gently tweaking his nose, "if no one strangles you first."

Stokes chose that moment to enter the room. Her mouth puckered and she bristled with disapproval.

"It'll serve you right if Master Rupert tells your mother you said that. Lady Westbury wishes to see you just as soon as you are dressed."

She disappeared into the dressing room on these dour words.

Rupert pulled a face. "Don't worry, I won't tell on you."

Georgianna's brows winged up. Her brother had frequently run to their mother with tales about her.

"Thank you, Rupert. I had not expected such consideration from you."

He shrugged and grinned. "I missed you, and I don't like Stokes."

A high-pitched, harassed voice screeched down the landing. "Master Rupert! Master Rupert!"

A petulant frown marred the young boy's brow. "And I don't like Mrs Tremlow," he said in accents of loathing.

"You don't like anyone who crosses you," Georgianna said dryly.

Rupert stuck out his tongue and ran from the room. Georgianna sighed and threw her covers back. Rupert's behaviour was disgraceful, but he was hopelessly overindulged. Although Lady Westbury never hesitated to punish her daughter for any perceived faults, she was ridiculously lenient with her son. But then, as she spent very little time in his company herself, she did not have to suffer his naughty ways. Georgianna felt sorry for Mrs Tremlow, his current nurse; how she was expected to exert any authority over her high-spirited charge when Rupert knew he would face no unpleasant consequences for his actions was beyond her.

A shrill scream brought her quickly to her feet. She ran out onto the landing.

"Lady Georgianna," Stokes squawked from her doorway. "You are not yet dressed!"

She ignored her maid and hurried to the top of the staircase. She gasped as she saw Mrs Tremlow sprawled in a heap on the half landing below. Rupert stood next to her, his face white.

"I didn't mean her to fall," he said in a small voice

as she hurried down the stairs. "I only wanted to go down to the stables, but she chased me and fell."

Mrs Tremlow groaned. "My ankle," she gasped.

"Rupert, go and find Adams. He will know what to do."

The little boy nodded and raced down the remainder of the stairs. Georgianna knelt beside Mrs Tremlow, her eyes widening as she saw the nurse's foot was sticking out at a very odd angle.

"I think it is broken," she said softly.

Mrs Tremlow opened her eyes and whispered bitterly, "I suppose I should be grateful it is only my ankle and not my neck!"

As the nurse raised herself onto her elbows, beads of perspiration glistened on her waxy skin.

"Lie still, Mrs Tremlow," Georgianna urged her.

One glance at the unnatural angle of her foot sent the poor woman into a swoon. Georgianna grabbed her shoulders as she fell backwards and lowered her more gently.

"Don't try and move her, ma'am," Adams said, coming swiftly up the stairs.

He took one look at Mrs Tremlow's foot and turned swiftly to the footman who hovered behind him.

"Pick her up very gently, Marcus, and take her to her room. Then you must fetch the doctor."

"Georgianna, return to your chamber and dress. You may leave Mrs Tremlow to me."

A very elegant lady stood at the top of the stairs. Golden curls peeped beneath her fetching lace cap. Her complexion was fair and still smooth, perhaps due to the regular applications of the juice of green pineapples that she treated it with. She was of average height but held herself very proudly. Her face was expressionless and her eyes chips of ice. Stokes hovered behind her.

"Yes, of course, Mama," Georgianna said, colouring, the presence of the footman making her conscious of her nightgown and bare feet.

As she came level with her mother, Lady Westbury reached out and pinched her upper arm.

"It seems you have been overindulging. There was no spare flesh there before you left. Come to my sitting room in half an hour; there is much I have to say to you."

On closer inspection, Georgianna noted that two fine lines had permanently etched themselves into her mother's brow as if she had been frowning a lot of late. Perhaps she had been more worried about Rupert than she had given her credit for.

Stokes brought out a plain, white muslin gown with short puffed sleeves. Feeling in need of something to bolster her confidence, Georgianna said, "I would prefer my sprigged muslin with the long full sleeves, Stokes."

"That's as may be, ma'am, but I'm afraid it has not yet been unpacked."

"I see," Georgianna said softly. "And why is that, Stokes?"

The maid paused in the act of tying the blue ribbon that marked the high waistline of her dress. "Because, ma'am, after my interview with Lady Westbury last evening, she said I was not to touch your trunks. Now, if you will excuse me, I have to take charge of Master Rupert whilst Mrs Tremlow is indisposed."

Georgianna sighed as her maid left the room. She was not sure who she felt most sorry for, Rupert or Stokes. She wandered over to the chair in the corner of the room and picked up her doll.

"Wish me luck, Peggy," she whispered.

As she walked along the landing towards her mother's suite of rooms, she considered the criticisms she might face and how she should conduct herself. The advice she had given to Marianne when she had felt a little overwhelmed at the grandeur of Cranbourne and its occupants whispered in her mind; *if you have taught me anything, it is that wealth or family history does not alone raise you above others. Such consequence and conceit is contemptible. Curb your unruly tongue, by all means, but do not be anything but yourself in whatever company we find ourselves. I think the thing that has impressed me most in all our dealings, is your honesty and your strong sense of who you are.*

She came to a halt outside her mother's sitting room door and gave a little nod. Georgianna realised that she did not have a strong sense of who she was, and much of what she did know, she did not like. She had spent so long trying to mould herself into the person her mother wished her to be, hoping to finally gain her approval and perhaps even her affection, that she had not developed her character as much as she should have. One trait she did share with Marianne and knew to be her own, however, was a sometimes too ready tongue. She had always had a tendency to voice her opinion. Neither beatings nor confinement had cured her of this fault, if fault it was. She would treat her mother with respect, but she would be honest and not cowed by anything she might say. She was no longer a child, after all.

She tapped lightly on the door before entering the chamber. It faced south and should have been bathed in sunshine, but Georgianna was not surprised to discover the curtains half drawn; her mother was always wary of the damage the sun might do her skin.

"Do not stand there in that awkward way, Georgianna. Sit down before you give me a stiff neck."

Georgianna sat on the edge of the chair opposite her mother, folded her hands neatly in her lap, and waited.

"I am most displeased with you, Georgianna," Lady Westbury said, her tone cold.

"What have I done to earn your displeasure, Mama?" Georgianna said calmly.

Her mother looked at her in astonishment. "Do not pretend you do not know, girl. Lord Wedmore's letter has reached us. Your father is away and so I opened it in case it was anything important. Always the gentleman, he has said nothing at all against you, merely that you both agreed you would not suit. But I would like you to explain to me why he would offer for the daughter of a mere viscount if you had done nothing to give him a disgust for you? Miss Ponsonby could hardly have been more beautiful than you."

"It is kind of you to say so, Mama," Georgianna said dryly.

"Do not be impertinent, daughter. That you are beautiful is an accident of birth, not an accomplishment."

"Indeed it is not," Georgianna agreed. "Miss Ponsonby is very pretty and fair where I am dark.

Perhaps it was that which attracted Lord Wedmore to her."

"Or perhaps it was her willingness to please," her mother said with some asperity. "Lady Strickland speaks of your dignity and reserve."

"I would have thought that would please you," Georgianna said evenly, "when you have been at such pains to instil these qualities in me."

A flash of anger sparked through Lady Westbury's eyes. "They can be taken too far. Tell me, did you make any effort at all to attract Lord Wedmore?"

"No," Georgianna admitted. "But you should not be surprised; I had already informed you that I could not like him."

"What has that got to do with anything?" her mother snapped. "Liking is not necessary in a marriage. It is far more important to be comfortably and respectably established."

"But I would not be comfortable in such a marriage."

"That is for your family to decide. Where is your sense of duty? Do not tell me you harbour ideas of *love*?" Lady Westbury said scathingly.

"No. For what do I know of love? But I do not think it unreasonable to wish to feel some degree of respect and affection towards my future husband."

Lady Westbury stood and in a rare display of agitation, paced back and forth in front of Georgianna. "I knew I should never have allowed you to go to Fanny Brancaster. I expect it is she who has put these foolish ideas into your head, or perhaps it was her niece, Miss Montagu. Lady Strickland wrote that she has been making sheep's eyes at Lord Cranbourne." She gave a hard little laugh. "Much good it will do her. She is far more likely to find herself without a reputation."

"Marianne is guilty of neither of the accusations made against her," Lady Georgianna said quietly. "And Lord Cranbourne always behaved with the utmost propriety towards her."

Lady Westbury did not appear to have heard her. She came to a stop in front of her daughter. Georgianna felt her stomach churn as she saw the bitter, almost malevolent gleam in her mother's eyes. She started to rise but Lady Westbury put a hand on her shoulder and pushed her firmly back down.

"And then there is this morning's debacle."

"But what has that to do with me?" Georgianna asked, bemused.

"It has everything to do with you," her mother said. "You threatened to strangle your brother causing him to run from your room, too frightened to hear Mrs Tremlow's calls. It might have been Rupert and not his nurse who had fallen down the stairs!"

Georgianna wondered if her mother had run mad. Her manner had always been cold towards her, some might even say cruel, but rarely had she displayed such brittle anger. Lady Westbury prided herself on being in control of her emotions at all times.

"Please, calm yourself, Mama," she said gently. "It is not true. I was joking with him and I did not say *I* would strangle him. He was not at all disturbed but ran out of the room because he wished to escape Mrs Tremlow and go down to the stables. It was his naughtiness that caused the accident, although I think he is very sorry for it now."

Her head snapped back as Lady Westbury dealt her a resounding slap. She bit her lip determined not to cry out and rose to her feet, taking some comfort in the fact that she towered over the bitter woman before her.

"You lie. How dare you blame your brother?" her mother said from between gritted teeth.

Georgianna stood tall, resisting the urge to lift her hand to her smarting cheek. "I spoke the truth and I shall speak some more. If you had dealt Rupert such a smack or allowed any of his nurses to, today's events would never have happened. Why is it, Mama, that he can do no wrong in your eyes and I can do no right? You act as if you hate me."

"I do!" Lady Westbury hissed.

Georgianna felt somehow relieved to finally hear her admit it.

"Would you mind telling me why?" she said dispassionately.

Georgianna's coolness seemed to fan the flames of Lady Westbury's anger. Her eyes blazed. "Because you were not a boy! I had to go through the horrific pain and indignity of childbirth only to present your father with a girl. Then I had to endure years more of his mauling before I conceived again and finally presented him with an heir! No one can say of me that I did not do my duty. I take every care of Rupert so I do not have to endure your father's attentions again and can let him take his pleasure elsewhere. He is in Town as we speak, visiting his latest mistress no doubt."

Once she had absorbed the shock of these frank words, Georgianna said gently, "I am sorry for you, Mama."

"Reserve your pity for yourself," Lady Westbury snapped.

Her anger finally spent, she sank back into her chair and said in a low trembling voice, "You have gone directly against my wishes and you might have caused your brother serious injury by your wicked words. You have also been extremely rude to Stokes; it is beneath your dignity to be rude to the servants. I had not quite made my mind up what to do with you, but this morning's events have decided me. I am sending you to your father's elder sister. You shall leave tomorrow."

Georgianna felt her heart sink. It was not only the prospect of another long coach journey that caused her dismay; she hardly knew Lady Colyford but what she remembered of her did not give her much hope of a kind reception. She had only been twelve when her aunt last visited and she had quarrelled with both her brother and his wife before leaving in high dudgeon, saying she would not step foot inside her old home again.

"I thought Aunt Hester had washed her hands of the whole family and moved to some remote spot in the north?"

"She has. Cumberland. She has set up home in a cottage or some such thing. It will do you good to learn some humility, Georgianna. A few weeks in her company should give you a taste of how bleak life can be when you have no male to protect you. It may even bring you to a realisation of how I have tried to take care of your interests. Your aunt made an imprudent marriage to a man of little means. She is now an impoverished widow who can barely afford any of the elegancies of life. She thought Westbury might allow her to come and live here, but I made it clear that she must live with the consequences of her actions. Perhaps when you have experienced her situation, you will be more amenable to the next man we deem a desirable connection for you. You will go without Stokes; I have need of her now Mrs Tremlow is injured. I will send one of the other maids with you for propriety's sake as you will be some days on the road. Now, leave me."

CHAPTER 2

A tense silence hung in the air of the study at Rushwick Park. Two gentlemen, one in his mid-twenties, the other approaching seventy, sat in the deep leather chairs that were placed on either side of the wide fireplace. The logs in the grate burned fitfully as if smothered by the thick atmosphere.

Although many years separated the two men, the resemblance between them was marked. The eyes that were locked in a battle of wills were of a rare golden hue. They also shared an aquiline nose and a strong, dimpled chin but the elder man's skin was deeply grooved and pale, whereas the younger's was dark and swarthy due to years of campaigning. Their temperaments were as similar as their features; both had a will of iron and a desire to have their own way.

Alexander Knight, Marquess of Somerton, broke the silence first.

"I have barely been home three months, sir. Do

you really think it necessary that I look about me for a wife quite so soon?"

The Duke of Rushwick's brows snapped together. "Your brother died nine months ago. Why it took you six to return is your own affair, but do not complain that you are being rushed. You have been a very loyal soldier to Wellington, but it is time you were a loyal son to me!"

"I have ever been a loyal son to you, sir, if you would but realise it," Alexander said softly. "But I would not return until we were safe from Bonaparte."

His Grace snorted. "If your idea of loyal was to argue with me on every point and persuade your brother to help you purchase your colours directly against my wishes, then our understanding of that term differs widely."

A wry grin twisted Alexander's finely sculpted lips. "But it was because we argued on every point that I went, sir. I had no wish to send you to an early grave."

The duke gave a reluctant chuckle. "I would not have given you the satisfaction. We are too alike, Somerton, that is the problem."

"Then why do you wish to shackle me so soon? You were beyond forty when you wed."

Although he felt the question reasonable, Alexander wished he could call the words back. His father seemed to shrink in his chair, his age suddenly weighing heavily upon him.

"I wondered when you'd throw that in my face," he said wearily.

"I am sorry," Alexander said gently. He reached for the brandy decanter that sat on the table beside him, poured a small glass, and passed it to his father. "I should not have reminded you of Mama."

His father took the glass and drained it. He soon rallied and sat a little straighter. "Why not? She should be remembered. Everything went to pieces after she died," he said gruffly. "A house needs a woman." A small reminiscent smile curled his lips. "And what a woman Eliza was."

Alexander grinned. "I've never met her like. She did not have a mean bone in her body and yet she was painfully honest. Do you remember when I spent a hefty part of my allowance on that blue and gold waistcoat I was so proud of?"

Rushwick gave a dry crack of laughter. "I do. What a fashionable young sprig you thought yourself."

"Not for long," Alexander said ruefully. "Mama informed me, quite kindly, that if I wished to look like a popinjay, I had succeeded to admiration."

His Grace sighed. "Your mother never raised her voice or kicked up a fuss, yet she could always handle you better than I."

"She handled all of us," Alexander said. "Even you."

"As you say. She had a rare understanding and an incisive tongue. I am fully aware that I ran mad for a short while after she died. I am not proud of that; you and James felt her loss as much as I did. I should have been more understanding."

"We should all have been that, sir. None of us behaved well."

"Perhaps not. But if I hadn't snapped and snarled at the pair of you like a wounded animal, you would not have bolted for Portugal and your brother would not have turned into a rip!"

"Was he that bad, sir?"

"Yes," the duke said frankly. "He ran wild for a time, but I brought him to heel in the end. He was shaping up nicely until, until…" He shaded his eyes for a moment.

Alexander was relieved that the subjects they had both been studiously avoiding for the past three months were finally coming to light.

"Well, going into the army was the best thing I could have done, sir. It suited me. I never had any great desire to go up to Oxford, you know. I could not have borne to have had my nose in a book, or to be kicking up some silly lark when there was some real adventure to be had on the continent."

A hint of pride came into the duke's eyes. "You must have learned some discipline, at least, to rise to the rank of major."

"I wouldn't have lasted five minutes without it," Alexander acknowledged. He frowned. "That I should have come through six years of action relatively unscathed whilst James should have been taken in a stupid accident seems nonsensical. And to have drowned on a fishing trip of all things when he had survived mad curricle races and drunken excursions to some of the seediest dives in Town. He was staying with his friend Allerdale wasn't he?"

His father nodded. "I didn't like him going above half; Allerdale was a bad influence. He has always been shockingly loose in the haft and rumour has it he's even worse now. But James pointed out he would be hard-pressed to get up to any mischief in the Lakes and promised he would look about him for a wife when the season began."

"And so we come full circle," Alexander murmured.

"I am not getting any younger, my boy," his father said querulously. "I have a desire to see you safely shackled and to have a bevy of grandchildren cutting up the peace of this mausoleum before I'm given notice to quit!"

Alexander raised a wry brow. "I already feel sorry for my prospective wife!"

The duke looked more hopeful. "Then you will at least consider it?"

"I will give it some thought, sir."

"That is all I ask! I do not expect you to marry for duty alone. Pick a gal who you admire not only for her appearance but her character also."

Rushwick reached for the ebony-handled cane that lay against his chair and began to rise. Alexander stood, firmly resisting the urge to put out a helping hand. Not for the first time since returning home he felt a swift stab of sadness that his father could no longer look him in the eye without peering up at him. He had always been an unusually tall man, with a strong body to match – yet another trait they shared – but now the duke was thin and stooped.

"You'll need to have that mop of yours cut before you go to Town."

Alexander knew that in his father's mind he had already capitulated. He supposed he had. He would make the old man happy if he could.

"That will not be for some time yet," he said. "And

you can hardly blame me for this mad riot of tawny curls when it is thanks to you I have them!"

The duke grinned. "You do remind me of what I was forty years ago. But I always wore a wig, my boy, or had my hair tied neatly. You're not as up to snuff as I was, though; you've not even spent one season in Town so let me give you some advice. There will be plenty of young ladies falling over themselves to attach you but don't let yourself be taken in. They'll all smile and show you their pretty society manners, but you need to dig a little deeper. You're a fine-looking fellow, Alexander, but it is the one who is not impressed by your status and looks that you want. Your mother would have none of me at first, you know."

Alexander quirked a brow. "Dare I ask why?"

"My reputation was not pristine," his father admitted.

"You surprise me, sir."

"Impudent cub! I admit I was as much a wastrel as Allerdale when I was young," the duke said bluntly. "I'm not proud of it now but I can't regret it; I would never have found your mother if I had settled down earlier. But don't you think that lets you off the hook. She very nearly didn't have me for reputation aside, I was eighteen years her senior!"

"What made her change her mind?" Alexander asked.

His father's eyes lost focus as he gazed into the past. "We had a connection," he said softly.

"Attraction is certainly important—"

"That is not what I mean. We had that too, but it was much more. She saw through my polish and posturing. Indeed, she obliterated it with her unguarded tongue. She told me in that matter of fact way she had that if I were going to try and woo her with ridiculous compliments and expensive trinkets, I would bore her to death. She wanted to know my past, my opinions, my aspirations, how I saw my wife's role in my household... in short, she wanted to know Sebastian Knight rather than His Grace, the Duke of Rushwick."

His father had given Alexander much food for thought. It was not only his desire to ensure the duke's last years were happier than the several that had gone before that had led to his capitulation on the matter of his marriage; Alexander's recent years had been spent in a quagmire of death and blood that he would be very happy to forget. He needed a fresh challenge and a new beginning. Bringing a new life that he could protect and guide into this world would perhaps be the very thing.

Alexander was pleased to see his father make a good breakfast the following morning.

"I've been thinking," Rushwick said when he was finally replete. "Why don't we invite your aunt Miriam to stay. We could hold a dinner party or two—"

"Hold fire!" Alexander said, exasperated. "If it isn't just like you to open your opponent's guard and then go for a home thrust! If you think I wish to have anyone and everyone who has a daughter of marriageable age paraded in front of me for the next two months, you are much mistaken."

"Not *anyone*," his father protested. "They would have to be suitably respectable."

"No! I said I would give it some thought but I will not have my hand forced in any way."

"Far too like me," the duke grumbled.

Alexander was relieved to see the butler enter the room carrying a silver salver. As his agent was away on business, his father had taken to opening his mail himself before it was vetted. He only hoped this missive would help divert his father's thoughts; he had no desire to be constantly brangling with him.

"Thank you, Benson," His Grace said, accepting the letter and swiftly opening it.

Alexander polished off the last of his coffee, glanced over at his father, and frowned. The duke's eyes were fixed on the words before him and his complexion had an unhealthy grey pallor.

"Sir?"

He handed him the letter in silence, a stunned look upon his face.

The Reverend R L Simpson

Buttermere 4th August 1814

My Lord Duke,

I hope you will forgive my taking the liberty of writing to you. It is with some hesitancy that I take it upon myself to do so, but any diffidence I might feel at the audacity of communicating with someone of such an exalted station as yourself, and what is more, someone completely unknown to me, must be overcome in the interests of Christian charity.

I have no wish to cause you pain, but I must refer to the sad events of last October when your son met his untimely end by accidental drowning. That tragedy will live long in the memories of those who dwell here, but there is another unfortunate event that will ensure he is not easily forgotten.

Molly Tweddle, a girl in the village, has recently given birth to a boy. She has finally seen fit to confide in me and has named your son as the father of her child. Her family have not cast her out, but they are very poor and will not find it easy to provide for the boy as he grows. As none of the family can write, they have asked me to inform you of the child's existence and to enquire if you would be willing to offer them some support. Molly has no desire to give the child up but sorely needs some help with the cost of his upbringing.

My anxiety for the family as well as my duty to my flock, has persuaded me to promote their welfare. I will press you no further on this matter but rather leave it up to your conscience to dictate your actions. If I do not hear from you in the coming weeks, I will know your answer.

Your obedient & humble servant,

R L Simpson

Alexander let out a long, low whistle. "Then James did manage to get up to some mischief, after all."

"So it would appear," the duke said grimly.

"Or did he?" Alexander mused.

"I hardly think Mr Simpson would take a hand in the business if he did not believe this girl's story to be true."

"He may well believe it but that does not necessarily make it true. I have learned to treat unverified reports with caution."

"I suppose you have," Rushwick acknowledged. "And what course of action did you take to verify them?"

"I sent someone to sniff out the truth, or I conducted a reconnaissance of the enemy's position myself."

"All very well. But with James not here to validate the truth of this matter, there is very little we can do. *If* the girl is lying, she is hardly likely to tell you the truth just because you ask her. She has nothing to gain and everything to lose."

"Do not underestimate me, sir. I shall not go as the Marquess of Somerton, but plain Mr Knight, a gentleman of no consequence. James took after Mama; he was of medium height with eyes of an unremarkable brown, so there is no fear anyone will make the connection. I have been away so long and the place is so remote, it is very doubtful I will bump into anyone who might recognise me. Besides, I have a desire to visit the place where my brother died and pay my respects."

"You can pay your respects in our chapel! I do not wish to risk losing another son in that godforsaken place."

"You won't, sir. I am a very hard man to kill. And if I do not go how else will you discover the truth of the matter? Do you really want to pay to bring up some other man's child?"

"Of course I don't. If the child proves to be James', I will bring him here."

"But Molly does not wish you to," Alexander reminded him.

"She will have no say in the matter," he said. "Besides, if the family are as poor as Mr Simpson claims, they will be glad to be relieved of the boy."

"Probably," he agreed. "But the point is moot until I have discovered the facts of the matter. I shall go tomorrow."

"Oh, very well! But do not linger there any longer than you need to and stay out of that lake!"

Alexander strode into his room, swiftly untied his neckcloth, and laid it neatly over the back of a chair.

"Lay out enough clothes to fill two saddlebags will you, Johns?"

The valet picked up the neckcloth and shot his master a knowing look. Having served as his batman, he knew him as well as anyone.

"I thought you'd be off looking for mischief before long," he said. "You've been as restless as a caged lion for some weeks. Where are we going?"

"I am off to Lakeland, Johns, to discover if my brother left an unexpected legacy."

The valet whistled. "That's the way of it, is it? Perhaps you should take me along, sir. I might be able to ferret out the truth a little easier than you."

"I will be incognito, Johns, and will do very well without you."

Alexander grinned as his valet looked disappointed.

"Feeling a little hemmed in yourself, Johns?"

"I admit I wouldn't mind a little adventure, sir."

"Another time," Alexander promised. "I want you to stay here and keep half an eye on my father. He did not look that well this morning and I shall rely on you to send word if he becomes ill."

CHAPTER 3

Georgianna had been eight days on the road before she caught a glimpse of the mountains that hinted that she might be approaching her destination at last. She was beyond weary. Although she found the company of Kate, the young maid who had been chosen to accompany her, far more pleasant than that of Stokes, the gulf between them ensured that their conversation was severely limited in its scope. Georgianna was very grateful for her presence, however. Not only was Kate very willing to please and eager to learn her new duties, but her presence in her room each evening was reassuring.

Today's journey had been more trying than most; the roads had seemed littered with ruts and holes, jolting the occupants of the carriage mercilessly. Georgianna sat slumped in the corner of the carriage, dozing fitfully. The rumbles issuing from her stomach finally roused her from her lethargy. Risking the dust from the road, she pulled down the carriage window and poked her head out. She was rewarded by the sight of a small but neat looking inn. Leaning a little further out, she turned her head and called up to her coachman.

"Please let us stop here, Jack. I cannot go another mile."

Jack Coachman slowed the horses to a walk and called down, "What was that, ma'am?"

"I wish to stop here."

"But, my lady, it's only a few more miles to Lancaster. You'll find a better quality of inn there."

"I do not care," Georgianna said wearily. "I am hot, tired, and hungry. You must be just as fatigued."

"I must admit I've been dreaming of a nice tankard of ale for I don't know how many miles," Jack said wistfully.

"And I am sure you have earned it," Georgianna said. She felt some sympathy for the old coachman. Her mother had acquired a much newer coach and a younger man to drive it, but it seemed not to have occurred to her that a ten-day journey, twenty if you included the return stretch, might be too much for Jack.

"I'll pull in and see what sort of place this is, ma'am. If it's clean and respectable we'll stay – but if it's not – we'll go on to Lancaster. I can't say fairer than that."

He swung into the small but tidy yard behind the inn, climbed down from the box, and passed the reins to a lad who came running from the stables.

"I do hope he finds it suitable," Georgianna sighed.

"As do I, my lady," the maid agreed. "If anyone

had ever told me that sitting down all day was exhausting, I would have said they were talking hogwash. I can't tell you how excited I was to be going on a long journey; I've never been further than Bristol before. But it's not so very exciting after all, and I hope we get there soon for it can't be good for your insides to be jiggled about hour after hour. I swear I'll never complain about a hard day's work again."

Both occupants of the carriage were relieved when the coachman reappeared with a grin on his weathered face.

"It'll do, ma'am. They have two guest chambers and both are free so you can take your pick. There's no private parlour to be had, mind you, but there's a coffee room that will be set aside for your use. Once I've seen to the horses, I'll be in the taproom across the way until you've had your dinner and gone up to your room."

A buxom lady with rosy cheeks awaited her at the bottom of a narrow staircase.

"Mrs Florry, ma'am," she said, curtseying. "We don't generally have the quality putting up at our inn, but you'll find our rooms as clean and comfortable as any other and a deal quieter, I'll be bound. And you don't need to worry about our customers; Mr Florry don't let any riffraff in."

"Thank you, Mrs Florry. A warm meal and a soft bed are all that I require."

She chose the room that looked over the stable yard as it was the slightly larger of the two and already had a second, smaller bed set up under the window.

Seeing that Mrs Florry was looking at her in some

expectation, she said, "It is a very pleasant chamber and will do very well."

Judging by the wide smile that spread over the innkeeper's wife's face, she had said just the right thing.

"You are very kind, my lady." She assumed a motherly tone. "Now you put off your bonnet and pelisse and I'll show you to the coffee room. I'll send my girl up to fetch your maid down to the kitchen when her supper's ready."

There was one highly polished large round table in the coffee room, a fire had been lit in the hearth, and the floral curtains that were set above the window seat had been drawn to afford her more privacy.

"You are clearly a very fine housekeeper, ma'am," Georgianna said when Mrs Florry again looked enquiringly at her.

"I don't hold with sloppiness," the woman assured her. "Now, I've a nice chicken and a roasted ham if that would suit?"

"It would suit very well," Georgianna assured her.

Unwilling to sit just yet, she wandered over to the window seat and pulled the curtains back a little. A lilac haze sat on the hills in the distance. Her thoughts turned to Lady Colyford. When she had come to Avondale, she had enjoyed very little conversation with her. Her mother's eyes had been upon her on the two occasions she had been admitted into her presence and she had known better than to put herself forwards or answer any enquiries directed at her in anything other than monosyllables. She hoped that her aunt would not reject her unexpected visitor out of hand, for the prospect of making the journey home again did not bear thinking about. But why Aunt Hester should take her in when her mother had refused to offer her a home was not immediately clear to her.

Mrs Florry soon bustled in again, two huge trays full of a variety of dishes balanced in each hand. "I think you will find something to tempt you here, my lady," she said, placing them on the table and beginning to offload joints of meat, a tureen of soup, and platters of steaming vegetables.

"The soup was made fresh today. I picked the peas myself this morning."

Georgianna's eyes widened at the feast set before her.

"I'll never eat the half of it, Mrs Florry."

"Nonsense. You get stuck in; you look like a breath of wind could knock you flat!"

Georgianna tucked into her dinner with a relish her mother would have deplored. She had just finished a bowl of the delicious pea soup when she heard voices in the passage that separated the tap and coffee rooms.

"But, sir, if you will but wait half an hour, the lady will have finished her dinner and you can have the coffee room to yourself!"

"No! I'm damned if I will! My stomach feels as if my throat's been cut!"

The door was thrust open and a man strolled into the room. His dark hair was swept back from a face that might have been handsome if it were not for the petulant expression that marred it. As he divested himself of his dusty greatcoat, eyes that were so dark they appeared almost black scanned the room before coming to rest on Georgianna.

She dropped her gaze, laid down her spoon, and rose to her feet. Ignoring the newcomer, she addressed the thickset man who stood in the doorway, a worried frown furrowing his brow.

"You must be Mr Florry," she said calmly. "Do not concern yourself on my behalf. I have finished my soup and that is all I require."

His brow smoothed and he looked at her in some relief. "Well, if you're sure, ma'am."

He was pushed none too gently out of the way as Mrs Florry came barrelling in, carrying a rolling pin still dusted with flour in one hand.

"What's all this? I told you the lady was not to be disturbed, you great lump!"

"But, Becky, this gentleman has turned up and wants his dinner."

Mrs Florry surveyed the interloper. The cut of his mulberry swallow-tailed coat was very elegant, and his neckcloth was tied with exquisite precision in a style any man of fashion would have immediately recognised as the waterfall. Although Mrs Florry might be ignorant of this sartorial detail, she knew quality when she saw it. Her rather fierce expression gentled a little and softened even further when the gentleman suddenly grinned, his eyes glinting in amusement.

"My good lady, I hope you do not intend to chase me out with your rolling pin! My reluctance to suffer such an indignity aside, it would be the height of cruelty for you to do so when the unmistakable smells of a delicious dinner have been assailing my nostrils for the last few minutes. I really am very hungry, you know."

"But I promised the young lady she would eat her dinner alone," she said, clearly torn.

"I have finished," Georgianna said, beginning to move towards the door.

"That you have not, my lady," Mrs Florry said sternly, waving the rolling pin, causing fine particles of flour to whirl about her. "You've only swallowed a mouthful of soup!"

"Might I suggest we share the table?" the gentleman said, bowing. "I am Allerdale. You will be quite safe in my company this evening, I assure you."

Georgianna raised a brow. "Only this evening, Mr Allerdale?"

His eyes lit with sudden interest.

"I promise no more," he said with a devilish grin. "And it is Lord Allerdale."

Georgianna inclined her head politely. "Lady Georgianna Voss."

"So this is where the delicious smells are coming from."

All eyes turned to a modestly dressed but clearly respectable gentleman who now stooped in the doorway.

"My you're a big 'un," Mr Florry said.

The newcomer smiled. "And I have a big appetite, sir, so I hope there is some dinner left for me."

"Well that settles it," Mrs Florry said, turning to Georgianna. "There's safety in numbers, ma'am. I'll leave the door ajar and you only have to call and we'll be sure to hear you."

A most unladylike rumble issued from Georgianna's stomach. She blushed as a pair of golden eyes turned towards her, glowing with amusement. The tall gentleman offered her a small bow.

"Mr Knight at your service, ma'am. It seems you are as hungry as I."

He strode to the table and held out her seat for her.

"Thank you, sir," she said, moving back to her chair.

It would seem churlish, not to mention cowardly to argue the point anymore, and Georgianna found that she did not feel afraid of either of these strangers. Although Lord Allerdale must be ten years her senior, he somehow reminded her of her little brother; sulky one moment, charming the next. Mr Knight, though huge, seemed to have gentle manners.

"Right, I'd best set some more places," Mrs Florry said, rushing from the room.

Mr Florry looked from one gentleman to the other in some perplexity. "I'm afraid I've only one room left if either of you gentlemen were thinking of staying."

"I was hoping for a bed, I must admit," Mr Knight said, glancing across at Lord Allerdale. "I'm quite happy to share, however, my lord."

His lordship did not seem overly enamoured by this idea judging by his raised brows. "Do not concern yourself with my arrangements, Mr Knight. I shall go on to Lancaster after dinner."

Mr Florry smiled. "That's all right and tight, then. You'll be more comfortable there, I dare say."

"As you say," Lord Allerdale said, a slight sneer curling his lips. "I don't suppose you've got any decent wine about the place?"

"No, sir. But I have some very good ale. I'll send some in."

"Are you still here?" Mrs Florry said, rushing in with more plates and cutlery. "You best get back in the tap before they start serving themselves!"

It was not Mr Florry but Jack who came in not very many moments later with two tankards of foaming ale. He put them down on the table and glanced at Georgianna.

"Everything alright, ma'am?"

"Yes, Jack."

He caught the coin Lord Allerdale sent spinning carelessly in his direction and placed it back on the table, sending him a keen stare from under his shaggy brows.

"Well, just you holla if you need me," he said sternly before leaving the room.

"What strange servants they keep here," Lord Allerdale drawled, pocketing the coin.

"He is my coachman, sir," Georgianna said coolly. "And if it is strange for him to be concerned for my welfare, then I suppose he is guilty as charged."

"A good servant who can't be bribed is worth his weight in gold," Mr Knight said, rising to his feet and reaching for the carving knife. "May I serve you some chicken, Lady Georgianna?"

"Yes, thank you, sir."

She felt Lord Allerdale's black eyes upon her. "I do not think I have seen you in Town, ma'am?"

"You could hardly have done so, sir, when I am not yet out."

One black brow winged up. "Forgive me. I took you to be older. You are very self-assured for such a young lady. Who is your father, if you don't mind me asking?"

"Lord Westbury."

A curious grin twisted his lips. "You don't say. I bumped into him in Town only last week. You are a long way from home."

"Yes. I am going to visit my aunt, Lady Colyford."

She smiled primly at Mr Knight as he passed her an amply laden plate.

"You have my sympathy," Lord Allerdale said softly.

Georgianna looked at him in surprise. "You know her?"

He grimaced. "I do. She is great friends with my mother, Lady Brigham. She is also my godmother. She is extremely forthright and always gives the truth with no bark upon it whether one wishes to hear it or not."

"So I believe," she said, her eyes holding his with speculative interest. "But then, if she speaks the truth, what has one to cavil at?"

Lord Allerdale gave a harsh laugh. "Truth is subjective."

Georgianna's brow wrinkled as she considered these words. "No, that cannot be right. The truth is the truth. It is only when someone wishes to bend it to suit their convenience that it becomes subjective."

Lord Allerdale frowned. "You do give your opinion freely, but you are too young to know what you speak of."

"What a convenient answer," Georgianna said with a small smile. "I may have only lived seventeen years upon this earth, sir, but I have already learned that if someone finds the truth unpalatable, myself included, it is often because they do not wish for a mirror to be held up to their actions."

Mr Knight had been silently consuming a healthy portion of every dish but at this, he raised his head from his plate and said, "There is some wisdom in your words, Lady Georgianna, but you must allow for the disparity in age and experience between yourself and a man of the world. Your behaviour is prescribed by societies strict rules, his path is often littered with more difficult choices."

"That may be true," she conceded. "But if his conscience is clear, what has a man of the world to fear from the truth? Surely his respective freedom, if used wisely, is a chance to do some good in the world?"

Mr Knight's eyes deepened from gold to amber. "But sometimes doing good in the world, as you put it, involves facing unpalatable truths. I wonder, Lady Georgianna, if you have ever read Machiavelli's, *The Prince*?"

"As a matter of fact, I have." She repressed a smile at his look of surprise. "I have always felt that a study of history might give me some insight into the human character. It is not enough to be a part of this world; I wish to understand it also."

"And do you believe that the ends justify the means?" Mr Knight asked softly.

Georgianna felt a little out of her depth. "I cannot give you a definitive answer, sir. It must be dependent on the ends. If they are noble and cannot be achieved by any other means, perhaps. If they are not, then no."

Lord Allerdale made no effort to disguise a yawn.

"I perceive we have a budding bluestocking in our midst."

Scorn laced through every word. Georgianna stood and speared him with her icy gaze. "Thank you, sir. If you have treated my aunt to such poor manners as you have shown me, it is no wonder you have heard some scathing truths. It has been an interesting evening, but I will bid you both good night."

Alexander stood and bowed as she left the room; Lord Allerdale merely inclined his head.

"What a proud, impertinent chit. She would be better learning the art of flirtation than trying to understand the motivations of mankind from a history book. If she knew her father was happily escorting his latest mistress about Town, she might not be so prosy and preachy."

"It would be quite shocking if she knew of it," Alexander said calmly. "And if you found her prosy and preachy then I fear she must have, quite inadvertently, struck a little too close to home for your liking, sir."

Lord Allerdale's brows rose haughtily. "Has she caught your interest, Mr Knight? She is undoubtedly a beauty but too cold for my liking. I prefer a cosier armful."

"And a less challenging one, I suspect," Alexander murmured.

Lord Allerdale gave a cynical laugh. "Very true. Where are you headed, Mr Knight?"

Alexander's eyes fixed firmly on his fellow guest as he said, "Buttermere."

That gentleman frowned, his eyes dropped to the table, and something that might have been pain or distaste twisted his lips. After a moment he said, "Painter or poet?"

"What makes you think I am either of those things?"

Allerdale shrugged. "We seem to be inundated with them."

"You do not admire their works?"

"No. They romanticise everything. A century ago the Lakes were a wild and desolate place with nothing to offer the traveller, but now dozens turn up with a Claude glass in their pocket and a guidebook in their hands. They are told where to go and what to think of the view. I think wild and desolate describe it far more accurately."

"You are not fond of your home?"

Lord Allerdale drained the last of his ale and got to his feet. "I visit it as little as possible but sometimes needs must."

"I see," Alexander said. "Been drawing the bustle a little too freely, eh?"

"Precisely. I bid you good evening, Mr Knight."

Alexander moved to the chair by the fire and spent some time staring into the flickering flames. He had meant to keep a low profile and would have taken his supper in a quiet corner of the taproom if he had not happened to have heard Allerdale speak his name on his way there. He might have satisfied himself with just a glimpse of the last man to see his brother alive if he had not seen the striking young lady standing a little uncertainly in the middle of the room. Chivalrous instinct had overcome his natural caution; he could hardly leave her to dine alone with a man of Allerdale's reputation.

He would search him out and reveal his identity when he had discovered the truth of Molly Tweddle's claims, for he wished to hear first-hand the account of his brother's death. It was a pity Allerdale had dropped his eyes when he had mentioned Buttermere; he would very much like to have seen if his expression had held guilt or regret.

CHAPTER 4

K ate sprang up from her narrow bed when Georgianna entered her room.

"I hope you enjoyed your dinner, my lady," she said, hastily brushing down her skirt and blinking the sleep from her eyes.

"Indeed I did, Kate. But I must admit I am more than ready to retire."

"I should think you are," the maid said, helping her out of her dress. "I've got everything ready and there's some warm water in the basin."

Georgianna washed and sat in the room's solitary chair. She closed her eyes as Kate pulled out the pins that held her hair.

"I hear as you had some unexpected company, my lady. They were full of it in the kitchen. I hope they were respectable gentlemen. I hear one was dressed very fine."

"Mmm," Georgianna murmured, enjoying each stroke of the brush through her thick, dark hair. "But I have a feeling he may have been the least respectable of the two."

The maid's eyes widened. "I hope he offered you no insult, ma'am."

"None of any import and he assured me I would be safe in his company, this evening at least."

Kate tutted. "The saucy devil!"

A small smile tugged at Georgianna's lips. "Better an honest rogue than a dishonest gentleman. But I was in no danger once he discovered that not only am I very free with my opinion, but worse, a bluestocking! I have a feeling I am not just in his style."

"Just as well by the sounds of it."

Georgianna shook her head as the maid reached for her nightcap. "Not tonight, Kate. I will wear it down for once."

"As you wish, ma'am."

The sound of hooves on cobbles floated through the slightly open window. Georgianna knelt on the maid's bed and peeped between a gap in the curtains just in time to see Lord Allerdale spring up into his curricle. As he flicked his whip, he glanced up. Perhaps it was just the reflection of the lamp that lit the yard, but she thought his eyes glittered rather wildly and reared back, embarrassed. She shivered, suddenly very glad that Mr Knight had joined them for dinner.

"Come away from that window, my lady. You've barely got a stitch on and will catch your death."

"Of course," she murmured rather absently.

She awoke to a grey sky from which a light, constant mizzle fell. Georgianna welcomed the cooler conditions and if the road beyond Lancaster remained uneven in parts, once they had passed Kendal, the glimpse of wooded valleys, rocky peaks, and long ribbons of water, made up for it. They spent the night at Keswick. A lofty, forbidding peak rose behind the small town and a lake encircled by an amphitheatre of smaller mountains lay before it.

The air was heavy with the threat of rain, but keen to stretch her legs, Georgianna donned a thick woollen cloak and strolled down to its shore, Kate following close behind. From a distance, the still water had appeared an opaque sheet of grey, as if a pewter lid had been placed over it, but as she came to its edge, she discovered the water was clear and pure. A mosaic of pebbles in a variety of hues stretched beneath the glassy surface. A sudden breath of wind sent ripples skittering along the water, obscuring them. Raising her eyes, Georgianna saw that dark clouds now obscured the tops of the hills on the opposite shore and a heavy mist was drifting across the lake towards her.

"It's downright eerie, my lady," Kate said, shivering. "Nature's all well and good, but I'd say there's a mite too much of it here and it don't feel friendly."

Georgianna smiled. "It is not nature that is the interloper, but us. If you must imbue it with human qualities, I suppose the prospect does have a brooding, slightly menacing quality today but it is only the weather. On a sunny day, I think you would find very little to object to."

"Well, it ain't sunny, ma'am. And if I'm not much mistaken, those black clouds are about to drop their load."

Even as she spoke, a strong gust of wind blew back the hood of Georgianna's cloak, little white-capped waves began to scurry across the lake, and a few heavy drops of rain began to fall. The thought that the inhospitable weather might be an omen of things to come whispered in Georgianna's mind, but she ruthlessly silenced it. She did not deal in superstition but facts; her aunt's reaction to her arrival would depend on her character alone, not the vagaries of the elements.

The sky had cleared by the morning. As they made their way up into the hills at the end of the valley, Georgianna glanced down at the lake and saw it reflected the trees and mountains that surrounded it with all the efficacy of a polished mirror. As they travelled on, signs of civilisation dwindled and only the odd shepherd's hut spoke of man's incursion into the ancient landscape. The road rose steeply for some time, and Georgianna's eyes widened with awe as they reached the top of the climb and she saw the wild, savage beauty before her. They were now bounded by mountains on both sides and a white, roiling river cut through the deep, shadowed valley below. Not a tree or bush softened the barren landscape, only great lumps of rock, some almost as large as the carriage, littered the ground on either side of the narrow winding road. When they neared the floor of the pass, the river roared and hissed around the boulders as if angered by their presence.

"It's as if we've gone to the ends of the earth," Kate said. "This place feels uncanny."

Georgianna did not disagree but after another steep climb, they began their descent into the Vale of Buttermere and the prospect gentled. Although the valley was still rimmed with mountains, it was wide enough to be flooded with sunshine. Two lakes, separated by a fertile strip of land, glinted in the sunshine.

A huddle of houses was set between them. As they reached the valley floor, they came to a farm and Jack stopped to ask directions.

They made their way along the road that skirted the water and turned onto a rough track that was barely wide enough to accommodate the coach. They followed it through a small wood for about a quarter of a mile and then slowed to a crawl as they squeezed between two stone pillars with only inches to spare. A rather weathered sign bore the appropriate, if rather unoriginal appellation, Lake Cottage.

They pulled up on a circular gravel sweep. A large barn lay to their left, and a long two-storey white-washed house to their right. Georgianna was surprised; she had expected to find a more modest dwelling.

As she approached the house the door opened. A small lady wearing a pair of spectacles squinted up at her.

"Is that you, Lydia?" Her myopic gaze turned to the dusty coach. "Your mother sent the carriage, how kind. If you just give me a moment, I will fetch my shawl. It is another fine day to be sure, but one can never be too careful. I wonder who we will meet in the park today? Mr Antsy showed me a flattering degree of attention last week, you know. He is such a kind gentleman with the most distinguished manners." On these words, the lady turned and hurried back into the house.

Feeling rather nonplussed, Georgianna turned her head and said, "Are you sure we have come to the right place, Jack?"

"Yes, ma'am, you'd best ring the bell. That lady

seemed a tad confused; never mind you're not Lydia, I'd bet my boots there is no park to drive carriages in anywhere near here! If I hadn't got forty years' experience under my belt, we'd never have made it through those mountains."

Georgianna nodded at her maid but as Kate reached for the bell pull, Georgianna heard the crunch of footsteps on gravel. She turned her head and breathed a shallow sigh of relief. A tall willowy lady carrying a basket hooked over one arm had come around the corner of the house. Her thick white hair, tanned skin, and light blue eyes made a striking combination. As she saw Georgianna, she paused in her tracks. She glanced from Jack to her niece and back again before approaching them.

"You did well to get that great lumbering tub down my drive, Jack," she said dryly.

The coachman doffed his hat. "I'm not sure I'd go so far as to call it a drive, milady. I'm pleased to see you looking so well."

Small creases fanned out from Lady Colyford's eyes as she smiled. "I'm brown as a nut and wrinkled as a prune, you old fool. I don't have a groom, but you'll find everything you need in the barn. When you've seen to the horses go to the kitchen and cook will give you some refreshments."

As Jack nodded and moved off, she turned to her visitor, her eyes cooling a little. It was not often that Georgianna looked another woman directly in the eyes, but her aunt was almost the same height as herself.

"I see you have turned from a rather awkward

tangle of limbs into a beautiful young lady, Georgianna."

"Thank you, Lady Colyford," she said, a small smile edging her lips. "I may no longer be a tangle of limbs, but I am still awkward, I assure you."

Her aunt raised a finely shaped brow. "In what way are you awkward?"

"I am no good at small talk, nor do I have the knack of making myself agreeable to others," Georgianna said honestly.

"That is hardly surprising," Lady Colyford said. "Both the art of conversation and pleasing manners are not inherited like your height or eye colour, Georgianna, they are skills that need to be learned and practised. Tell me, are you also proud like your father and conceited like your mother?"

Georgianna did not flinch but considered this question carefully, feeling that her welcome here might depend on her answer.

"I do not believe I am conceited, Lady Colyford, but I have, at times, been guilty of being proud. I am, however, trying to rectify the fault as I have come to realise that it is not a person's birth but their accomplishments that merit such a feeling."

Lady Colyford nodded. "Quite right. You had best come in, but you may leave your pride at the door; we are a humble household. You may also address me as Aunt Hester."

Georgianna followed Lady Colyford into a long, narrow hallway. A maid was polishing the banisters of the staircase until they gleamed.

"Sally, take my visitor's maid to the kitchen and ask cook to draw a glass of cider for their coachman."

The maid dropped a rather clumsy curtsy. "Yes, ma'am."

Lady Colyford glanced down at her basket and laid it on the small table at the foot of the stairs.

"Take this basket of eggs with you. Cook should be pleased; the hens are laying very well at the moment. Oh, and bring a tray of tea to the drawing room."

She led the way into a large square room that was flooded with sunshine. It had a fine view of the lake, the mountains on the far side seeming to drop straight into the water. Bare rock grazed the sky at their summit, but the lower slopes were dressed in dense woodland, the greenery occasionally interrupted by foaming waterfalls cascading down clefts in the rock.

"Beautiful," Georgianna murmured. "Neither the house nor the location is quite what I had anticipated, Aunt Hester. I expected both to be far humbler when Mama said that you lived in a remote place in a cottage."

"Did you expect to find me living in a hovel?" she said, an amused glint in her eyes. "My circumstances are not quite so desperate. I have a cook, one live-in maid apart from my own, and two girls from the village who act as maids of all work. A local man helps with the gardens, but we do most of it ourselves. I take it you are on a tour of the Lakes and have dropped in to satisfy your curiosity? I am not surprised your mother has not accompanied you; we do not see eye to eye. Where are you both staying?"

Georgianna retrieved a letter from her reticule. "You had better read this."

Lady Colyford took it and sat down but before she

could open the missive, the lady who had first greeted Georgianna came in, a parasol swinging jauntily from one hand, a straw bonnet set upon her grey locks, and a shawl dangling from her skinny elbows.

"There you are, Lydia. Thank goodness! I thought you had gone when there was no sign of your coach. I thought it rather odd, for I am sure I have not kept you waiting above a few minutes."

Lady Colyford rolled her eyes. "It is not Lydia, Miss Ravenchurch, but my niece, Lady Georgianna Voss. You are no longer in Town but in the Lakes, remember?"

The little lady's face fell. "Oh yes, of course, I had forgotten. How silly of me."

She turned and walked with lagging steps from the room, the shawl, which had slipped from one crooked elbow to the floor, trailing behind her.

"Miss Ravenchurch is a distant relative of ours and my companion. She is easily confused and seems to live in the past more and more frequently."

"Who is Lydia?" Georgianna asked.

"I have no idea," Lady Colyford said. "Probably some friend from her youth. I believe she had one season in Town as a girl and it is to that time she most often reverts."

Georgianna observed her aunt anxiously as she read the letter, resisting the urge to fidget. It seemed it was not a very long missive for Lady Colyford soon came to its end. She gave a rather bitter laugh, folded it, and stared off into the distance as if deep in thought.

"Aunt?" she said after a moment, eager to know her fate.

Lady Colyford sent her a searching look. "I'm trying to read between the lines, but it is not easy. Your mother never was one to waste words."

"Perhaps if read it, I can help you," Georgianna suggested quietly.

The maid hurried into the room and plonked the tray down on the table beside Lady Colyford, the cups rattling in their saucers and a little milk slopping onto the tray. Georgianna's mother would have given her a sharp dressing down for her carelessness, but her aunt seemed not at all concerned.

"Thank you, Sally," she said, passing the letter to Georgianna. "Make up the bedroom next to mine for Lady Georgianna, will you? And another for her maid in the attic."

Georgianna smiled gratefully and glanced down at her mother's neat writing.

Dear Hester,

I have been meaning to write to you for some time but have been quite distracted of late; Rupert has been very ill with a bad case of chin cough. At one time, his fever mounted so high I feared he would not survive it. Fortunately, Georgianna was exposed to no danger as we had sent her to Miss Wolfraston's Seminary for Young Ladies to round off her education. She has also enjoyed a few weeks stay with her friend, Miss Montagu.

My troubles have made me think of yours. I am sure it cannot be comfortable to be so far from your family and friends. Although she has only just returned to me, I have sent Georgianna to you for a visit in the hope that she might offer you some companionship. I have, of course, sent with her enough money to pay for her keep; it is in Jack Coachman's possession. As you are unlikely to be able to accommodate him or the maid I have sent with her, they will return to Avondale.

You must not hesitate to put Georgianna to work in any way that is useful to you.

Your affectionate sister,

Serena

Georgianna flushed with embarrassment.

"Do not worry, Georgianna; I shall not ask of you anything I myself would not do, nor will I send your maid or Jack back," Lady Colyford assured her. "Apart from it being ridiculous to expect a man of his age to attempt the return journey so soon, he shall come in very useful. I cannot justify the expense of keeping a carriage as we seldom leave the village."

"I am sorry, Aunt Hester," Georgianna said in some mortification. "How Mama can write such stuff when it is thanks to her that you are so far from your family, I do not know."

Lady Colyford looked a little startled. "What has she told you?"

"Only that you wished to live with us, but she would not countenance it. She said you had made an improvident marriage and must live with the consequences."

Georgianna would not have been surprised if her aunt had looked a little angry at this rather blunt statement, but it was relief and not anger that briefly flickered in her eyes.

"I see. Well in that, at least, she speaks the truth. However, I did not wish to stay at Avondale permanently, but only for six months or so whilst I regrouped and thought about where I wished to go next. I could not remain in the dower house at Colyford; the estate had to be sold to pay my husband's debts. I still had a little money of my own, but I did not wish to waste it on renting rooms and so I went to Avondale. Nothing would have prevailed upon me to stay there permanently; my brother is a pompous fool and your mother… well, never mind. Mercifully, I received a letter from my friend Lady Brigham, which led me here. I have a fondness for the Lakes and her husband, the Marquess of Brigham, agreed to rent this house to me for a very reasonable sum. Miss Felsham and I share the costs."

"Miss Felsham?"

"Yes. I am far more fortunate in my friends than my family. Miss Felsham was my neighbour at Colyford. She has been a constant source of support to me for many years. She kept house for her father, Viscount Turridge, but when he died not long after I moved here, she came for a visit. She fell in love with Buttermere and never left. It is an arrangement that suits us both."

"So, you are not in need of companionship, after all," Georgianna said, a little wanly.

"Perhaps not, but I think you may be," Lady Colyford said. "What on earth have you done for your mother to send you to me? You must have displeased her greatly, I think."

"Yes," Georgianna said in a flat voice. "My first transgression was to have been born a girl, my latest is to have thwarted her plans to marry me to a gentleman for whom I felt no regard."

Lady Colyford frowned as she saw an icy coldness redolent of her mother, glitter in her niece's eyes.

"That Serena should be annoyed by the second misdemeanour, is perhaps understandable, although I do not see why she is in such a hurry to see you wed, but she can hardly blame you for being female."

"I assure you she does," Georgianna said. "My mother hates me for it and wishes to be rid of me as soon as she can."

The ice in those large, deep blue eyes suddenly melted and they swam with tears. Georgianna hastily brushed at one or two which escaped and fell onto her ashen cheeks.

"You must be mistaken, my child," Lady Colyford said gently. "You are tired after your journey and have perhaps taken some harsh words too much to heart."

To Georgianna's surprise and horror, her tears now fell as fast as the rushing waters of the waterfalls she had so recently admired.

"I am not mistaken," she choked out. "I have suspected as much for some time and now she has finally admitted it."

Blinded by her tears, Georgianna did not see the look of profound shock that momentarily held her aunt immobile. She heard a rustle of skirts and then stiffened as two long slender arms wound about her.

"Come, have your cry and then tell me all about it."

Her warm, sympathetic tone melted Georgianna's reserve. Her head dropped onto Lady Colyford's shoulder and she abandoned herself to the rather alarming heart-wrenching sobs that spoke of years of unhappiness and loneliness more eloquently than any words could have.

CHAPTER 5

Three days after Georgianna's arrival, Alexander came through the pass that had so impressed her with its wild beauty. He was not quite as awed by the scenery as she had been, but then he had spent years fighting in mountainous terrain, some of it far less hospitable than any to be found in Cumberland. His horse, a sturdy stallion of seventeen hands, was as experienced as he and made short work of the steep inclines.

As he came to the lake, Alexander dismounted and led him down to a small stony beach. His gaze roamed over the still, smooth water. It was, he acknowledged, a picturesque and tranquil scene, but then appearances could so often be deceptive. Although the lake was modest in circumference, his experience of mountain lakes told him that it would likely be very cold and deep at its heart.

He bent and picked up a pebble and with a flick of his wrist, sent it skipping across the surface. He watched the ripples spread out with each hop and frowned as an image of his brother thrashing about in the water swam into his mind. He knelt and dipped his hands into the cool, clear liquid, scooping up great handfuls and throwing it over his face. His mind was playing tricks on him; by all accounts, James had dived into the water and not resurfaced. His body had been found a few days later. He trailed his fingers in the water for a moment and murmured softly, "Rest in peace, James."

He rode to the village at the far end of the lake and found a small inn by a swiftly flowing brook. He entered a dark taproom, grateful to be out of the hot sun. Although the inn was modest, it was clean and doing a healthy trade. He was surprised to see a few tables were occupied by smartly dressed gentlemen. He had not expected to find this remote spot frequented by visitors. One swift glance about the room reassured him that they were all strangers. He had hoped to stay at the inn but was to be disappointed.

The innkeeper shook his head and sighed. "I'm that sorry, sir, but there's nowt available. Ever since that feckless, deceivin' rogue, John Hatfield, married our local beauty, Mary, pretendin' to be Colonel Hope, brother to an earl, it must 'a bin twelve years since now, we get hordes of visitors who come to see where it all 'appened. He was hung for his imposture; never mind he already had a wife and two bairns."

"Poor Mary," Alexander said with a small smile.

"Aye, it was a bad do. But all's well as ends well, and she's properly married now and lives at Caldbeck. Any road, we only 'ave two rooms and between those interested in Mary's story and those as comes to fish –

for the tarn is full of char and trout as fine as you'll find anywhere – we're always full in summer."

"Is there anywhere else hereabouts that might have a room?"

"Well, you could try Lorton, t'other end of Crummock."

Alexander frowned. "I had hoped to stay at Buttermere."

"Only thing I can suggest is you go back along the tarn aways and ask at the farm. They 'ave been known to take in the odd visitor."

Alexander accepted this with good grace, enjoyed a swift tankard of ale, and went to fetch his horse. Needing to stretch his legs, he led the stallion back along the road. If members of the gentry frequently visited Buttermere, it was perhaps just as well the inn was full. A humble farmhouse would suit him just as well and afford him far more anonymity. He paused as he came to a track that led towards the lake and benefited from the shade of a small oak wood. He had assumed the innkeeper had referred to the farm he had passed at the top of the lake, but perhaps there was another.

The shade tempted him in. He soon came to the house, and if it was a little larger and smarter than he had expected to find, the barn encouraged him to believe that his instincts had not erred. He led his horse towards it; there was no point disturbing anyone until he had made sure it could adequately house his mount. What he saw there gave him pause. There were already two horses stabled and an antiquated carriage that he could not imagine belonged to any local farmer. A set of steps set against one wall led to another floor, which he assumed contained housing for the stable hands. Even as this crossed his mind, they creaked under the weight of a man's tread.

His brows winged up as the man turned towards him. "Jack, isn't it? Lady Georgianna's coachman?"

"You have a good memory, sir," he said. "That's a fine horse you've got there."

Alexander patted his mount. "There's none better."

"Have you come to call on my lady?"

Alexander glanced down at his dusty coat. "No," he said wryly. "I had no idea she was staying here."

A faint prickle started at the base of his neck and instinct caused him to look over his shoulder. Two ladies stood in front of the house, their arms linked. It was obvious to him that they were related; not only were they both unusually tall, but they shared a delicate bone structure with high cheekbones, perfectly straight noses, and a narrow chin. They made a striking picture: one with hair of the purest white, the other's black as a raven's wing; one with skin as brown as an acorn, the other's as pale as alabaster; one with eyes of the lightest aquamarine, the other's of a deep sapphire blue.

"Mr Knight!" Lady Georgianna said. "How did you know I was here?"

"I did not," he said. "They could not accommodate me at the inn and suggested I try my luck at a farmhouse. I mistakenly thought that I might have found one here."

Alexander regretted that he had embarrassed her but thought the delicate pink tinge that infused Lady Georgianna's cheeks suited her.

"I did not mean to sound conceited, sir. It is just such a strange coincidence that you should come to the very house that I am visiting."

"I do not think you conceited," he said gently. "If I had found a room at the inn and discovered you were also staying in the village, you may be sure I should have called on you."

Georgianna turned to the woman at her side. "I met Mr Knight at an inn on the way here. I was in a rather awkward position until he arrived."

Alexander found himself on the end of a wide, amazed stare and wondered if he appeared more dishevelled than he had realised. Allerdale had called Lady Colyford forthright, yet she stood mute, staring at him as if she had seen a ghost.

"Aunt?" Lady Georgianna said, gently squeezing her arm.

Lady Colyford started and gave a shaky smile. "What awkward position were you in, child?"

"I had been promised the coffee room to myself but Lord Allerdale insisted he dine with me. I did not feel quite comfortable but then Mr Knight arrived."

Lady Colyford's eyes sharpened. "I am very grateful to you, Mr Knight. I would not have liked my niece to dine alone with a stranger, particularly not Allerdale."

Alexander gave a lopsided grin. "She was in no danger, ma'am. Between Jack, the innkeeper, and his wife, Mrs Florry, she was far better chaperoned than many a young lady at a ball."

"I am pleased to hear it. Did I hear you were looking for accommodation, Mr Knight?"

"Yes, ma'am."

"I cannot allow you to sleep in the cottage," Lady Colyford said. "We are a female-only household."

"I did not think for one moment—"

"However," Lady Colyford interrupted him, "there is a free room in the barn should you wish to take it."

"I would not wish to impose—"

"You will not be imposing, Mr Knight. Apart from charging you for your board and lodging, for you may, of course, join us for meals, I will expect you to carry out any tasks that require a stronger arm than we can provide."

"But, Aunt," Lady Georgianna protested, "you surely cannot expect a gentleman to sleep in the barn with Jack?" She looked quickly at her coachman. "No offence intended, Jack."

"And none taken, ma'am. I'm in agreement with you, so I am."

"Nor can you expect Mr Knight to carry out menial tasks more fitted to a servant."

"Why not? Everyone in this house contributes to its upkeep."

"I accept your offer, Lady Colyford," Alexander said, offering her a small bow. "I have been a soldier and slept in far worse places, I assure you. Besides, the secluded situation so near to the lake will more than make up for a simple lodging."

Lady Colyford glanced at his bulging saddlebags. "That's settled then. We dine at six, Mr Knight. I see you have no valet with you, and as you have been so accommodating, you may send any laundry you have up to the house."

"You are very kind, Lady Colyford," Alexander said.

A sardonic smile spread over that lady's face. "When you have chopped wood, mended fencing, and moved a few very inconvenient, not to mention huge boulders from my garden, you may change your mind."

He grinned. "It would take a great deal more than that to daunt me."

As the ladies disappeared into the house, Jack shook his head. "Lady Colyford has always had an odd kick in her gallop."

Alexander led his horse into the stables. "As long as it is dry, I shall be content."

"Oh, it's dry enough," Jack said taking the reins from him. "You leave your horse to me, sir. There's a broom in the corner over there; you'll want to give your room a sweep and get rid of the cobwebs."

Alexander rather liked his room. It was large, airy, and had a window which looked down to the lake. Its only drawback was the bed; it was rather narrow and his feet would surely dangle over the end. This was not an unusual occurrence; his father had had to have special beds made to measure for both himself and his son.

He presented himself at the house promptly at six o'clock in fresh linen, buff pantaloons, and a dark blue coat. He was a little surprised when Lady Georgianna answered the door.

"Good evening, ma'am," he said, bowing. "Have you taken on the role of housekeeper in this unusual household?"

She stepped back to allow him entry. "I am hardly

qualified to do so," she said coolly. "Lady Colyford organises the house but we all do whatever is needed."

As she shut the door behind him, he noticed that one long, curling lock of hair had escaped its confines, snaked along the length of her slender neck, and settled in the hollow between her shoulder blades. He was aware of an urge to reach out, wind it around his finger, and discover if it was as soft and silky as it looked.

He filled the narrow hallway and as Lady Georgianna turned, she stumbled against him. Two wide, startled eyes flew to his and he reached out his hands to steady her. Even as he registered the warm smooth skin beneath his palms, he felt her flinch as if the contact was distasteful to her. He immediately released his grip on her arms and took a hasty stride backwards. His heel came into sharp contact with the bottom step of the stairs, his knee buckled, and his weight sent him toppling backwards. He was grateful that the stairs were carpeted, but even so, he winced as his back came into contact with their hard edges.

"What a clumsy fellow I am," he said with a rueful grin, pushing himself to his feet.

Lady Georgianna's eyes dropped to the floor and for the second time in their short acquaintance, a delicate blush stole over her cheeks. "I do not believe the house was designed with someone of your size in mind, sir," she said. "Come this way please."

He followed her into the drawing room.

"Good evening, Mr Knight," Lady Colyford said. "Allow me to introduce Miss Felsham and Miss Ravenchurch."

He bowed politely to the two ladies who had risen at his entrance.

"I am pleased to make your acquaintance."

Miss Felsham merely smiled and nodded, but Miss Ravenchurch burst into a tangled, rather breathless speech.

"How do you do, sir? How splendid it is to have some company, for we do not receive very many visitors you know. My, how big you are, if you were any taller your head would almost brush the ceiling. I noticed that you had to stoop when you came through the doorway; it must be a sad inconvenience for you."

"Not at all, Miss Ravenchurch. One becomes accustomed."

"I am glad to hear it, sir, for it would be a great deal too bad if you had not; to be permanently banging your head would be most injurious to your health. I once knew a man—"

"Shall we go in to dinner?" Lady Colyford said.

Alexander offered her his arm. "I hope you will forgive me coming in my boots, ma'am. I had not expected to be in company on this trip."

"Do not give it a thought," she said, taking his arm. "We are very informal here."

She proved the truth of her words not many minutes later when she ladled out the soup herself and passed the bowls along the table.

Alexander had not been aware of quite how hungry he was until he took his first sip of the broth. He had to overcome the urge to wolf it down but was aided in this feat by his awareness of the frequent covert glances Lady Colyford sent his way. As he finished, she said, "What has drawn you to the Lakes, Mr Knight?"

"I heard there was some good walking to be had here, ma'am."

"Then you will not be disappointed, although it might be wise to take a guide. The weather can close in extremely quickly in these parts, and the hills become shrouded in mist before you know it. We had such a case, last year. Fortunately, the gentleman was discovered by a shepherd and so returned safely."

"I will bear that in mind, Lady Colyford."

The soup was followed by some fresh trout.

"This is very good," Alexander said. "It is from the lake, I presume?"

"Of course," Lady Colyford confirmed. "If anyone catches more fish than they need, they often bring the remainder of their catch to us. We generally have all we need here; we grow most of our own vegetables and keep a few pigs and chickens, and there are plenty of sheep in these hills, so mutton is never in short supply. There is also a local man, Mr Peeks, who delivers the post to Cockermouth, as well as collecting any parcels for Buttermere and Lorton and he will do any odd bits of shopping we require."

"It seems then, that you want for nothing. I noticed a rowing boat tucked away at the back of the barn and a fishing rod. I would be happy to catch you some fish."

"That is very kind of you," Miss Felsham said.

He turned his gaze to her homely face. "Not at all. I will enjoy it."

"Oh," Miss Ravenchurch gasped, "do be careful.

There was a poor gentleman who drowned in the lake only last year."

Alexander took an unhurried sip of his wine. "Is it so dangerous?"

"Not generally in the summer months if you stay close to the shore," Lady Colyford said. "But the water further out must be very cold in winter."

He would have liked to ask more but could think of no reasonable excuse to do so. He did not feel quite comfortable in his deception and considered for a moment whether he should take them into his confidence. He dismissed the notion almost immediately; he doubted Miss Ravenchurch could be relied upon to keep his secret and if he were to discover the truth of Molly Tweddle's claims, he must remain anonymous. Besides, he found he was enjoying the refreshing lack of deference with which they treated him. The respect he had earned from his men had been hard won and well deserved and he had still not accustomed himself to the rather fawning attention his new position had accorded him. He could not move at Rushwick without a footman rushing to open a door for him and on the few occasions he had accompanied his father to a dinner hosted by one of the local families, everyone had been overly eager to please him.

"I am afraid we cannot take it upon ourselves to entertain you in the evening," Lady Colyford said. "We generally read or sew after dinner."

"I would not dream of disrupting your routine," Alexander said with a measure of relief. He did not relish the idea of parrying questions into his history or of having to listen to Miss Ravenchurch's ramblings. When the ladies withdrew, he took his leave.

"You can see yourself out," Lady Colyford said. "And do not bother with the bell when you come for breakfast or dinner; the door is always unlocked until we retire for the evening. I will ask cook to pack you up something to sustain you on your rambles."

"Thank you, ma'am. But please do not expect me at breakfast, I like to be away early."

"I must say I am very impressed with Mr Knight," Miss Ravenchurch said, as they settled in the drawing room. "He has such charming manners and seemed very pleased with our simple dinner."

"And why should he not be pleased, Agnes?" Miss Felsham said softly. "That he is a gentleman cannot be in doubt, but he is one of modest means, I suspect."

"You may be right, Leticia," Miss Ravenchurch agreed, "but he has a certain air about him that speaks of good breeding. I have often observed that it is not always present in those of much higher rank. I remember when I made my come out…"

Georgianna filtered out Miss Ravenchurch's gentle prattle. She sat a little apart on the window seat so she could benefit from the fading light outside as she decorated the hem of a small gown. It was for a baby that had recently been delivered to a local girl out of wedlock. Georgianna had heard of her plight when the vicar, Mr Simpson, had visited the day after she had arrived to inform Lady Colyford that he had discovered the identity of the child's father.

"And can he be persuaded to marry her?" she had asked.

"That is out of the question, I am afraid. He is nobly born. I have, however, written to his family in the hope that the girl might receive some support for the boy. The parish can ill afford to support them."

Miss Ravenchurch had been quite affected by this news. "That was very well done of you, sir," she had said in admiring tones. "That poor girl is ruined. It is quite her own fault, of course, but even so, one can't help but feel sorry for her and her poor child. And it does not seem fair that she should bear all the consequences of her folly when the gentleman in question is just as much to blame."

When Lady Colyford had naturally enquired as to the identity of this gentleman, he had given her a rather condescending smile and said, "I am sure you will understand when I tell you I cannot, just at present, oblige you with his name. If any support is to be forthcoming it has occurred to me that the family might attach certain conditions, their anonymity being one of them."

"Then I assume they are a family of some note?"

The vicar had wagged a finger and said in indulgent tones, "You will not trip me up quite so easily, my lady. I will admit that they are a very distinguished family, but you must press me no further."

"I doubt there is any need for me to do so," Lady Colyford had said dryly. "It is very difficult to keep a secret in such a small community."

Georgianna set the last stitch in the garment. She hoped the father would honour his obligations to Miss Tweddle; in her view, an educated man of the world bent on his own pleasure was far more to blame than an ignorant, young country girl, who had probably had visions of a much grander future for herself.

"It is finished," she said, holding the garment up before her.

Miss Felsham smiled. "It is lovely. Your stitches are very neat."

"We shall visit the Tweddles tomorrow, Georgianna," Lady Colyford said. "I am sure they will be very pleased with your gift."

Dusk had fallen and Georgianna stood and pulled the curtains. "I think I will retire."

Miss Ravenchurch had been gently snoring, but her eyes suddenly sprang open. "I was just thinking the same thing," she said, getting to her feet. "All these parties are quite wearing me out. I wonder who will call on us tomorrow?"

Georgianna smiled and took her arm. "Who would you like to call, Miss Ravenchurch?"

She giggled like a young girl. "Oh, Lydia, do stop teasing me. You know it is Mr Antsy whom I wish to see above all others."

"Agnes! You are dreaming again. It is not Lydia but Lady Georgianna. You must make an effort to overcome this habit of slipping into the past or one day you will find yourself stuck there."

The sharpness of Lady Colyford's voice recalled Miss Ravenchurch to the present. "Of course," she said, a little flustered. "It was just that I was having such a pleasant dream and I do not think I had quite woken up."

Lady Colyford sent Georgianna a rather stern look. "And you must not encourage her, Georgianna."

Georgianna flushed. "Very well, Aunt."

Miss Felsham smiled gently at her and held out the book she had been reading. "I do not know if you have come across this novel before, Lady Georgianna. It is very good."

Georgianna took the book and thanked her.

"I am sorry you were scolded," Miss Ravenchurch said in hushed tones as they mounted the stairs. "I do not mean to do it, but I slip into a daydream and then I think it is real for a few moments."

"Who was Mr Antsy?" Georgianna asked.

Miss Ravenchurch sighed. "He was a true gentleman. I did not tend to attract the attention of very many gentlemen during my season. I was a vicar's daughter, quite plain, and had no fortune. I would never have had a season at all if my aunt had not invited me. For some reason Lydia Horston befriended me; she was very tall like you, a beauty, and very kind. She always had a host of admiring gentlemen about her. Most of them took very little notice of me but Mr Antsy frequently paid me those little extra attentions that are always so welcome."

"Such as?"

"Oh, he would always hand me up into the carriage or help me over rough ground, and he never failed to notice if I wore a new bonnet."

"He sounds a very pleasant gentleman," Georgianna said. "Were you in love with him?"

"Oh yes," Miss Ravenchurch said softly. "But it was Lydia he married."

"I am sorry."

Miss Ravenchurch smiled. "Do not be. I never had any real hope that he felt the same way and I was very pleased for Lydia. She received several offers, some from gentlemen of far higher rank than Mr Antsy but she followed her heart and was very happy in her choice."

"And her parents did not object?"

"Not at all. Her father, Sir Graham Horston, wished only for her happiness. Mr Antsy was quite well off and had an estate somewhere in Somerset. She wrote to me for some time, but I was always moving from one relative to another and we eventually lost contact. I have been very fortunate in my relatives, Lady Georgianna, and should not complain, but I must admit that I sometimes wonder how different my life might have been if I had married and had a home of my own. Good night, dear."

"Good night, Miss Ravenchurch."

Georgianna had taken to sleeping with her curtains open for she had discovered that a very special, soft light lit the valley in the early morning. She lay in bed absently watching the last of the day fade away, but her mind was far from still.

Her mother had thought to punish her by sending her to her aunt, yet she found herself content. A combination of fatigue and emotions far too long repressed had led to her unseemly bout of weeping upon her arrival but it had cleansed her somehow. Feelings of inadequacy, hurt, and bewilderment that she had never openly acknowledged before had poured from her, leaving a sense of calm in their place.

She liked the simple life she was living and the novelty of feeling that she was of some value. Whether she was helping in the garden, darning sheets, or sewing a gown for one of the local families as she had been this evening, she felt as if she was an accepted and useful member of this household.

All the accomplishments her mother had ensured that she had acquired had been for one purpose only; to catch a husband. This was the way of the world, of course, and Georgianna acknowledged it. So why had she been so stubborn in refusing to fall in with her mother's plans? Georgianna sighed. She had feared that she was as cold as her mother, but unlike her, the prospect of living life with a man she could not like had been repellent to her. Georgianna did not wish to follow her parents' example; she would be trading one miserable life for another.

Apart from when they were entertaining, her parents led largely separate lives. They tolerated each other with cool politeness. Had it always been thus? Her mother's comments on the distasteful attentions of her father suggested it had. Georgianna certainly did not wish for a husband who would treat her only as a broodmare.

But what other options did she have? She now had first-hand knowledge of three ladies, apart from her old governess, who were not in such a fortunate position as herself. Lady Brancaster's companion, Miss Bragg, had spent her life like Miss Ravenchurch, being passed from one relative to another and never knowing a home of her own. Miss Hayes, her favourite teacher at Miss Wolfraston's seminary, was clearly a gentlewoman who had fallen on hard times, for someone of her grace, elegance and beauty would not otherwise be teaching in a seminary. She had always been good humoured and patient, but Georgianna had sensed a restlessness in her and had once caught her sitting in the garden, her thoughts far away and an expression of profound sadness in her eyes. Was this the life she wished for herself?

An ironic smile curved her lips as she watched the moon inch its way from behind a cloud; although this visit was not the punishment her mother had envisaged, it had nevertheless achieved her aim. The next time she was presented with a prospective suitor she would not make hasty judgements as she had with Lord Wedmore – who had turned out to be a far better man than she had given him credit for – but give herself time to get to know him. First impressions were obviously not a reliable indicator of a person's worth.

She grimaced. Who was she to judge someone on first impressions? The pride and reserve with which she had so far conducted herself in society were likely to attract the very sort of man she wished to avoid. Lord Cranbourne had had the wit to spar with her and she had liked him the better for it, but it had been Marianne's more open character that he had preferred. Her aunt was right; she must practise the art of being more pleasing in both her manners and conversation.

She chewed her lip. There was only Mr Knight. When he had grasped her arms to steady her, she had experienced the strangest feeling. She was as tall as most men, taller than some, but when she had looked up into those strange golden eyes and felt those huge hands encircling her slender arms, she had felt feminine, dainty even. She had been shocked and surprised by his proximity and he had released her as if she had been a hot coal, stumbled backwards and gone sprawling on the stairs. Her awkwardness had caused this reaction, yet he had shown none. Instead, he had laughed and blamed it on his own clumsiness.

Perhaps she could practise on Mr Knight, after all. She need not worry if her attempts were woeful; he was totally ineligible. Her parents would never agree to her union with a nobody.

Content with this plan, she closed her eyes and tried to sleep. The night was uncomfortably warm and after first sticking her feet out from under the blankets and then throwing them off altogether, Georgianna rose and padded to the window. She pushed it up, rested her arms on the sill, and drank in the peacefulness of the midnight blue water. Her eyes followed the golden trail cast by the waxing moon to the shore beyond the house. They widened as something suddenly erupted from beneath the calm surface. A man stood waist deep in the water, his silhouette now interrupting the moon's path. As he walked slowly towards the shore, Georgianna gasped and took a step away from the window. Her eyes were not so disciplined; they roamed over the broad shoulders and down the well-defined torso to his narrow waist. Only when the water reached his hips did she turn away.

Her hand rose to her mouth, hiding a secretive smile. She had always thought the images of Greek Gods that she had seen were idealised, exaggerated. Mr Knight might be a nobody, but he would not look out of place next to any of them!

Georgianna climbed into bed and reached for the book Miss Felsham had kindly loaned to her. *Sense and Sensibility; a novel in three volumes by a lady.* Her father's library did not contain any novels and she soon became engrossed in the story. It was only when her candle began to gutter that she marked her page and closed it, feeling a pang of guilt that she had been so thoughtless. She had no idea of the cost of candles but felt sure her aunt could do without any extra expenses. The younger Dashwood sister reminded her of her own Marianne in her impulsiveness, outspokenness, and honesty, but was not as kind and considerate of others. She hoped her friend had received the letter she had written before she left Avondale; she would like to know if she was happy.

CHAPTER 6

Alexander arose with the light, dressed, and trod as lightly as a man of his size could down the stairs. His consideration proved to be unnecessary; Jack was already sweeping the floor of the barn.

Without turning his head, he said, "You're up with the lark, sir. There's a pot of coffee keeping warm on the brazier if you'd like a cup."

Alexander laughed. "I was trying not to wake you, Jack."

"There's not much chance of that," the coachman said, resting his chin on his broom and grinning. "When you've been in service as many years as I have, risin' early is as natural as breathing. Apart from that, you'll find as you get older you don't need near as much sleep as you did when you were a young 'un."

Two tin mugs were set beside the brazier. Alexander poured the coffee, handed one to Jack, and sat on an upturned wooden box.

"You can tell you were a soldier, Mr Knight. You seem as at home in this barn as a rat!"

Alexander looked up quickly. "I have been compared to many things, Jack; an elephant, a giant, an ox, but never a rat. I hope you do not mean to imply I am an unwelcome intruder."

Jack gave him a long, considering stare. "I'm not saying that, sir. I flatter myself that I'm a good judge of character and I've seen nothing as yet to make me suspect you're a wrong 'un. I don't know what your game is, but I've been around the quality all my life and I'd go bail you're no Mr anything."

Alexander looked down into his coffee for a moment, his lips twitching into a wry smile. "What gave me away?"

Jack nodded approvingly. "If you'd tried to bamboozle me, I'd have reconsidered my opinion."

"I'm an old campaigner," Alexander said softly. "I know when I've been rumbled."

"Aye, I know you are, sir. The way you unpacked your saddlebags and organised your room as fast as I could blink told me as much, never mind the quality of your horse. And if you didn't rise to at least captain, you may call me a nodcock!"

"Major, Jack. But I don't mean to tell you more than that at the moment and I hope you will keep it to yourself. My business here does not concern any of the ladies at Lake Cottage and they stand in no danger from me."

"I'm of a mind to believe you," Jack said. "I only hope it's the truth for both Lady Colyford and Lady Georgianna have had their crosses to bear and I wouldn't like to see either of them troubled further."

Alexander looked surprised. "For Lady Colyford to be living in such a retired and strange household, I can well believe it. But Lady Georgianna is barely out of the schoolroom."

"It don't mean she hasn't suffered," Jack said feelingly. "Best thing her mother ever did for her was to send her to her aunt; she's always been a cut above the rest of the family. They're a cold bunch; why, you show more affection to your horse than that young lady's ever known and so any servant at Avondale would tell you."

"I'm sorry to hear it. No wonder she is a little unusual."

Jack finished the last of his coffee and got to his feet. "Unusual she may be, but she's a good gal for all that. I don't know why I've opened my budget to you, Mr Knight, but there's something about you that inspires confidence. I won't say nothing at present, but if you give me any reason to doubt you, I won't hesitate to do so. Would you like me to saddle your horse?"

Alexander shook his head. "No, I shall be walking the fells today."

The coachman nodded to a parcel wrapped in muslin. "Cook gave me that for you when I fetched the coffee."

Alexander picked it up and pushed it into his small knapsack. "I'll see you later, Jack."

"You will if the good Lord wishes it," he said, picking up his broom. "And if you really do wish to remain incognito, sir, I'd suggest you take that ring from your finger. Can't say as I recognise it but there's no saying Lady Colyford won't."

Alexander lifted his hand and glanced at his gold signet ring. The bloodstone had a lion carved into it and his initials set below. His father had had his own ruby signet designed after he had fallen out with Alexander's grandfather, but he had named his second son after him and gifted him the ring on his eighteenth birthday. He viewed it as a lucky talisman. He did not remove it but twisted it so only the gold band faced forwards.

Alexander did not know quite how he was going to proceed in his quest to find out more about the Tweddles, but old habits were hard to break, and his first impulse was to understand his location. He started by walking around the far side of the lake and then made his way up into the fells that rose behind Buttermere.

His eyes automatically scanned the terrain whilst his mind dwelled on what he had learned of Lady Georgianna. She had been so outspoken on their first meeting, yet she had been far more awkward and quiet last evening. He had already seen her blush twice; the first time when she had thought herself conceited, and the second when she had bumped into him. He was beginning to suspect that she was not as confident as she had at first appeared. Which was the real person; the girl who was logical and literal, unafraid to challenge, or the girl who was easily embarrassed and shied away like a nervous filly?

She was certainly unlike any other beautiful young lady he had met. He might not have spent a season in London but he had not lived as a monk and had been to enough social functions abroad to understand what his father meant when he spoke of society manners. Lady Georgianna did not appear to have them;

neither mind-numbing trivialities nor false flattery tripped off her tongue. He shrugged. Lady Georgianna Voss was nothing to do with him and he must not let himself be distracted from his main purpose in coming here.

He climbed until he was surrounded only by scree and rock before he sat down on a boulder by a mountain stream and pulled out the package from his knapsack. A thick slice of pork was wedged between two slices of bread liberally smeared with butter. He ate it quickly before drinking from the clear, cold waters of the stream. He glanced up as a series of short high-pitched calls pierced the air. A golden eagle soared towards the summer pastures below.

"Perhaps you are right," he murmured, as cold fingers of wispy mist drifted down from the peak above.

He followed the stream and before long heard the dull clink of sheep's bells. Rough grass now softened the earth beneath his feet and he soon spotted the hardy animals below him dotted on either side of the stream. They were not of a kind he had seen before; their faces and legs were white, but their fleeces ranged from dark brown to grey and the males boasted impressive curling horns. A rough hut was set some way from the stream, huddled under an outcrop of rock. The shepherd, who sat on a bench outside smoking a pipe, got to his feet as he approached.

"I'd get down into the dale if I were you. The weather's turnin'; you won't be able to see your hand before your face soon."

Alexander nodded. "I thought as much. Will you go down?"

A series of deep grooves spread across the man's forehead as he frowned. "Nay, ask anyone an' they'll tell you John Tweddle sits up 'ere in all weather. I take the sheep down just 'afore dark, have a spot of supper and go to bed. I'm up with the dawn and brings 'em back up here to graze. Routine's the same every day, in summer."

"I commend you for your dedication to your duty," Alexander said, his mind searching for a way to turn this chance encounter to his advantage.

"Aye, I know my duty well enough. No one will take my grazing land or water on my watch."

"Is there a danger of such a thing happening?" Alexander asked, surprised.

"It 'appened 'afore in me granfer's day." He nodded at the stream. "Jacob Mossop blocked the stream up aways and sent it over his land. Granfer went to 'ave it out with him and they settled it with their fists. Granfer was knocked down and smashed his skull on a rock, or so *they* say. Our families have been enemies ever since."

"That's a long time to hold a grudge, Mr Tweddle."

"We've long memories up 'ere. Any road, the stream was unblocked an' I'll mek sure it stays that way."

"Forgive me for saying so, Mr Tweddle, but you're not a young man. If there was any trouble, how would you get help?"

"Bless you, lad," he said, picking up the long crook that rested against the wall of the hut. "I may be t'other side of fifty, but I can still inflict some damage with this if need be. Besides, you'd be surprised how far a whistle carries in these hills. My son would hear it down at Lane End Farm, no trouble."

"I'm glad to hear it," Alexander said. "I will bid you good day, Mr Tweddle."

"If you pass a young lass dawdling up the hill, it'll be my Molly bringin' me luncheon. I'd be obliged if you tell her I said for her to get a move on."

Alexander followed a well-worn track down the mountain, but he passed no one. However, when he was still some fifty yards above the road, he came to a small lane cut into the hillside. Sure enough, the rough, uneven track led to two long, low buildings that squatted next to each other, hidden from the road by a stand of trees. As he approached the house a door opened. Lady Colyford and Lady Georgianna stepped out, followed by a young dark-haired girl carrying a baby.

He strode up to her and smiled. "You must be Molly."

"I am," she said hesitantly.

"That's a fine-looking child you have there."

The girl clasped the baby to her as if afraid he might snatch him away.

"How do you know my name? I'm sure I've never set eyes on you 'afore."

Alexander smiled reassuringly. "I met your father up on the fell. He asked me to remind you that he is waiting for his luncheon."

A stout lady with greying hair appeared in the doorway. "Here, give me the child." She took the infant and pushed a package into the girl's hands. "Hurry or there'll be no end to his grumbling."

Molly scowled. "Why can't Ada go? I've got a bairn now too!"

She received a swift clip around the ear for her protest. "And who's fault is that, missy? You're lucky you've still got a roof over your head. Now mek yourself useful and get up the hill!"

As she scurried off, Mrs Tweddle regarded Alexander. "It was very obliging of you to deliver Mr Tweddle's message, but he should have known better than to have asked a stranger to go to the trouble."

"It was no trouble," he assured her.

A little girl chased a young black and white puppy from the house.

Mrs Tweddle frowned. "Martha! How many times have I told you dogs stay in the yard or the barn, not the house! Where have you been hiding her this time?"

The girl hung her head. "Under me bed."

"I can see you have your hands full, Mrs Tweddle," Lady Colyford said with a sympathetic smile. "We shall take up no more of your time."

"There's not a moment's peace to be had," she said. "It was very kind of you to call and for the young lady to make a gown for the bairn."

The little girl had scooped up the puppy and now stood regarding Georgianna with her large brown eyes.

"That's a very pretty ribbon, lady."

Georgianna smiled down at the child and reached up to disentangle the slender blue satin strip that Kate had somewhat inexpertly wound through her hair that morning. She held it out to the girl.

"Here, take it."

"Put the dog down first," Mrs Tweddle said sharply. "Or she'll tear it to shreds."

Martha promptly dropped the puppy, snatched at the ribbon, and raced back into the house, shouting over her shoulder, "Thank you! I must go and show Ma!"

Mrs Tweddle shook her head. "You shouldn't have given it to her, milady."

"Why not?" Georgianna said. "I have plenty more. If I had realised there were two children in the house, I would have brought another gift anyway; it does not seem fair to favour one over the other."

Mrs Tweddle sighed. "There'll be three soon, for my Ada's increasing again and we've hardly room to move as it is."

"I take it Molly is in some disgrace," Alexander said as they walked back down the lane.

"It is only to be expected," Lady Colyford said. "It is not unheard of for a country girl to be with child before wedlock if the couple are promised to each other, but if she is to avoid disgrace, she must be wed before it is born."

"The father is not local?" Alexander asked.

"No," Lady Colyford said. "If he was, he would, in all likelihood, have been dragged to the altar by now. Apparently, he is a gentleman, but the family are remaining very tight-lipped about his identity."

Alexander nodded. It seemed he was not much farther forward. Any hope that he might be able to recognise the child as a Knight at a glance had been firmly dashed. It had, he acknowledged, been ridiculous to expect it; one baby looked very much another.

Mr and Mrs Tweddle seemed honest, hardworking, and straightforward, but their daughter had seemed sullen and resentful. This might be explained by the disapproving cloud she was under, of course, yet he still found himself reluctant to accept her story. Perhaps it was because he did not like to think that one of his brother's last acts upon this earth had been a careless and less than honourable one.

Molly Tweddle had barely outgrown her childhood, if she was more than sixteen, he would be surprised. She also belonged to a respectable local family and there was certainly nothing of the trollop about her. He somehow doubted that she would have given up her innocence unless she had been promised something in return and he refused to believe that James would have led her on in such a way, especially when he had made up his mind to finally marry and settle down.

"Mr Knight?"

Alexander had been so deep in his thoughts that he had not even noticed he had come to a standstill at the end of the lane.

"Forgive me, Lady Georgianna. I was woolgathering."

"Clearly," she said dryly. "Yet I would not have thought you a daydreamer. Surely a soldier has to keep his wits about him?"

"But I am no longer a soldier."

"I had not thought old habits so easy to break," she said, a little tartly.

"They certainly are not where you are concerned, Georgianna," Lady Colyford said sternly.

Alexander watched with interest as their gazes

locked. Lady Georgianna's was the first to drop. Lady Colyford turned back to him.

"What plans have you for your future, Mr Knight?"

He smiled ruefully. "If my father has his way, I will marry and produce a bevy of grandchildren for his amusement."

Lady Colyford's laugh did not quite disguise her niece's unladylike snort. "And so you have picked up your heels and taken to the hills. You are in retreat, Mr Knight."

His smile widened. "I do not admit to it, Lady Colyford. Rather I am pausing hostilities and softening the ground for future negotiations."

"A cunning plan," she acknowledged. "And where will these negotiations take place? Where is your family home?"

"Near the Malvern Hills, ma'am." Eager to change the subject, he held out both elbows. "Please, take an arm, ladies, the path is very steep here."

Once he had seen them safely to the road, he glanced down at Lady Georgianna. "What was it you said to me whilst I was daydreaming?"

"Nothing of importance," she said, disengaging her arm. "I merely asked if you had enjoyed your walk, but now I wonder if you had your head in the clouds the entire time."

"Not in the sense you mean, ma'am. But the mist did begin to descend; it is why I came down so soon."

Lady Georgianna and Lady Colyford glanced upwards and saw the truth of his words. The thickening mist had already crept halfway down the mountain.

"You were wise to do so," Lady Colyford said. "It may or may not sink as far as the valley, but it is likely to hang on the hills all day. I must admit it is my least favourite sort of weather; it oppresses my spirits."

"Feel free to assign me any unpleasant duties you wish, if it will alleviate them somewhat," he said.

When Lady Colyford laughed he caught a glimpse of the girl she had once been. She must have left many a man languishing at her feet in her youth. It was a pity her niece did not share her sense of humour.

"Done," she said. "As the weather has cooled, you may chop some logs for the fire."

CHAPTER 7

"Has Mr Knight done something to offend you, Georgianna?" Lady Colyford asked as they entered the house.

"Was I so very rude?"

"If not rude, certainly prickly. A well-mannered young lady should not show a gentleman that she is piqued, especially when he has given her no real cause."

Georgianna frowned. "You are quite right, Aunt Hester. It is just…"

Lady Colyford raised her brows.

"I am too sensitive," Georgianna said, colouring. "When I was in Cheltenham, I was quite impressed by Lord Cranbourne, but he showed no interest in me. It was hardly surprising, for I was stiff and… prickly, whereas Marianne was natural and engaging. I was intentionally rude to Lord Wedmore at Cranbourne to discourage his interest in me, and yet when he transferred that interest to another with remarkable ease, although I was relieved, I could not help but feel a little deflated. I can have no interest in Mr Knight as both Mama and Papa would consider him ineligible but decided only last night that I would try to be more pleasing and practise my society manners on him. But when I attempted to draw him into a conversation, he did not even seem to be aware of my existence. I am a hopeless case," she said. "I had racked my brains for a suitable conversation opener, and he chose that moment to be wool-gathering!"

"I can see that you might have found that a little annoying," Lady Colyford conceded. "But every gentleman you meet should not be seen as someone whom you must either repel or attract. You must learn to like and accept yourself for who you are and then you will be more natural in any company. If you must practise anything on Mr Knight, practise being your-self. You have many fine qualities, my child."

"Such as?"

"A swift intelligence, a keen wit, and honesty, for a start. Apart from that, you have a kind heart when you are not on the defensive. Look how swiftly you gave little Martha Tweddle your ribbon, and you have shown many small kindnesses to Miss Ravenchurch. You have also taken on any task I have set you; nothing has been beneath your notice."

"I have enjoyed feeling that I am of some use."

"And so you have been. You overthink things, Georgianna. I never suffered much from self-doubt when I was a girl; I suppose I had my share of the abominable Voss pride!"

"I suspect that you were surrounded by a host of admirers, Aunt Hester."

"I was," she admitted. "And yet I made some very poor choices."

"You mean Lord Colyford?"

"Oh no," Lady Colyford said softly. "By then I did not have any choices left at all."

A dozen questions were hanging on Georgianna's lips, but Miss Ravenchurch chose that moment to run down the stairs.

"I thought I heard voices. I am so pleased you are back. Poor Leticia is not at all well; she has a terrible headache."

"It is probably the change in the weather," Lady Colyford said.

"I have bathed her head with vinegar; my mother always swore by it, you know, but it does not seem to have helped at all."

A door at the end of the hall inched open. Sally pushed it wider with her back and turned. In her hands she carried a small tray with a teapot and a cup balanced upon it, the pink tip of her tongue protruded from the side of her mouth as she concentrated on not spilling a drop. When she saw Lady Colyford she attempted a curtsy and the tray's contents began to slide. Lady Colyford stepped swiftly forwards and relieved the maid of her burden.

"Cook has made some willow bark tea for Miss Felsham," Sally said, curtsying again.

"Thank her for me, will you?" Lady Colyford said. "It is just what I would have suggested myself."

"Your hair looks very pretty, Sally," Georgianna said.

The maid grinned and twirled one of her ringlets around her finger. "Thank you, ma'am. You can't make a silk purse from a sow's ear and so I told your Kate, but she had me up at the crack of dawn anyways; said she had to practise." She glanced quickly at her mistress. "She helped me catch up with my chores afterwards, my lady. I hope I did right."

"As long as your chores got done, I have no complaints, Sally."

Mrs Ravenchurch came down the last of the stairs and took the tray. "I shall take it up to Leticia; I know just how she likes to be treated at times like these."

As she turned away, Georgianna's eyes met her aunt's. They both suddenly smiled.

"Quite," Lady Colyford said softly. "We must hope that if the tea does not do the trick, Miss Ravenchurch's soft ramblings will send her to sleep. Now, I really must do an inventory of the still room."

"May I help?"

"Of course. You may make a list of what we most need."

Georgianna followed her aunt towards the kitchen. Before they reached it, they turned into a long narrow room that she had not yet explored. She stood for a moment eyeing the shelves laden with jars and the dried herbs that hung from the ceiling before wandering slowly about the room, picking up and examining the objects that were neatly laid out on the large wooden table.

Lady Colyford looked at her in some surprise. "Georgianna, anyone would think you had never been in a stillroom before."

"I have not."

"Do not tell me that your mother has never taught

you how to make a poultice, a saline draught, lavender water, oh, or a dozen other things?"

"No. Is it so important? Mrs Adams always attended to such things."

"That is all very well, but the mistress of any establishment should make it her business to know not only how to make them, but which remedies will best alleviate a specific ailment, be it a headache, a rash, an insect bite—"

"What is this?" Georgianna asked, holding up a curved bowl in one hand and a club-shaped object in the other.

"A pestle and mortar, for grinding roots, seeds, and herbs."

"And this?" she asked, pointing with the pestle at an upturned pot with a strange spout that sat in another bowl."

"It is a still."

Georgianna's eyes brightened with interest. "What is it used for?"

"To distil the essence of things."

Georgianna looked blankly at her.

"I shall show you." Lady Colyford reached for a long shallow basket which hung on a hook by another door. "This way will take you directly to the herb garden. Fill the basket with lavender."

As Georgianna stepped into the garden, she shivered. The air was noticeably cooler yet heavy; the mist had continued its descent, enveloping the trees on the far side of the lake in its wispy tendrils and a brooding silence hung over the valley. Georgianna's lips quirked into a smile. Kate would no doubt tell her it was unnatural and eerie, but she felt cocooned and protected by it somehow.

As she walked towards the lavender bed, a repetitive dull thud disturbed the peace. Curious, she made her way towards the sound. It led her into the woodland behind the barn. She had only walked a few yards into the trees when she discovered what and who was responsible for the disturbance. Several logs were stacked up on the far side of a small glade and in its centre, a wide, circular stump jutted from the earth.

Mr Knight had placed a log vertically upon it and was vigorously attacking it with an axe. He had discarded his coat, but even so, his exertions had caused his white shirt to cling to his broad back. It seemed that chopping wood was hard work. This impression was confirmed when after the next downward stroke he left the axe embedded in the trunk, wiped his forearm across his brow, and hauled his shirt over his head.

Georgianna's brows shot up and she stepped quickly behind the trunk of an old oak that bordered the clearing. She had already witnessed the splendour of his muscled body, but she stifled a gasp as she saw the thick ridge of raised scar tissue that extended from one shoulder and swept diagonally across his back to his hip. She waited until he raised the axe once more and beat a hasty retreat.

Georgianna's skin felt tight and hot and she was strangely unsettled. She hurried back to the herb garden, knelt, and inhaled the sweet fresh scent of the lavender. She doubted very much that Mr Knight had forgotten his soldiering instincts; that wound must be a constant reminder to be vigilant. She could not help but wonder what he had been thinking about earlier. As she began to snip the lavender, she decided that if such a thing happened again, she would simply ask him.

As Georgianna came back into the stillroom, Lady Colyford replaced a jar on a shelf, walked over to a small desk, and wrote something down.

"It is only the buds we require," she said, without looking up. "Put them in the bowl I have prepared and then add one quart of water for every cup of buds."

They worked in companionable silence until Georgianna had removed all the buds. She then watched, fascinated as her aunt put the mixture in the still and lit a small fire beneath it.

"The water will turn into steam and when it cools, we shall have our first distillation. Then we shall repeat the process a second time and pour the water into a jar and seal it well. It is very useful for soothing insect bites and minor wounds or as a light scent."

"How wonderful that something so beautiful and natural can be used for so many things."

Lady Colyford smiled. "It seems your imagination has been caught, Georgianna. I have a journal full of recipes and their uses; you must read it."

"You may be sure I will."

"Pick up your basket, my dear," Lady Colyford said, reaching for another. "It will take some time and we must collect some lavender for drying whilst the buds are still tight."

All their efforts filled only two small jars. Lady Colyford labelled them and went to place them on a shelf. She paused after she had done so and reached up again to retrieve one. She returned to Georgianna and held it out to her.

"As we have a good harvest this year, I shall be generous. Take this and use it to rinse your hair, it will not only add shine and make it smooth but give it a lovely delicate scent."

"Thank you, Aunt Hester," she said, a lump in her throat. "You are very kind."

Lady Colyford cupped her cheek. "Ridiculous child. Anyone would think I had given you a great gift. You remind me of the lavender; willowy and beautiful, delicate yet strong, even if you do not yet realise it."

"Your hair smells lovely," Kate said, as she brushed out Georgianna's long tresses. "I only hope I can do it justice; I was that mortified when you came up last night with some of it trailing down your back."

"You are doing very well considering you are settling into a new role. Keep it simple," Georgianna suggested. "A knot on top and a few trailing ringlets will be perfectly acceptable. Just make sure you pin it well."

Kate took her words to heart and Georgianna needed all her fortitude not to grimace as she scraped her scalp again and again with the pins.

There were only three of them for dinner as Miss Felsham had some soup in her room and Miss Ravenchurch refused to leave her side until she was quite recovered.

"I'm not sure I approve of you leaving your house open as you do, Lady Colyford," Mr Knight said, as the first course was removed.

"Whether you approve or not is immaterial. We

are a small community, Mr Knight. There is no crime here."

"Yet Mr Tweddle informed me only today of the feud between his family and the Mossops."

"Ancient history," she said. "The families may not have anything to do with each other, but there has not been any trouble that I know of since I have been here."

"But would you know if there had been?" he asked.

Lady Colyford smiled. "Our vicar keeps me tolerably well informed on local events. He is a pompous fool, but he does keep an eye on his flock, and they are a God-fearing bunch. Will you come with us to church tomorrow?"

"I will," he said. "I should like to see this pillar of the community for myself." He reached for the wine. "Shall I pour?"

"Please do."

"If you do not wish to lock your house, perhaps you should at least consider employing a footman."

Lady Colyford raised her brows. "How disappointing. I had thought you were not quite in the common style, Mr Knight, but now I see you are like so many others of your sex; you do not think a group of women can survive without a man. If I had wished for a footman, I would already have employed one."

"The gardener, the postman who does your shopping, and the fishermen who bring you their spare catch aside, if you had wished to show that you could survive without a man, I think that you have already proved your point. But why continue to labour it when a footman could only add to your comfort?"

"How long do you intend to stay?" Lady Georgianna asked hastily, noticing the flash of annoyance in her aunt's eyes and for some strange reason wishing to shield Mr Knight from her ire.

"Oh, a while yet," he said. "There are many more fine walks to be had, I am sure."

She smiled wistfully. "I envy your freedom to roam where you will."

"You enjoy walking, ma'am?"

"Yes," she said. "Our grounds are extensive at Avondale, but although they are very pleasant, they are manicured and tamed."

"There is no reason you should not walk around the lake if you take your maid with you," Lady Colyford said. "I would not wish you to go alone at this time of year for you are likely to stumble upon visitors."

Georgianna smiled. "I think I shall."

"I would be happy to walk with you around the lake if Lady Colyford does not object," Mr Knight said. "If you are not afraid to climb a little, there is a lovely spot by one of the waterfalls."

"Thank you, Mr Knight. Perhaps after church tomorrow."

Sally hurried into the room carrying a tray. She placed it on the side and began transferring the dishes to the table.

"Do not place them all in a huddle, Sally," Lady Colyford snapped.

It was the first time Georgianna had heard her aunt show any degree of impatience with the maid. The girl flushed and began to spread them a little further apart and in her haste, she knocked Mr

Knight's wine glass over. She froze, watching the deep red liquid spread over the cloth and drip into his lap.

"I'm that sorry, sir," she gasped, snatching up a napkin and dabbing at the cloth in an attempt to stem the flow. She then hurried over to the sideboard and grabbed another. Returning to the table, she folded it into a pad and made as if to treat his pantaloons to the same treatment.

Mr Knight caught her arm and removed the napkin from her grasp.

"Thank you, Sally," he said, unfurling it with a flick of his wrist and placing it over the stain.

"That will be all," Lady Colyford said in a rather strangled voice.

She had barely left the room when Lady Colyford raised her hand to her mouth, not quite managing to repress a hoarse snort.

"I apologise, Mr Knight," she gasped. "She is a good girl really."

"I am pleased you found the episode so amusing," he said, a little stiffly.

"I am sorry," she said, raising her napkin to dab at the tears now leaking from her eyes, "but if you could have seen your face when she went to mop up the wine from your lap…"

Georgianna felt her own lips twitch but wishing to restore some harmony, she rose impulsively to her feet and reached for the glass jug which housed the wine. "Let me refill your glass, sir."

It seemed that the enthusiasm with which Kate had pierced her scalp had been for nothing; the lavender water had done its job too well. The suddenness of her movement combined with the smooth silkiness of her hair caused it to escape the pins that had been somewhat haphazardly aimed at the large coil of hair behind her head. Without the benefit of any braids to further anchor it, it fell in random clumps about her shoulders.

As a flush of mortification began to brighten her cheeks, her gaze turned towards her aunt who had now fallen into unrestrained whoops of laughter.

"I am sorry, my dear," she wheezed, clutching her sides. "But p-perhaps Mr Knight has a point, a-after all; we do seem to be housing a m-most inept group of s-servants."

Georgianna's eyes met their guest's. As his shoulders began to shake, she felt the corners of her mouth tilt upwards. She replaced the jug with a shaking hand as ripples of laughter swept through her, sank back into her chair, and abandoned herself to the general mirth.

CHAPTER 8

Alexander lay with his hands behind his head watching the soft buttery light that heralded the new day, a lazy grin upon his lips. What an extraordinary household this was; an earl's sister who eschewed men and permitted the clumsiest of girls to wait on her, an earl's daughter whose maid could not successfully dress her hair, a spinster who came for a holiday and never returned home, a garrulous companion, and now a duke's son travelling incognito, living in the barn! His father would never believe the half of it!

He chuckled as a picture of Lady Georgianna drifted into his mind, her ridiculously deep, blue eyes wide with shock as her hair tumbled about her shoulders. With his own lap drenched in wine, dinner had turned into a roaring farce and Lady Colyford had enjoyed every moment. Her unrestrained laughter had been quite outrageous but infectious, nevertheless. He had half expected Lady Georgianna to run from the room in confusion or freeze him with an icy glare for daring to laugh at her, but she had surprised him; he had not thought her capable of laughing at herself. The transformation had been quite breathtaking. The light of laughter in her eyes had warmed them and he had discovered two engaging dimples beside her delicately curved lips when they spread into a wide smile.

He rolled off the bed as he heard Jack moving about downstairs. The old man had intimated that Lady Georgianna had known very little joy in her life and Alexander discovered that he felt quite privileged to have witnessed the change in her last evening. He would, he realised, quite like to see those dimples again.

He was to be rewarded with this sight sooner than he had expected. Lady Colyford led the way to church with Miss Felsham, who had recovered from her indisposition, on one side and Miss Ravenchurch on the other, leaving Lady Georgianna and Alexander to follow behind.

"I am pleased to see you had a spare pair of trousers, sir," Lady Georgianna said softly, a smile in her eyes if not on her lips.

He answered with mock solemnity. "It is indeed fortunate, ma'am. And let us hope that with the added protection of your rather fetching bonnet, your hair will not escape its confines."

Her smile widened and her dimples obligingly peeped.

"It would not dare. This morning, I enjoyed the services of Grantley, my aunt's maid."

"And was your own maid's nose not put out of joint?"

"Not at all. Kate watched with close attention and has gratefully accepted Grantley's kind offer to teach her. She was a general maid at home and was only meant to accompany me on the journey."

"I see," Alexander said.

But he did not see. Although Lady Georgianna's words had explained her maid's incompetence, he could not understand what Lady Westbury had been about to send a girl barely out of the schoolroom so far with only a young maid as ignorant in the ways of the world as her mistress, and a coachman who should have been retired by now. It showed a shocking negligence of duty on her part.

Mr Simpson read both a morning and evening sermon on a Sunday in summer, for although the local population was not large, the chapel was extremely modest in size. Lady Colyford had rented a pew for her small entourage, but it was not long enough to accommodate Alexander, as she explained to him as they entered the chapel.

"Do not concern yourself, ma'am," he smiled. "I shall take an empty pew towards the back for I will need to sit sideways if I am not to break my knees."

There was no obstacle to this plan as there could not have been more than twenty-five in the congregation. The Tweddles were ranged on one side of the aisle and were exchanging greetings with some of the people on the other side. He found it interesting that the small group who were squashed into a pew immediately opposite them, kept their gazes fixed directly ahead during these exchanges. His brows rose as the Tweddles then turned to the front and the family who had studiously avoided greeting them, turned and exchanged a few smiles and nods with various acquaintances who sat in the Tweddles' half of the chapel. It was like watching a highly tuned dance. He could only assume that the unknown family were the Mossops.

His gaze shifted to the lectern as Mr Simpson mounted the steps and placed a book upon it. He looked to be somewhere in his forties, but his sandy hair was already thinning, emphasising his round, pink face. Once he had opened his book, he regarded the congregation and nodded repeatedly, causing his rather short neck to disappear behind an impressive double chin.

"Almighty and most merciful Father, we have erred and strayed from thy ways like lost sheep; we have followed too much the devices and desires of our own heart; we have offended against thy holy laws…"

Alexander's attention began to wander and as his eyes brushed over the people in front of him, he saw Molly Tweddle, who sat at the end of her pew, tilt her head to the side and reach up to smooth her hair. Simultaneously, the young man opposite lifted his hand to rub his cheek and as he lowered it, Alexander saw that he briefly held four fingers up. He was in no doubt that they had communicated something to each other. A wolfish grin curved his lips. He was not yet sure what the signal meant, but he was on the scent of something. Could it be that he had stumbled upon a case of forbidden love? It was a tale as old as the hills that surrounded this valley, after all. Had Molly been too terrified to admit that she had lain with a Mossop and so laid the blame at the door of someone who could not gainsay her?

"When the wicked man turneth away from the wickedness that he hath committed, and doeth that which is lawful and right…"

Alexander observed the Mossop boy drop his head at these words. He watched the couple carefully for the rest of the sermon, but nothing more passed between them and he began to doubt what he had seen. But as the young man left his pew, he sent a swift sideways glance towards Molly before striding down the aisle, a scowl marring his dark, brooding features.

Lady Colyford's party were the last to rise. The vicar accompanied Lady Colyford down the aisle. She leaned down and said something in his ear. Alexander thought the smile that played about her mouth when she rose, rather mischievous. That she had been relaying some information about him became clear when Mr Simpson sent a surprised glance in his direction and a small frown puckered his otherwise smooth forehead. He was a man of short stature and as they came to a stop in front of Alexander, he was forced to tilt his head and lean slightly backwards to meet his gaze.

"I am happy to see you here today, Mr Knight," he said. "It is not often that any of the visitors who pass through Buttermere take the time to pay their observance to the Lord."

"I would not have liked to miss your sermon, Mr Simpson. I have found the last hour most illuminating."

Mr Simpson's frown was replaced with a self-satisfied smile. "I like to think that my observations on the human condition are both instructional and apposite. I must admit that when Lady Colyford informed me that she had a man who was not a member of her family staying with her, I was a little alarmed."

"It would be more accurate to say that I am staying in her barn or stable, Mr Simpson."

For a brief moment the vicar was speechless, a rare event, Alexander felt sure.

"The barn?" His amazed gaze turned to Lady Colyford. "Whilst I fully understand and approve of your reluctance to welcome a stranger into your house, ma'am, having now met Mr Knight, I cannot but feel that he deserves better. He is clearly a gentleman of some discernment."

Lady Colyford raised her brows, the smile still playing about her mouth. "But surely it was my Christian duty to offer succour to a weary traveller when the inn was full. Was not Jesus born in a stable? Surely if it was good enough for the son of God, it is good enough for Mr Knight?"

The vicar bristled with disapproval but unwilling to offend someone of Lady Colyford's rank, he managed an unconvincing smile. "Very amusing, Lady Colyford." He turned to Alexander. "Perhaps it would be better if you came to stay at the vicarage, sir. I have more than enough room."

"Thank you, Mr Simpson, you are very kind, but I am quite content with my situation at present. I think it is good for a man to occasionally experience more humble conditions than is his wont."

The vicar nodded approvingly. "Very true, Mr Knight, very true. You seem a very sensible young man. I hope you will pay me a visit, at least, before you leave the area."

"You may be sure I will, sir."

"You seem to delight in teasing the vicar, ma'am," he said to Lady Colyford as they strolled back.

"I must take my amusement where I can, Mr Knight. If he would refrain from offering us both his company and advice quite so often, I would be less tempted to do so."

"Ah," he said with a rueful smile. "Now I understand. I realised last evening that I had taken a misstep when I offered you some."

"Indeed. But at least I later admitted that you had a point."

"But only, I think, because Sally proved it for me."

Lady Colyford smiled ruefully. "You are very perceptive, Mr Knight; I have always been a stubborn creature."

"Do you require a rest before we take our walk about the lake, Lady Georgianna?" he asked as they reached the house.

"Not at all, sir. I will go and change my shoes for something sturdier and will be with you in a moment."

Kate brought the requested half-boots with a lagging step. "It seems to me, ma'am, that you've already had as much exercise as any lady could wish for today."

The maid stepped back in surprise when she encountered a frosty stare.

"I have given you a great deal of leeway thus far, Kate. I see that I have perhaps been too lenient. It is no part of your duties to inform me when I have or have not had enough exercise or anything else for that matter."

Kate immediately tipped into a swift curtsy. "No, milady. I meant no offence."

She rushed forwards and knelt by Georgianna's feet.

Georgianna sighed. "Get up, Kate. I can put on my own boots. I do not wish to be overly harsh with you, but I will tolerate neither impertinence nor disrespect. I realise that you have no great love for the outdoors, and I would not ask you to come if it was not necessary. Mr Knight is to show me a local beauty spot and I cannot go with him completely unattended."

The maid looked penitent. "No, that you can't, ma'am. I'm sorry if I seemed disrespectful when you have been so patient with me."

"You have been thrust into a role that you were ill-prepared to take on and I have been very impressed with your attempts to learn. I heard how you got up at the crack of dawn to practise on Sally."

Kate rolled her eyes. "And a fat lot of good that did."

"It did more good than you realise, Kate," Georgianna said softly. "It made me laugh and laughter has not played a great part in my life."

The young maid frowned, knelt, and began to lace Georgianna's boots.

"There ain't a servant at Avondale that don't know that, ma'am."

Georgianna's eyebrows rose in surprise. Although she knew the butler and housekeeper to be her allies, she had not known that she had the sympathy of the remainder of the servants.

Misreading her expression for one of censure, Kate flushed. "I'm sorry, ma'am. There I go again, speaking out of turn. Please don't say anything to Lady Westbury; she might well turn me off."

"You need not fear, Kate. I am not angry. Although I cannot like being the subject of gossip at Avondale."

"Not gossip, ma'am, never that. We might be told to be invisible, but that don't make us deaf and blind! I may not have been at Avondale above two years but even I could see how much you were to be pitied. The way you've all but been locked away in the school-room or punished for the slightest thing ain't right. I was glad when I heard that you were going to that seminary, for if you've ever had a friend, I've never heard of it. Everyone was right glad that you were going on a visit with another young lady, although it put the mistress in a right temper. And Stokes is not liked; no one approves of the way she runs to her with tales about you."

"I can't say I'm overly fond of her myself. I much prefer you as a maid, Kate."

The girl flushed with pleasure. "I might speak out of turn every now and then, ma'am, but it is my plea-sure to serve you, and you may be sure I'll never betray you. I'd rather cut out my tongue first!"

Georgianna felt quite touched and a little unwor-thy. "I do not feel that I deserve such loyalty, Kate. You say you have been at Avondale for two years, yet I am ashamed to admit that I did not even know your name."

Kate laughed. "And why should you? There are more servants at Avondale than you can shake a stick at."

A reminiscent smile curved Georgianna's lips. "I did make a friend at the seminary, Kate. Her name was Marianne. In my place, she would have known your name."

"It seems as you were fond of her, ma'am."

"I am," Georgianna said. "I had hoped to receive a letter from her by now. I wrote to her before I left home."

"I wouldn't fret about that, my lady. Goodness knows how long it takes a letter to reach here."

"Perhaps I am being impatient," she acknowledged, rising to her feet. "Now come, we have kept Mr Knight waiting long enough."

With no more complaint, the maid followed her from the room. She was to be delayed a little longer as her aunt pulled her to one side before she left the house.

"Keep your wits about you, Georgianna. Remember we hardly know Mr Knight and people are not always what they appear to be."

"I thought you liked him?" she said, surprised.

"I do. I'm not past the age of appreciating a handsome young man. But remember he is ineligible. He has a singularly charming smile and it would not do for you to develop a tendre for him."

"You need not worry, Aunt. I do not believe I am of a romantic disposition. However, the fact that he is ineligible combined with the humour we shared last night, has somehow freed me from my inhibitions. I shall be myself in his company for good or ill."

"Very well. Go and enjoy your walk but leave your parasol. The lake is surrounded by trees enough to provide you with shade."

Miss Ravenchurch tripped into the hall. "I thought I heard voices. Are you going for a walk in the park, dear?"

Mindful of her aunt's feelings on Miss Ravenchurch's lapses, she said, "No, I'm going for a walk around the lake with Mr Knight."

The little lady looked bemused. "But, Lydia, I do not believe we know a Mr Knight."

Lady Colyford gave a long, low sigh, before taking Miss Ravenchurch by the arm and leading her back into the drawing room.

The first part of the walk was very pleasant and relatively flat. But as they reached the opposite shore, they turned onto a narrow path that wound beneath the trees and soon climbed steeply. Forced to walk in single file she did not immediately notice that Kate had dropped behind. When she did turn, she saw her sitting on a rock some distance below, her shoe in one hand.

"I'm sorry, ma'am," she called up, her voice barely discernible above the rushing waters that were not yet visible, but clearly close at hand. "I've got a stone in my shoe and my legs are trembling like you wouldn't believe. I can scrape a grate or bash a carpet without breaking a sweat but walking up this hill has floored me."

Georgianna caught the gist of her words and observing her maid's pink cheeks and glistening fore-head, said, "How much further, Mr Knight?"

"Only another hundred yards or so."

Georgianna nodded decisively. "It seems a shame to climb all this way and not be rewarded with a sight of the waterfall." She cupped her hands around her mouth and shouted, "Wait for me there, Kate, we won't be long."

The hiss of the waters became a thundering roar and Georgianna quickened her step, eager to see the torrent. Mr Knight turned and smiled at her and she stumbled over a protruding root. She gasped as the ground came quickly towards her, sure she was about to suffer the indignity of sprawling in the dirt, but hard, firm hands suddenly gripped her arms and she was hauled upwards before that humiliating event occurred.

She found herself pinned against Mr Knight's body for a moment and discovered she could not breathe. Her startled eyes flew to his and widened as she saw they had turned from golden to liquid honey. They were not lit with amusement but some other emotion she did not recognise. She frowned as she registered alarm and relief in equal measures. How could she feel afraid and yet safe in the same moment? This time he did not release her but bent his head.

"Careful, Lady Georgianna," he said, his voice strangely gruff. "I would not have you suffer any injury on my watch."

His warm breath tickled her ear and whispered against her neck. It was not an unpleasant feeling and she felt herself shiver. Deciding she would analyse her strange reactions later, she pulled herself together and smiled. "I have suffered no injury, sir, and I thank you for saving me from a fall."

He released her arms and held out his hand. "Come, it is only a few more steps."

Her gloved hand became lost in his as he led her to a break in the trees. Her mouth parted in wonder as she witnessed the raw power of the tumbling white waters before her. They hurtled down a deep ravine, foaming scornfully over and around large boulders whose hard edges had been smoothed and burnished to a bright shine by their clamorous passage. If Mr Knight made her feel feminine and small, this splendid example of nature's magnificence reminded her of how completely insignificant she was in this landscape.

She turned to her companion, her eyes sparkling. "Thank you, Mr Knight. From afar the falls look pretty and quite benign, I am glad that I have seen their true nature and majesty."

He had stooped to catch her words and she saw his eyes also shone with exhilaration. A slow smile curved his lips and her gaze dropped to them. Her aunt had called his smile charming and she supposed it was, but it was also disturbing and quite mesmerising. She felt the strangest urge to lift her finger and trace their finely sculpted edges.

"My heart's drumming fit to bust, milady, but I made it!"

The strange spell that had briefly gripped her was broken. Georgianna smiled at her maid. "And what do you think of the view, Kate? Was it worth it?"

Kate dutifully looked at the gushing cataract. "My, what a lot of water. It's a pity it's so far away, for what I wouldn't give for a drink of it right now."

Georgianna's eyes sought out Mr Knight's and she

was pleased to see her amusement at this prosaic response was shared.

"The waterfall feeds a stream further down," he said. "I shall take you to it so you can quench your thirst."

CHAPTER 9

Alexander stripped off his coat and neckcloth before strolling to the clearing where he had chopped the wood. He scanned the stacked trunks for a moment before selecting a long one that was not too thick. Hoisting it over his shoulder, he strode to the vegetable garden and regarded the three lumps of rock that sat in the bean, potato, and cabbage beds. Not only were they unsightly but they significantly reduced the planting area of the beds.

Dropping his log by one of the boulders, he strode into the woodland that surrounded the cottage and chose a rock that was of a reasonable size but that he could lift without too much exertion. He placed it close to one of the boulders and wedged his log between it and the offending object. Pressing his not inconsiderable weight upon the end of the log, he managed to lift the rock and turn it over. By the time he had shifted it to the edge of the woodland, he was coated with sweat.

Undaunted he went back for the second boulder. He had moved it halfway across the garden when he glanced up and saw Jack leaning against the corner of the house, a tankard in his hand.

"You're as strong a man as I've ever seen, sir, but pause a moment and take a drink of this cider. It might not be what you're used to, but it's refreshing for all that."

Alexander grinned, dropped the log, and strode over to the coachman. "Thank you, Jack. It will be most welcome."

He drained the tankard in a few thirsty gulps.

"Never tell me Lady Colyford asked you to move those great boulders on such a muggy, hot day and a Sunday to boot?"

"She did not," Alexander confirmed. "But I have been used to a great deal of physical exercise, Jack. A walk to church and a little excursion up to the waterfall has left me still restless."

"Has it now?" Jack said. "I 'eard as you took Lady Georgianna up there. Cook says Kate has been moaning that she's got a blister as big as a hen's egg."

"I can well believe it. She found the climb quite challenging, I think."

"And Lady Georgianna?"

"She made no complaint, Jack. And she certainly enjoyed the view. I have never seen her so animated."

The coachman nodded. "I'm pleased to hear it, sir. And have you discovered what you came for, yet?"

"Not quite, Jack, but I believe I have made a little progress."

"Well, if there's anything I can do to help, let me know."

Alexander considered his words. "There might be something, Jack. I am a little reluctant to show my face at the inn as it seems to be a beacon for visitors. If you do happen to find yourself there, perhaps you could keep an ear out for any gossip about two local families; the Mossops and the Tweddles."

"I reckon I could do that, sir. I haven't much else to do of an evening and I'm rather partial to a tankard of ale."

Alexander went back to work, an ironic smile on his lips. It seemed he had the coachman's trust, but he was not sure he deserved it. If Jack knew how close he had come to kissing Lady Georgianna earlier, he might sing a different tune. His motivation in hauling her against him had been pure; he had only wished to prevent her fall and steady her. He had half expected her to flinch as she had before, but she had not. Those large eyes had held surprise and confusion. He had felt a little tremor run through her when he had whispered in her ear that had certainly not been caused by disgust. His pulse had quickened at her response and only the calm composure with which she had thanked him had recalled him to his senses. Shaking his head, he again applied himself to his lever. He must not be distracted from his purpose or his father would begin to fret.

When he let himself into the house that evening, he found only Lady Colyford and Lady Georgianna in the drawing room.

"I hope Miss Felsham is not indisposed again?"

"No, she is in good health," Lady Colyford assured him. "It is Miss Ravenchurch who is not quite herself.

117

Miss Felsham is watching over her. I shall relieve her after dinner."

"I hope it is nothing too serious, ma'am?"

"Let us hope not," Lady Colyford said pensively.

"I can always ride for the doctor if you wish," Alexander offered.

Lady Colyford smiled. "You are very obliging, Mr Knight, but I hope that will not prove necessary." Swiftly changing the subject, she said, "When I stepped outside earlier, I could not help but notice that you had removed all three rocks from my vegetable garden. Thank you."

"It was my pleasure, Lady Colyford. I am not used to being idle."

"No, I don't suppose you are. How long is it since you left the army?"

"A little over three months, ma'am."

"And what position did you hold?"

Alexander found himself reluctant to tell an outright lie to his hostess and frowned.

"Perhaps you do not enjoy speaking of that time Mr Knight?" Lady Georgianna said. "I expect it holds some painful memories for you."

He smiled gratefully at her. "Indeed, it does, ma'am."

Sally came into the room holding a letter. "A groom has ridden over from Brigham, ma'am. He brought this with him and is waiting for a reply. Cook has put dinner back half an hour so you have time to answer it as he wants to get back before it gets dark. He says the moon won't be full for another four days and he won't attempt these roads at night without its full light."

"Thank you, Sally. I shall answer it directly." She took the letter rather gingerly, avoiding a large splodge of grease transferred by the girl's fingers, went over to a desk that was set in a discreet corner of the room, and began to peruse its contents.

Alexander felt his senses heighten and his mind whirled. Four days! The Mossop lad had held up four fingers. In four days, the moon would be full and as long as the night was clear, it would be the perfect opportunity for a secret assignation.

"Mr Knight?"

He laughed. "You have caught me wool-gathering again, Lady Georgianna. I deserve to be flogged for my rudeness!"

She smiled. "I do not think that punishment would match the crime, sir. I will settle for knowing your thoughts."

"Georgianna, we have been invited to visit Lady Brigham for a few days. Her son has told her of your chance meeting upon the road and she wishes to meet you. I am tempted; I am very well aware that I have little to offer you in the way of entertainment and I have not seen her for some months now."

Georgianna reluctantly turned her gaze away from Mr Knight.

"I am very happy here, Aunt, and do not need to be entertained. However, if it will afford you some amusement to visit with your friend, I am happy to go with you."

Alexander felt his bubble of excitement burst. "Do you think Allerdale is the man to entertain Lady Georgianna?"

Lady Colyford raised haughty brows. "I find you presumptuous, sir."

"I do not mean to be," he said. "I have met him only once, but his reputation is not unknown to me."

"He is a very different creature when he is under his mother's eye," Lady Colyford said sharply. "I do not approve of the way he conducts himself when he is in Town but I would ask you to remember that he is my godson. He has not always been as troublesome as he is now, but he took the death of the young man who drowned in the lake very much to heart and has sought distraction in a variety of foolish ways. Lady Georgianna will certainly be in no danger from him now he knows she is my niece."

"I bow to your superior knowledge, ma'am," he said coolly, suddenly every inch a marquess.

Lady Colyford stared at him intently for a moment, a ghost of a smile curving her lips. "Do not get upon your high ropes, Mr Knight, or you will be a very uncomfortable dinner companion. The truth is I am a little distracted this evening. I would very much like to visit Lady Brigham; I was rather fond of Allerdale before he became quite so wild and I would help him if I can. Perhaps Lady Brigham and I could put our heads together and discover a way of keeping him at home where he is always more manageable. But I must admit, Miss Ravenchurch's condition is worrying me."

Alexander unbent a little. "Perhaps you should send for the doctor."

"It is not her physical health that concerns me. She sometimes slips into the past and thinks herself a young girl again. I can usually recall her from these starts by a few sharp words but today she only became upset and more confused. She is sedated at the moment and I hope that after a rest she will be herself again. If she is not, I am not at all sure I should leave her."

"Miss Felsham will take good care of her and you may be sure I will make myself available if she needs any assistance."

"Thank you, Mr Knight, that does put my mind at ease a little. Leticia is certainly more patient with her than I, and if you would agree to sit with Miss Ravenchurch in the event Leticia needs a rest, I would feel much happier."

"Consider it done, ma'am."

"And if her condition worsens, would you ride over and let me know? Brigham is only two hours away."

"Yes, Lady Colyford, I will."

"Very well, I shall write our acceptance."

"When do we go, Aunt?"

"Wednesday," she replied, her quill already flying across the paper.

Alexander did not know quite how he had gone from disliking the scheme to ensuring it went ahead but acknowledged that Lady Colyford had been quite right to reprimand him for his presumption; Lady Georgianna was no concern of his. Besides, he would do much better without the distraction.

"Mr Knight?"

He looked ruefully at Lady Georgianna. "I was wondering if you were looking forwards to renewing your acquaintance with Lord Allerdale. After all, your first meeting did not go as smoothly as it could have."

"Perhaps not," she acknowledged. "But I cannot in all good conscience lay all the blame for that at Lord Allerdale's door. My own manners were not all they should have been."

"You certainly put him in his place," Alexander said dryly.

Georgianna grimaced. "Yes, and I delighted in giving him as poor an opinion of me as I had of him. But I think everyone deserves a second chance, don't you?"

"Do you refer to yourself or Allerdale?" Alexander asked, not entirely satisfied with her answer.

"Both," she said. "If my aunt was fond of him at one point, he cannot be all bad."

"There, it is done," Lady Colyford said, rising from her chair. "Take it to the kitchen will you, Georgianna? I would ring for Sally, but I would rather it reached Lady Brigham without any chicken fat, soup, or anything else marring its appearance."

"Of course, Aunt Hester."

Having decided that he would do better without the beautiful distraction that Lady Georgianna provided, Alexander found himself racking his brains for another excuse to be in her company before she left.

When she returned he said, "If you would like to go for another walk tomorrow, Lady Georgianna, we could take a stroll to Crummock Water."

"Thank you, Mr Knight. I would like to very much, but only if it is an easy walk for Kate's feet are rather sore."

"Yes, I heard she has a blister the size of a hen's egg."

Lady Georgianna laughed. "I have discovered she is prone to exaggeration; it is not as bad as she has professed. I have treated it with an ointment made from bifoil which I found in the stillroom."

"Well done, Georgianna," Lady Colyford said.

"Do not sound so surprised, Aunt! Did I not say that I would read your recipes?"

"Indeed, you did, child, but what people say and what they do are not always the same thing."

"I hope I always do what I have promised," she said. "I must admit I find the recipes fascinating. Have you a book that explains why the herbal remedies work?"

"I am afraid I have not," Lady Colyford admitted. "I have merely copied any recipes I have come across but there is an extensive library at Brigham, perhaps you will find what you seek there."

Georgianna retired to bed early keen to consider the day's events. She dismissed Kate as soon as she had helped her undress and sat at her toilet table slowly brushing out her hair. She had been surprised when she had discovered that Marianne did not wear a nightcap but ever since that night at the inn, she had also broken the habit. She found it not only more comfortable with her long locks unrestrained but also comforting somehow.

When she was satisfied that no more tangles roughened her hair, she placed her brush carefully on the table and looked into the mirror. A slow smile spread across her face at what she saw. No longer did she dwell on the thinness of her face or the jutting bones of her shoulders; they had been superseded by the softening of her expression, the delicate colour that had bloomed in her cheeks, and the new self-awareness that lurked in her eyes.

She had always felt awkward and unassured; she had covered these feelings at the seminary by holding everyone at arm's length until Marianne and Charlotte had somehow broken through her defences. She had thought Charlotte's terrible shyness a weakness to be despised, but when her fellow pupil had received a letter from her great aunt inviting her to visit and she had seen the disbelief, hope, and fear in Charlotte's eyes, she had realised that they shared the same disease; a lack of self-esteem and extreme loneliness. She had felt ashamed of the superior mantle she had thrown over her own weaknesses and quick-witted Marianne had not been slow to lay her hypocrisy bare.

That she had done so with humour rather than cruelty spoke volumes about her character. Georgianna had discovered that she shared Marianne's humour if not the freedom with which to express it. But then Marianne had grown up secure in the love of her parents and had been encouraged to form and voice her opinions, however outrageous.

Only now that she had become acquainted with her aunt, could Georgianna truly appreciate the value of family. There was a bond between them that could not be denied. Their physical similarities were clear, but that was not what bound them. Her aunt had an independent spirit and straightforwardness that she admired and recognised in herself, even though her mother had tried to extinguish these traits at every turn.

Georgianna's smile widened and her expression softened even further. She could not deny that Mr Knight had also played his part in her transformation. She had witnessed both Lady Brancaster and Marianne blossom under the attentions of a gentleman, but she had not fully understood their reactions. She had certainly not envied them; they had seemed to her illogical, uncomfortable, and contradictory; one moment they were the best of friends, the next they barely acknowledged each other.

Now she thought she understood these reactions a little better. Mr Knight made her feel feminine, attractive, and protected. She was very aware of his size, his smell, and his manliness. She was, she acknowledged, attracted to him and it was not an unpleasant experience, but armed with the knowledge that he was completely ineligible, she had not allowed her heart to rule her head.

She would walk with him tomorrow and enjoy their burgeoning friendship, as well as these new sensations. The fear she had briefly experienced when he had held her so close was because these feelings were new and strange, but she felt sure they were natural. She wished to explore and examine them more closely. If she could feel this way about a mere nobody, surely there was hope that she might meet a more suitable marriage prospect who might also inspire such feelings?

Although she was not completely clear on what happened between a man and a woman in the privacy of their bedchamber, she felt sure a mutual attraction must make it far more bearable. Her mother's disgust at what she called her father's mauling, must stem from not only her cold nature, but a lack of respect and attraction to him. She would not make the same mistake.

CHAPTER 10

Georgianna picked up her parasol and left her bedchamber. She had not gone more than a few steps when she heard the sound of a door opening further along the landing. Turning, she saw Miss Ravenchurch step out of her room dressed only in her shift.

"Lydia," she said querulously. "I do not mind you borrowing my parasol, I am sure, but you really should have asked me first."

Georgianna rested it against the wall, bade Kate wait for her downstairs, and went quickly towards her, concerned. Never had she heard the little lady speak in such a manner.

"Miss Ravenchurch, you are mistaken, the parasol is certainly mine."

She took her arm and tried to steer her back into her chamber but stepped back quickly when Miss Ravenchurch shook her off with surprising strength, a scowl on her usually kindly face.

"You are going for a walk with Mr Antsy, aren't

you? Not only have you stolen my parasol you wish to also rob me of my hopes and dreams."

"No! It is Mr Knight who is to accompany me."

Miss Ravenchurch looked confused. "Mr Knight?"

Georgianna took her arm more firmly this time, led her back into her chamber, and took her over to the window.

"I am not Lydia, and we are not in Town but at Buttermere. Look out of the window and you will see the lake."

Miss Ravenchurch stared blankly out of the window, fear and confusion in her eyes. After a few moments, she turned back to Georgianna and smiled.

"Good morning, dear. How nice of you to pay me a visit. I must have overslept this morning. How shocking that I am not even dressed yet."

"How are you this morning, Agnes?"

They both turned to Miss Felsham, who stood in the open doorway.

"I am very well, thank you, Leticia. Although I do not understand how I came to sleep in so long this morning."

Miss Felsham's understanding smile held more than a hint of relief. "It is of no matter, Agnes. I shall leave you to get dressed. I believe Mr Knight is waiting for you downstairs, Lady Georgianna."

"Thank you. I shall come directly."

Miss Felsham closed the door softly behind them. "Lady Georgianna, would you mind telling me what you were doing in Miss Ravenchurch's room?"

Georgianna briefly explained their encounter.

"Oh dear," Miss Felsham said gently. "She is getting worse."

Georgianna voiced the suspicion that had more than once occurred to her. "Is she going mad?"

"I suppose it is a sort of madness," Miss Felsham sighed. "My father also suffered from it for quite some time. I prefer to think of it as a disease for which there is, unfortunately, no cure. His last years were very difficult and troublesome. I came here for a rest when it was finally all over but found it so peaceful, I remained, and then, I like to be needed, you see, and at that time, I felt that Hester needed a friend."

"At *that* time?"

"Yes, I am beginning to think, however, that rather than helping her, both myself and now Miss Ravenchurch, are rather hindering her."

"I do not understand," Georgianna said.

Miss Felsham smiled gently at her. "Your aunt has a very kind heart and takes her obligations very seriously. But obligations can sometimes prevent a person from seeking their own happiness."

"I am sure my aunt does not see you as an obligation, Miss Felsham. She told me it suited her very well to have you here."

"That is nice to know, Lady Georgianna. Now, I have kept you long enough. Do not let this morning's episode dampen your spirits. Go and enjoy whatever the day has to offer you."

Georgianna picked up her parasol and ran lightly down the stairs. She found Mr Knight waiting for her outside the house.

"I am sorry if I have kept you waiting, sir."

"It is a lady's prerogative, I believe," he said with a small smile.

She arched a brow. "I am usually very punctual, I assure you."

The episode with Miss Ravenchurch had disquieted her a little and she strode next to her escort in pensive silence, her eyes fixed on the path ahead.

"You are an energetic walker, ma'am. It is refreshing to walk with a lady who does not move at a snail's pace."

She glanced up, surprised to discover they were already approaching the end of the drive.

"I must apologise, again, sir," she said ruefully. "It is I who have been wool-gathering this time."

"You do seem rather preoccupied," he acknowledged. "What is troubling you?"

"Miss Ravenchurch. She became confused and angry this morning. She thought I had stolen her parasol and the gentleman she once held a tendre for."

"Did she frighten you?" he asked, frowning.

Georgianna was quick to deny it. "No. I felt saddened and surprised, but not alarmed."

"I have seen men lose a limb and others who have lost their wits. I think the former injury preferable. Life can have no meaning once a person has lost all sense of who they are."

"Did any of the men who lost their wits recover?"

"For some it was only a temporary madness."

He smiled so gently at her that Georgianna unconsciously took a step closer to him as if looking for further reassurance.

"But it was a different sort of madness to that which Miss Ravenchurch suffers, I think," he said gently. "She has suffered no great shock or witnessed events that might play on her mind long after they are over. The body inevitably weakens with age, does it not?"

Georgianna cocked her head as she considered his words. "Are you suggesting that the mind does also?"

"Certainly not inevitably; my father is as sharp as he ever was. But I have heard of two other cases with symptoms similar to Miss Ravenchurch's. One of the soldiers I served with received a letter informing him of his grandfather's death. He had begun behaving as if he were twenty again, rather than eighty. He had not ridden for some years but one morning he rode off telling one of the stable hands he was going hunting. The hunt was only in his mind and he came to grief trying to jump over a hedge."

"Perhaps you are right," Georgianna said thoughtfully. "It does make some sort of sense. If a person no longer has very much to look forward to, it is not inconceivable that their minds might prefer to dwell on happier times. What happened in the other case?"

"When I was at school, I had a friend whose great aunt was housed in a cottage on his estate. She was provided with two attendants to look after her. When he visited her, she often mistook him for someone else and would introduce him to people who were not there and include them in the conversation. But she was apparently quite happy as long as no one tried to contradict her."

They had come to the road. Glancing over her shoulder, she saw that Kate was some way behind and limping quite badly.

"I'm sorry, milady," she said, "but I really don't think I can go much further."

Georgianna felt a stab of disappointment. She had found their conversation interesting and stimulating. "No, of course not, Kate. We will return to the house immediately and I will take another look at your heel."

She sent a sideways glance at Mr Knight. If he too was disappointed, he hid it well. He regarded the maid for a moment and then looked down and smiled.

"I have a suggestion," he said. "I took the boat down to the water earlier; I have not yet fulfilled my promise to catch Lady Colyford some fish. If you do not think the idea dull, I could row us a little way into the lake and try my luck. If your maid sat upon the bench at the end of the garden, she would be able to both rest her foot and keep you in sight."

"I think it a splendid idea, Mr Knight. I have never been on the water before."

They each took one of Kate's arms so that she could take most of the weight from her injured foot. Their progress was necessarily slow and after a few moments Mr Knight said, "I could carry you if you would permit it, Kate."

"Well I don't permit it," she said sharply. "I don't mean to be ungrateful, sir, but I'd rather hobble if it's all the same to you. I won't be hauled over your shoulder like a sack of potatoes. I have my dignity to consider now I am a lady's maid."

Gratified by the implication that Mr Knight was eager to be alone in her company, and amused by Kate's newfound dignity, Georgianna chuckled.

"You are quite right, Kate. But have you considered that as we are both much taller than you, your feet keep leaving the ground altogether like a small child who is being swung between two adults? I think you will find Mr Knight is quite capable of carrying you before him in a quite unexceptionable manner."

Kate squawked as, waiting for no further encouragement, he scooped her up before him and quickened his pace. The day was warm, yet when he lowered her onto the bench not a single bead of perspiration dampened his brow. He bowed elegantly before the maid and grinned.

"I am happy to be able to inform you, Kate, that in no way do you resemble a sack of potatoes or any other vegetable."

Forgetting her dignity, the girl giggled. "Get away with you, sir!"

Georgianna settled into the bow seat, angled her parasol over her head, and smiled as Mr Knight efficiently wielded the oars. She nodded at the bucket that lay on the floor between them.

"I hope the presence of that object does not mean the boat has a leak. It would be beneath *my* dignity to have to bail the water out."

"Would it?" he said, a warm glow in his eyes. "You must forgive me if I take leave to doubt you, ma'am. It seems to me that you are happy to turn your hand to anything that requires doing, whether it be applying salve to your maid's heel or making a gown for a fatherless baby. You are both kind and practical."

"But then it is in my interests to ensure Kate's speedy recovery, and I made the gown at my aunt's instigation; she has some sympathy for both the mother and the infant."

"Of course, and I suppose you gave the other child your ribbon because you did not like it? You must learn to accept compliments and admiration more graciously, ma'am."

Georgianna did not miss the hint of gentle censure in his tone and coloured. With incurable honesty, she said, "Perhaps, but I am not used to either, sir."

"Then you must become accustomed. We shall play a game. We are not at the moment gliding noise-lessly over the lake but in a crowded ballroom. We are currently enjoying a waltz—"

Georgianna smiled, but said, "I do not know the dance, sir, neither Miss Wolfraston, whose seminary I attended, or my mother approved of the waltz."

"A pity," he said, "I think I would have enjoyed waltzing with you; we would have been able to hold a conversation without me developing a crick in my neck. Perhaps we are enjoying a cotillion or a reel… no, I have set my heart on the waltz. You will just have to use your imagination, Lady Georgianna."

Georgianna had not thought her imagination one of her strong points, yet somehow, she could easily imagine being twirled around the floor in his arms.

"Very well. We are enjoying a waltz. You have just stepped on my dress and torn my flounce—"

"I have not! I have never been guilty of such a clumsy manoeuvre."

"I am afraid you are mistaken. You have certainly just torn my flounce. Come, come, Mr Knight, use your imagination!"

"Touché," he acknowledged, briefly letting go of one oar to throw up his hand. He picked it up again but let them drift whilst he held her eyes. "I am morti-fied, ma'am. Never has such a thing happened to me before, but then never before have I gazed into eyes such as yours. They glitter like the finest cut sapphire."

"I quite understand, Mr Knight," Georgianna said politely. "How very inconvenient it must be for you; I am only just beginning to appreciate your bravery. Every ball you attend must be a severe trial for you if you lose control of your feet every time you encounter the glitter of a jewel."

He laughed. "I deserved that riposte, I suppose. My compliment was rather trite."

"Yes," Georgianna agreed. "But trite or not, I am sure many ladies would enjoy it. I preferred your first compliments because you were praising something useful I had done rather than my looks. I thank you for them. Now, let us end our game; I think I prefer gliding on this lake than on a ballroom floor."

"So do I," he acknowledged. "The bucket is not for bailing water but to put any fish I catch in until I get back to shore."

Georgianna watched him pull the oars in and reach for the rod that lay along the floor of the boat. As he prepared the line, she closed her eyes and tilted her face up to the sun. After a moment she repositioned her parasol so that it was again in the shade. She thought it a little ridiculous that a lady must always have a pale skin; both Mr Knight and her aunt looked attractive and healthy with their tanned skin. She sighed. If she returned home having displeased her mother yet again, she would not be surprised if she was locked in her room and only permitted out when her mother's next choice of suitor came calling.

She realised she knew very little about her companion and would have liked to ask him about his family, but that would only invite unwelcome enquiries about her own. Neither could she ask him about his time as a soldier as he had already intimated that he preferred not to dwell on it. She was not fond of small talk and neither it seemed was Mr Knight. They drifted in companionable silence until her attention was caught by a large bird that glided gracefully across the sky above them.

"What bird is that?" she asked.

Alexander glanced across at her, a small smile curving his lips. "You are always so curious. I should not be surprised; I remember when we first met you mentioned that you wished to understand the world."

"Is that so strange?"

"Not strange but unusual. My experience of the fair sex is not extensive," he admitted. "But most of the ladies I have met have been more interested in how to catch a husband or what colour bonnet would best compliment their dress rather than why a herbal remedy works or the name of a bird."

"Let us agree that I am a little unusual then. I have decided to embrace the fact rather than worry about it. Now, Mr Knight, I am still waiting for the name of that bird."

Alexander glanced skywards. "It is the enemy, Lady Georgianna."

She raised a brow.

"It is an osprey and it wishes to catch my fish."

Even as he spoke, it plummeted towards the lake, levelling out at the last moment so that its talons entered the water first. It rose triumphant, a fish caught between its claws, its tail wriggling in a futile attempt to escape.

"It seems the osprey has succeeded," she said dryly. "You must concede defeat, sir."

"Never!" Alexander cried, as his line went taut. "Now we shall see how practical you are, Lady Georgianna. I may need some help in landing him as I have no net!"

Georgianna glanced down at her white gloves in some dismay, shrugged, and hastily stripped them off.

As Alexander raised the line from the water, a large trout wriggled on the end of it. He swung it towards the boat, but the fish somehow leapt off the hook, somersaulted through the air, and landed only inches away from Georgianna's boots. Taking a deep breath, she reached down and grasped it in both hands, juggled it for a moment, and then tipped it into the bucket.

"Bravo," Alexander said. "And not one squeal or squeak."

Georgianna leant over the side of the boat and washed her hands in the water. "I am not prone to squealing or squeaking so go ahead and catch another; one trout will not be enough for dinner."

After they caught their third fish, Georgianna reached for her gloves. "We had better go back."

The breeze had been steadily rising and as a small wave rocked the boat, she dropped one. It floated on a thermal of air like a white dove for a few yards before gracefully diving to the water's surface.

Alexander reached for an oar and deftly caught it on the blade. He lifted it in the air like a medieval jouster raising his lady's token.

"Knight by name, knight by nature," Georgianna murmured, taking the wet item from the oar.

He grinned. "You may be sure I shall slay any and all dragons who threaten you, ma'am."

Alexander pulled the boat onto the beach and helped Georgianna alight. He did not immediately release her once she had stepped onto the shore but bent and placed a kiss upon the back of her bare hand. She stared at it for a moment, feeling it tingle.

"Thank you for your help, fair maiden."

She looked up and laughed. "Think nothing of it, Sir Knight."

Her smile slowly faded. The warm golden glow in his eyes mesmerised her. It spoke of admiration and something else she suspected might be desire. Was it reflected in her eyes also? If the touch of his lips on her hand could cause her to tingle, what would happen if they pressed against her mouth? She had a suspicion that she was about to find out as Mr Knight slowly lowered his head towards hers. Should she flee or satisfy her curiosity? When his lips were a mere whisper away, Georgianna took a hasty step backwards and shook her head.

"I must see to Kate," she said, her voice husky.

She picked up her skirts and hurried up the small bank that separated the lake from the garden, her heart hammering in her chest. What had she been thinking? She liked Mr Knight and had discovered that she enjoyed his company, but there could be no future for them. It was not like her to be so rash. Attraction was clearly a powerful and dangerous thing if it could override all sense and reason.

She flushed. Her reserve had always been her armour; it had shielded her from her mother's hatred and kept at bay painful feelings which might have destroyed her had she examined them more carefully. It was perhaps not surprising that she wished to explore the pleasant feelings Mr Knight aroused in her, but it was certainly foolish. With his golden eyes and tawny curls, he reminded her of a tame lion, but she was not so naïve that she did not know that when a man's passions were aroused, he could be dangerous. Look at Molly Tweddle's predicament or that of Miss Eliza Williams in the novel she had just finished reading. Not that she wished to draw a comparison between Willoughby and Mr Knight; he was no scoundrel she felt sure. Yet would a true gentleman have tried to kiss her on such a short acquaintance? She sighed. If he were a man of modest means, would not the dowry of an earl's daughter be quite as appealing as herself? She frowned. No, she would not believe that of him, that was the old Georgianna thinking. She would not put her armour back on, but she would make sure that her usual good sense held sway over her newfound sensibility and ensure she was not alone with Mr Knight again before they left for Brigham.

Alexander ran his hand through his hair, turned, and hauled the boat a little further up the pebble beach. He was undeniably smitten with Lady Georgianna Voss. She was like a rosebud that was slowly but surely unfurling her petals. He had no doubt that she was also attracted to him, and yet for the second time she had proven that she had more restraint than he. Her innocence should have been protection enough against a stolen kiss and he was a cad for wishing to take one without any serious intentions towards her. He could not help but wonder if she would have withstood the temptation quite so easily if she had known he was the son of a duke.

He stood staring blindly at the bottom of the boat. That thought was unworthy of him; there was nothing artificial about her. His father had spoken of having a connection other than attraction for his mother, was there something more between himself and Lady Georgianna? He certainly liked and even admired her. There had been no awkwardness in the silences that had fallen between them on the boat but a feeling of companionship. Should he confide in her? He was becoming increasingly uncomfortable in his deception.

He frowned and bent to retrieve the bucket from the boat. He stilled as something glinted between two of the wooden planks. His fingers were too large to prise it out and so he wedged the end of the rod beneath it. After a little jiggling, it popped up. He retrieved it and straightened, aware of the suddenly heavy thud of his heart in his ears. It was an enamel cufflink, depicting the lion from his family crest. He sat down on a nearby boulder and cradled it in his palm. It must have belonged to James. Lady Colyford's rowing boat had been the very one taken out on that fateful day. He supposed he should not be surprised; Allerdale's father owned the property and she was his godmother after all.

The urge to throw off his pretence and question her more closely was strong upon him but he knew better than to rush his fences. His hand closed around the cufflink and his mind cleared. There was no reason to suspect his brother's death had been anything but an accident and he would hear the full account from Allerdale himself before too long. There was also Molly Tweddle to consider. Both Lady Colyford and her niece had some sympathy for the girl. If he revealed that he had come to find out the truth of her claims they might view him with some hostility for doubting her. It was only another three days until the full moon and then he would hopefully have the proof he sought.

He took the fish to the kitchen and then returned to the barn to put the cufflink somewhere safe.

"I'm off tomorrow to take the ladies to Brigham, Mr Knight. Lady Colyford has decided to go a day earlier than planned. I'm sorry that I can't be of any more use to you."

Alexander nodded absently. "Think nothing of it, Jack."

"I shall go down to the inn tonight, however, and keep my ears open."

"That's very obliging of you, Jack. Just don't imbibe the ale too freely, will you? Apparently, it's only two hours to Brigham but the roads aren't all they could be."

The old coachman frowned. "I don't need you telling me my business, sir. I've never had an accident yet and I don't mean to start now."

Alexander held his hands up. "Lay your bristles, old fellow. I am sure you do."

They were a full complement for dinner that evening. Most of the talk was about the trip to Brigham.

"I have decided we shall go tomorrow, Georgianna. I have already given Kate instructions to pack your things. Brigham is very near Cockermouth and Mr Peeks will deliver a note for me informing Lady Brigham of our early arrival when he fetches the post."

"Yes, I know, Aunt. I found your maid instructing Kate on how to pack. It was very kind of her. She also said that she would look after me at Brigham."

"I think she is enjoying the diversion," Lady Colyford said. "We so rarely entertain or pay a visit to anyone that she usually has very little to do. Kate is going to wait on Miss Felsham in your absence."

"You need have no worries about Miss Felsham when you are gone," Miss Ravenchurch said. "I shall take very good care of her."

"Thank you, Agnes," Lady Colyford said.

The little lady nodded. "And then, of course, we have Lord Somerton to watch over us. I must say it is nice to have a man about the place."

Although his heart had just missed a beat, Alexander looked up with every appearance of nonchalance and raised a brow. Lady Colyford looked at him intently for a moment before saying, "I think you meant Mr Knight, Agnes."

Miss Ravenchurch became flustered. "Oh yes, of course. How silly of me. I do not know why it has not occurred to me before, but you bear a striking resemblance to Lord Somerton, Mr Knight, who was then heir to the Duke of Rushwick. I cannot have seen him above twice, but his eyes were so unusual he was not easy to forget. He must be the duke now, if he is not dead, for he was not a very young man, even then."

Alexander merely smiled, not wishing to perjure

himself further. Miss Ravenchurch then turned to Lady Colyford.

"Do you remember him, Hester?"

Lady Colyford shook her head and stood abruptly, signalling that dinner was over. "It was all so long ago, Agnes."

Alexander rose with the ladies and went to hold the door open for them.

"I wish you a pleasant journey and an enjoyable stay at Brigham, Lady Colyford."

"Thank you, Mr Knight. I am sure I can rely on you to keep an eye on things in my absence."

"Of course. Please feel free to assign me any tasks that will be helpful to you whilst Lady Colyford is away, Miss Felsham."

She smiled and laid a hand on his arm. "Thank you, Mr Knight. You may be sure I shall. It is a comfort to have you near; there is something very reassuring and dependable about you."

Lady Georgianna was the last to leave the room. As she passed him, he said softly, "Please take care, ma'am. Beware of Allerdale. He is in trouble and in my experience men who are already on the ropes can behave in unpredictable ways."

She raised an eyebrow. "And are you on the ropes, Mr Knight?"

He smiled ruefully. "I do hope not, ma'am. But if I am, I fear the blame must be laid at your door."

Her other eyebrow joined the first. "Then perhaps it is just as well, sir, that I am leaving."

The fragile harmony that had developed between them appeared to be at an end. Alexander strode back to the barn, swiftly changed, and saddled his horse.

He did not wish to sit twiddling his thumbs whilst he waited for Jack. Although dusk was approaching, there would be enough light from the moon when darkness fell if he did not stray from the road.

He rode through the village and followed the route that skirted Crummock Water, allowing his mount to enjoy a gallop. He turned when he reached the lake's end and made the return journey at a more sedate trot. The sun slipped behind the mountains and the burnt sky turned the lake amber. His father had not come here after James' death and had called the place godforsaken. He was mistaken. It was sublime. There was some comfort to be had in that. If his brother had to have been taken so soon, better here than in a seedy dive in Town or on a battlefield.

Jack had returned by the time he rode through the gates of Lake Cottage. He came out to meet him and took the reins after he had dismounted.

"I've some coffee brewing. You go and pour us both a cup whilst I see to this fine beast."

Alexander did as he was told, sat on the upturned box, and cupped the tin cup between his hands. Night had fallen and there was a chill in the air. Jack soon joined him.

"There's trouble brewing if you ask me," he said. "The young Mossop lad was there tonight; Thomas is his name."

"What did he tell you?"

"Nothing," Jack said.

"Then how do you know trouble's brewing?"

"He spoke to no one. Just sat on a stool by the bar, alternately staring into his tankard and drinking from it with a face like thunder."

"As if he were drowning his sorrows?"

"Exactly. And then the Tweddle lad came in. Thomas got to his feet, his fists clenched as if he were ready for a set-to. The landlord had his wits about him, I'll give him that. He leant over the bar, grabbed him by the shoulder, and told him to go home."

"And did he?"

"He did, but he kicked over a chair on his way out."

"And what about the Tweddle boy?"

"Sam Tweddle is a good sort," Jack said. "He just shook his head and ordered his drink. He was quite happy to talk in a general way. I asked him what was up with the young whippersnapper with the cloud hanging over his head, of course."

"And?"

"He told me that life was too short to hold old grudges, but there were some as knew no better, his father included." Jack stood, stretched his back, and yawned. "I best be getting to bed if I'm going to be fit for purpose tomorrow."

"You do that, Jack. I'll see to the cups and the fire."

CHAPTER 11

Lady Colyford delayed their departure until she was quite satisfied that Miss Ravenchurch was herself. It was mid-afternoon before they left for Brigham. Georgianna stared out of the carriage window but saw nothing of the passing landscape. She was surprised to realise that she was looking forward to meeting Lord Allerdale again; he had been quite amusing until Mr Knight had joined them and he had become surly. She imagined her brother might turn out very like him if he was not disciplined and instead allowed to think only of his own wishes. She was interested to see the change in his behaviour that her aunt had assured Mr Knight occurred when Lord Allerdale was at home.

She felt both relieved and perturbed to be leaving Mr Knight behind. Relieved because she knew it was wrong to encourage the undeniable attraction between them and perturbed because she liked the person she became in his company.

"I am very grateful that Mr Knight is watching

over things whilst we are away, but I think I shall ask him to move on when we return, Georgianna."

She glanced up quickly, the notion that her aunt could read her thoughts briefly crossing her mind.

"Oh?" she said, trying to sound indifferent. "Why is that, Aunt?"

"Do not be disingenuous, Georgianna. I saw you both standing by the lake from an upstairs window, just as I stood by another lake many years ago with a man who was the image of Mr Knight. A man who also bore the family name Knight, although he was titled."

Georgianna gasped softly. "Lord Somerton?"

Her aunt nodded. "Yes, although not long afterwards he became the Duke of Rushwick. For once, Miss Ravenchurch was not confused."

Georgianna was beginning to see why her aunt had asked Grantley to sit on the roof with Jack. "Then is Mr Knight related to this duke?"

"Undoubtedly. He can only be his son; I knew it the moment I set eyes on him."

Georgianna frowned. "But then why has he no title? And why have you not mentioned that you know his father?"

Barely had the words left her mouth when she gasped again, louder this time.

"Precisely. The only explanation is that he is Rushwick's natural son."

"But he talks of his father with fondness."

"It is not unheard of for the illegitimate children of highly born noblemen to be placed with an obscure member of the family and be brought up as their own. But the situation is even more complicated. The young man who drowned in the lake last year was his half-brother."

Georgianna's eyes widened. "And do you not think that he should be told of this?"

"No, certainly not, and you must not mention it to him. You can do him no good by informing him of it and might well cause him unnecessary pain. I am only telling you all this because I do not wish you to make a foolish mistake. I would never forgive myself if history repeated itself!"

"What happened, Aunt Hester?" Georgianna asked softly.

Lady Colyford closed her eyes for a moment. "Your mother does not even know the full story," she said softly. "If she did, she would never have sent you to me. Your father will be quite horrified when he hears that she has done so, but at least his pride has ensured that my secret has been kept safe."

Georgianna saw indecision and pain in her aunt's eyes. She leant forwards and took her hands. "Let there be no secrets between us, Aunt Hester. I will think no less of you whatever you did. I am thankful that Mama sent me to you. You have shown me only kindness and I… I have come to love you."

Her aunt smiled, a sheen of tears brightening her eyes. "And I you, child. When you turned up on my doorstep in disgrace; hurt, bewildered, and oh, so lost, you reminded me of myself all those years ago. The only difference was, I deserved to be punished for my foolishness. Having Mr Knight close by has brought it all back to me. I had thought I was over it all long ago, but yet I could not send him away. His charming smile reminded me of the blissful happiness I knew for a brief time as well as the painful time that followed."

Lady Colyford sat back, rested her head against the squabs, and began her tale.

"I was a hit during my season. I was well born, beautiful, and shockingly frank. The *ton* decided to be amused by me. It may have gone to my head a little. Although I had many suitors, I was drawn to Lord Somerton. Not because he was the son of a duke but because he was tantalising, elusive, wild, and made me feel frighteningly, wonderfully alive. He could have charmed the birds out of the trees, but he was dangerous, and I knew it."

"In what way was he dangerous?"

"Because although he sometimes amused himself by toying with the latest beauties, especially if he wished to snatch them from under the nose of a rival, he never offered for them. He had enjoyed a string of mistresses and it was well known that the widowed Lady Jaywick was his latest. I thought it would be quite a coup if I could make him fall in love with me."

"And did you?" Georgianna prompted gently.

"I thought so. I certainly amused him, for I dished him up none of the flattery he was used to. We exchanged witty insults rather than bland compliments and enjoyed a few weeks of heady flirtation, although I always made sure that I was not seen to favour him above another. He persuaded me to go with him to a masquerade ball one evening. It was a shocking affair and when an unknown and rather inebriated gentleman grabbed me about the waist, Sebastian was furious and knocked him flat. Fortunately, my disguise held, and the man never knew who I was."

"Then it seems he did care for you, after all."

"Yes, that was what I thought. He took me into the gardens and apologised for exposing me to such a loutish crowd. He seemed genuinely ashamed to have taken me there. We walked for some time in the moonlight until we came to a lake. He told me how much he admired me and promised to mend his ways. He kissed me under the stars and asked me to marry him. When I accepted his proposal, he kissed me again and I am ashamed to say I completely lost my head."

"You lay with him?"

"Yes. And although I should not admit to it, I cannot regret it. It was the most moving and wonderful experience of my life."

"But then what went wrong?"

"He promised to call on my father the next day, but he did not come. Nor the next day or the one after that. I went to a ball hoping he would be there, and Lady Arnsley, who was a great friend of Lady Jaywick, took great pleasure in informing me that her friend had gone to Paris, and was it not strange that Lord Somerton had also removed there?"

"You must have felt wretched."

"Yes, although I had not yet given up all hope. But the weeks passed, and he did not return to Town. Nor did Lady Jaywick. And then I discovered that our union had borne fruit."

Georgianna's eyes widened. "You were with child!"

"I was, although I did not realise it at first. I began

to be sick in the mornings and my maid told my mother, who of course, told my father."

"I never knew my grandfather. Was it terrible?"

Lady Colyford gave a bitter laugh. "It was extremely unpleasant. Your father is very much in the same mould. I was beyond disgrace. The wound to the family pride cut deep and he insisted that I tell him who the father was so he could make him marry me. But I would not, even when he threatened to beat the truth out of me."

"But you loved him!"

"Yes. That is precisely why I could not marry him. I can think of nothing worse than to be married to a man you love if he does not return your regard. He would have resented me and carried on as he had before the marriage. It would have destroyed me."

"But if your situation had become known, you would have been destroyed anyway."

Lady Colyford smiled. "You are always so logical, Georgianna. I had sunk into a terrible lethargy by then and did not care what became of me. My mother tried to persuade me to bring one of my other suitors to the point, press him for a quick marriage, and pass the child off as his own. But I would not play such a trick on any of them."

"Then how did your marriage to Lord Colyford come about?"

"My mother put it about that I was ill, which was no more than the truth, and rented a cottage deep in the countryside in Devon. She would not risk taking me home in case any of the servants discovered my condition. Lord Colyford lived in the big house close by. I had gone for a walk and had unknowingly wandered onto his estate. He discovered me crying." She gave a wry smile. "I had turned into quite a watering pot. He was some years my senior and very kind. Somehow my sorry tale poured out. He took me home to my mother and the next thing I knew they had come to an agreement. His house was in dire need of repair, but his father had left him with very little money. The estate was not entailed, and he feared he would have to sell it." She smiled fondly. "He loved his home and would have done anything to save it. He agreed to marry me and accept my child in return for a handsome settlement."

"And were you happy?"

"Not at first. I lost the child and was unable to have another. It was my ultimate punishment, I suppose. My husband remained kind and I eventually became content with him. But the repairs to the house alone swallowed up most of the money and by the time he died, we were deeply in debt. There, now you know it all. Miss Felsham is the only other person who knows who the father was."

Georgianna's head was reeling with all she had learned but she smiled. "Thank you for trusting me, Aunt Hester. I understand why you have confided in me, but I had already decided that I must keep Mr Knight at arm's length a little."

"You are a sensible girl," Lady Colyford said. "But he is as charismatic as his father. I do not say he would seduce you, but it looked very much to me as if he was about to kiss you."

Georgianna blushed. "Yes, he was. And I very nearly let him. Is that why you brought us to Brigham a day early?"

"Of course." Lady Colyford glanced out of the window as they turned through a gateway. "We are here."

The house sat on a plain, midway between the mountains of the Lakes and the sea. It was not as large as Avondale, but impressive, nevertheless. Lady Brigham herself came out to greet them as they pulled up in front of the house.

"I have been looking out for you, Hester. I am so pleased that you decided to come in time for our dinner after all, for my numbers are uneven."

Georgianna saw that she had the same dark eyes as her son. She was extremely petite, had dark, curling hair without a trace of grey, and an impish smile.

"Welcome, Lady Georgianna. You are very like your aunt before her hair turned white and she gave up on bonnets!"

Lady Colyford laughed. "I am sure a long-standing friendship with you is enough to turn anyone's hair white, Julia, and I am well past the age of caring about bonnets. I think the most freeing thing about being a widow fast approaching sixty, is that I may do as I please without caring a button for the conventions."

Lady Brigham embraced her friend. "When did you ever?"

Releasing her aunt, she took each of them by the arm and began walking towards the house.

"Your aunt's husband was a cousin of mine, Lady Georgianna. I will never forget the time Brigham and I visited them only to find the roof in our chamber had sprung a leak. And what do you think your aunt did about it?"

Georgianna smiled. "Move you to another chamber?"

"Not at all. She suggested I put a basin underneath it as she was sure that rainwater was good for the complexion!"

Lady Colyford laughed. "You must learn to take everything Lady Brigham tells you with a pinch of salt, Georgianna. What she says is perfectly true, but she has omitted to mention that at the time of her visit, every guest chamber at Colyford suffered from the same problem. The whole roof had to be replaced!"

Georgianna looked down at her hostess. "All I can say, ma'am, is that it certainly did your complexion no harm for it is flawless."

"I had a feeling I was going to like you."

Georgianna's brows rose in surprise. "Whatever gave you that idea?"

"When my son mentioned that he had met his godmother's niece at an inn, I naturally asked him for his impression of you. He merely informed me that you were a little unusual and I could not have been more delighted. I understood at once that you must take after your aunt and nothing could have pleased me more, for I love her dearly."

They had by now entered the house and stood in a huge entrance hall with a chequered marble floor. A door on the other side opened and Lord Allerdale strode through it, the frown that Georgianna had witnessed before marring his handsome features. It lifted as he saw his mama and was replaced by a warm smile.

"Come and greet our guests, my love," she said in caressing accents.

Georgianna watched with interest his reception of his godmother. She'd expected his greeting to be formal and cool but that was not the case at all. He took her hands, bent, and dropped a light kiss on her cheek.

"If you have come to rake me down with your acerbic tongue, Lady Colyford, you are too late. My father has beaten you to it."

She kept hold of his hands but took a step backwards and scrutinised his face closely. "You look as if you have been burning the candle at both ends for some time, Miles, but I am sure a spell in the country will soon restore you. As for raking you down, you have hardly had time to give me cause. That is unless you behaved in a less than gentlemanly manner when you met my niece upon the road?"

Lord Allerdale bowed and grinned ruefully at Georgianna. "Well, Lady Georgianna?"

She inclined her head and hid a smile. He had put his head in the noose but in this mood, he was charming, and she found she had no desire to tighten it. "Your manners were quite as good as my own, sir."

"Of course they were," Lady Brigham said. "I do not understand why everyone is always ready to think the worst of my poor boy. I am sure that Lady Georgianna's obvious quality ensured that she was safe in his company."

"Oh, Lord Allerdale assured me of it," she said, sending him a satirical glance.

Lady Brigham beamed at her son. "It was very thoughtful of you to put Lady Georgianna at her ease,

155

Miles. Now, let me show you to your rooms for our guests will be arriving within the hour."

Lord Allerdale fell into step with Georgianna as they mounted the stairs.

"Thank you, Lady Georgianna," he said softly. "I was not in the best of moods when we last met and you would have been well within your rights to hang me out to dry. I am very grateful that you did not; I do not like to upset my mother."

She sent him a sideways glance and saw contrition in his eyes.

"It was not my finest hour either, sir."

They had reached the top of the stairs and he bowed to her. "I underestimated you, I think. I look forward to knowing you better, ma'am. I hope we can be friends. I am rather fond of my godmother."

Georgianna cocked her head to one side and considered his suggestion. "Perhaps we can." A grin twitched her lips. "That is if you do not fall into a temper whenever I speak my mind. I am as forthright as my aunt."

"Forewarned is forearmed, ma'am."

Grantley gave her a new look, allowing one long curling tendril of hair to fall over her neck. It softened her face and the angular line of her shoulder.

"Thank you, Grantley. You are very accomplished."

The maid smiled. "I should be, my lady. I have been Lady Colyford's maid for nigh on forty years. Her hair was as dark as yours until ten years ago. She has been lucky mind you; pure white is so much more becoming than grey. Your eyes are much darker than my lady's, but anyone might easily take you for her daughter."

Georgianna wished very much that she had been. She was conscious of a feeling of pride when her aunt came to take her downstairs. Although Lady Colyford always changed into a clean dress for dinner, Georgianna had not yet seen her adorned in anything she would not be happy to do the gardening in. The silver silk she wore this evening emphasised her trim figure to perfection. Upon her head, she wore a black turban adorned only by a single white ostrich feather, and around her neck a rose gold necklace studded with gemstones of blue topaz, their shade a perfect match for her eyes.

"You look beautiful, Aunt Hester."

Her aunt kissed her cheek. "No, child, if you can look past my brown skin, handsome perhaps. It is you who are beautiful. The time you have spent outside has given you a healthy glow and that pale blue gown suits you to admiration."

"Is it to be a large party?" Georgianna asked as they made their way to the drawing room.

"Not overly so. I believe twelve of us will sit down to dinner. Lord and Lady Farr, their son Viscount Maudley, and their daughter Lady Priscilla have been invited." She dropped her voice to a whisper. "I don't like any of them; they remind me too much of our own family. It is why I originally declined the invitation to dinner and chose Wednesday as our day of arrival."

Georgianna hung her head a little. "I'm sorry, Aunt."

Lady Colyford squeezed her arm. "Do not be a

goose. Sir Gerard Hughes will more than make up for it; he is delightfully vulgar and a favourite of mine. You will also meet his daughter. Miss Hughes has a seemingly endless flow of nonsense on the tip of her tongue, but I would ask you to show some tolerance where she is concerned. She is amiable and not at all concerned with pomp or ceremony. I like her the better for it."

Georgianna smiled. "I will do my best, Aunt. It appears we are to be a rather unusual party."

"One cannot choose one's neighbours after all."

"Very true. By my reckoning, we are still one person short."

"Yes. I do not know who that may be as Julia did not mention him in her letter. I can only assume I do not know him."

CHAPTER 12

The person missing from her aunt's list was Viscount Devonan, a guest of Lord Farr. Georgianna judged him to be in his thirties. He had a good figure, a languid air, and regular features that seemed inclined to organise themselves into a sneering expression. Georgianna disliked him immediately. When he bowed to her from across the room, his eyes held a calculating look. They swept over her from head to toe, much as she imagined a man might look over a horse to assess its good points. She realised that she had been found wanting when he did not approach her but bent to catch something Lady Priscilla said. This lady's eyes were also upon her for a moment before they turned to each other and smiled.

"They are made for each other," Lady Colyford said in a low voice. "They are both so pleased with themselves that they cannot need the approbation of anyone else."

A satirical smile curved Georgianna's lips. "If I am

not much mistaken, they have just shared a joke at my expense. I do not begrudge them their enjoyment; I would rather be a maypole than a pocket Venus. If I am to look up to someone, I would rather it was because they have done something to earn my respect rather than my lack of inches."

"Well said, child."

Over Lord Devonan's shoulder, Georgianna saw Lord Allerdale stride into the room. He came to an abrupt halt as he saw him. The two gentlemen exchanged a brief, rather abrupt bow. It looked as if Lord Allerdale would walk straight past his guest but found himself detained when that gentleman briefly laid a hand on his arm.

"There is no love lost there, I think," Lady Coly-ford murmured. "Oh, unsheathe your claws, my dear, I do believe you are about to be honoured by the attentions of Lady Priscilla. According to Julia, she is still smarting because she did not achieve a creditable match last season. Apparently, she had set her sights on Rushwick's heir last September, who perhaps not unsurprisingly, given the family history, flirted outra-geously with her but did not come up to scratch. At least she has the consolation of knowing that she turned down three other eminently respectable gentle-men. Unfortunately, she was not as gracious as she could have been in her refusals and to top it all off, she upset a number of popular young ladies with her poisonous tongue. When she returned to Town for the main season, she found herself less than popular."

Georgianna raised an eyebrow. "I fear my claws are not as sharp as yours, Aunt Hester. Have you no sympathy for her?"

"You are an abominable girl," Lady Colyford said with an appreciative smile. "I might well have had some sympathy for her if she was not so set up in her own conceit. She has no heart to lose and was only interested in becoming a duchess. Quite understandable, of course." She groaned. "Julia is summoning me. I must go and pay my respects to Lady Farr."

Lady Priscilla sauntered unhurriedly towards Georgianna, a cool smile on her lips. "Lady Georgianna, how pleasant it is to meet a girl of my own standing in this wilderness. We owe it to our sex to band together and prove that some of us have more than hot air between our ears. I believe Miss Hughes will be here tonight and she is bird witted enough for a dozen of us."

"Is that so?" Georgianna said. "Let us hope then that she has some other redeeming feature that will ameliorate this grave fault."

Lady Priscilla gave a tinkle of laughter. "Such as?"

"Good nature, perhaps?"

A flash of anger briefly illuminated Lady Priscilla's eyes.

The butler just then announced Sir Gerard and Miss Hughes. Sir Gerard was a portly gentleman with a red complexion, comfortable rather than fashionable clothes, and a wide smile that was both genuine and infectious. His deep voice boomed across the room.

"Every time your butler announces me, Brigham, I feel like royalty, dashed if I don't!"

When Georgianna had been introduced to the marquess she had found him all that was polite, but he had been rather aloof and his grey eyes cynical. But they twinkled in amusement at this jocular greeting. He smiled and strode forwards to meet his guest.

"Sir Gerard, whilst I am happy that your consequence has been thus gratified, I can feel only relief that you are not royalty. If I had to entertain the Prince Regent, I fear it would take me a year, at least, to recover."

"Nonsense," Sir Gerard said, shaking his host's hand. "Any man who would complain about the hospitality to be found in your house is either a fool or beyond being pleased by anything!"

Sir Gerard bowed to Lady Farr who inclined her head by the smallest fraction. He then spotted the lady by her side.

"Lady Colyford!" he bellowed, hurrying over to her. He took her hand and kissed it reverently before clasping it between both his own. "Make me the happiest man alive and say that you'll be mine, ma'am."

Lady Colyford laughed. "Be careful what you wish for, Sir Gerard. One of these days I might say yes and then you will be in a pickle. I would put you on a strict diet and forbid you to drink port!"

"You would not be so cruel!" he cried. "I should feed you such sweet delicacies that you would put some flesh on your bones, at last."

"How nauseating," Lady Priscilla said. "I do not know why your aunt does not snub him!"

Lady Brigham swooped down upon the young lady still standing in the middle of the room with an indulgent smile upon her face. She was a little on the plump side but had a countenance as congenial as her father's.

"Let me introduce you to Lady Colyford's niece, Lady Georgianna, Miss Hughes."

"I am very happy to meet you," she said. "Your aunt and my father are old friends. They are only funning and play this game every time they meet. It is a shame Lady Colyford never takes him at all seriously for I am persuaded she would do him a great deal of good. He really should go on a reducing diet."

Lady Priscilla's eyes rested a moment on Miss Hughes' rather full bosom which was putting the seams of her dress under severe pressure.

"Perhaps you could show him the way, Miss Hughes."

This barb did not quite have the intended effect. Miss Hughes laughed. "You are right, of course. I have had to let out this dress for the second time. Fortunately, Mr Tucker does not mind at all. He says he much prefers a plump armful."

"Who is Mr Tucker?" Georgianna asked.

"He is Baron Feathercotte's son," Lady Priscilla drawled. "And a halfwit if ever I saw one."

It appeared that Miss Hughes, whilst happy enough to take any insult aimed at herself in good part, was not so forgiving of any directed at Mr Tucker.

"It is not common knowledge as yet, but I will take leave to inform you, ma'am, that we are to be wed. I will not stand by and hear you disparage him."

As her bosom swelled with indignation, a slight tearing sound dropped into the silence that had fallen at this direct attack. Miss Hughes reddened and snatched at the side of her dress just below her armpit. Lady Priscilla's scornful laugh drew the enquiring gazes of the other guests. Georgianna hastily took Miss Hughes' arm and led her from the room.

"Do not worry. It will be but the work of a moment to repair it."

"Thank you, Lady Georgianna. I should not have allowed myself to rise to the fly. Lady Priscilla is like an angry wasp who will sting anyone who gets in her path. I usually feel sorry for her; how miserable it must be to only be able to raise yourself up by putting others down. But I will not have my Finlay so maligned."

Miss Hughes might rattle on a trifle, but Georgianna was impressed by her insight into Lady Priscilla's character. She was no fool.

"Congratulations on your forthcoming marriage," she said.

Miss Hughes turned a face suddenly radiant with happiness in her direction.

"Thank you. I have known Finlay forever. He doesn't mind my prattle and never makes me feel gauche or foolish. We are very comfortable in each other's company; I think it would be very unpleasant to be married to someone if that were not the case, don't you? He may not be cleverest of gentlemen, but he is no halfwit. He'll roar with laughter when I tell him I nearly burst out of my dress!"

Georgianna smiled. "You sound perfect for each other."

When they returned to the drawing room, Sir Gerard strode up to his daughter and pinched her cheek.

"If it isn't just like you to be here no more than five minutes without causing a rumpus, Puss."

He turned to Lady Georgianna, a warm look in his eyes. "Thank you, ma'am, for helping my girl out of her scrape. I'm not surprised though; you have a look of your aunt about you so I would expect you to have quick wits. I must say I am delighted you have come to visit her; it is about time one of her family did."

"Yes, it was very well done of you, child," Lady Colyford said, just then coming up and taking Sir Gerard's arm.

He unconsciously patted her aunt's hand and smiled down at her with such affection that Georgianna realised that for all his funning, he genuinely admired her. What was perhaps a little more surprising, was the fond smile that her aunt gave him in return.

She had the dubious pleasure of being escorted into dinner by Viscount Maudley. He had an air of proud detachment, a receding chin, and a tendency to interview her as if she had applied for the post of becoming his wife. After only ten minutes in his company, she thought she would rather starve in a gutter.

When they had at last exhausted the scope of her talents, he said, "It seems you are very accomplished, Lady Georgianna."

"Thank you, sir. And what of your accomplishments?"

He turned an uncomprehending look upon her. "My accomplishments?"

"Yes. What particular skills have you developed to ensure you will be able to step into your father's boots when the time comes?"

A supercilious grin twitched his lips. "I am very familiar with our estate, ma'am."

She nodded encouragingly. "I imagine you must be. But have you taken an active interest in the running of it?"

"My father would not appreciate me trying to take too active an interest just yet. He is hardly in his dotage. Besides, we have a very good steward, ma'am."

"Oh, I see. So how do you spend your time, sir?"

"Like any other young gentleman of fortune, I expect."

She tilted her head and sent him a look of innocent enquiry. "As I am not yet acquainted with many young gentlemen of fortune, I think you will have to elucidate a little more if I am to understand your habits, sir."

He gave her a condescending smile and lifted his wine glass to his lips. "You need not concern yourself with my habits, ma'am. They can be of no interest to you."

She raised an eyebrow. "I think on that point, at least, we can agree, sir."

Viscount Maudley choked on his wine and suffered an unseemly bout of coughing. It was perhaps just as well that Lady Brigham chose that moment to rise from the table. As Georgianna got to her feet, her eyes met Lord Allerdale's. They were alight with laughter and something which looked very much like approval.

The gentlemen had not long joined the ladies when the butler made a discreet entrance and had a quiet word with Lord Brigham. He strode over to the window and pulled back the curtain.

Lady Priscilla had been looking quite discontented for some moments, her eyes darting now and then to where Lord Allerdale and Lord Devonan stood in private conversation. She suddenly jumped to her feet.

"Shall I play, Lady Brigham?"

"I am afraid we must forgo that pleasure this evening, Lady Priscilla," Lord Brigham said. "It looks like a storm is coming."

She pouted. "But the night is yet young, and I have had no opportunity to catch up with all Lord Allerdale's news. Is it so very close?"

Sir Gerard frowned and strode over to the window. "You are right, Brigham. We shall have to leave whilst we can still see the moon." He returned to Lady Colyford's side. "I had hoped to enjoy a long chat with you, my dear. Promise me you won't run away too soon?"

"We will be here a few days, at least."

Miss Hughes turned impulsively to Georgianna. "Please come and visit us before you leave. It is so nice to make a new friend."

Georgianna smiled. "I would be glad to if we have time."

They all went outside to wave the guests off. As they returned to the house, Lord Brigham summoned his son to the library.

"Oh dear," Lady Brigham sighed. "I wish I knew what was between them but neither of them will tell me."

"Lord Allerdale mentioned that he did not like to upset you," Georgianna said. "Shall I pour the tea?"

"Thank you," Lady Brigham murmured absently.

"I wish they would understand that keeping me in the dark upsets me far more."

"Stop fretting, Julia," Lady Colyford said. "I imagine he is run off his legs and wishes his father to advance him his allowance early. You know how cross Brigham becomes over such matters. I remember when you were always in a quake if you lost too much at Loo or Faro."

Lady Brigham laughed. "Do not remind me!"

"I do not believe I know either of those games," Georgianna said, interested.

"I should hope not," her aunt said dryly.

"Oh, do not be so priggish, Hester. Sir Gerard's good humour has been the only leaven in an otherwise tedious evening. It will be fun to teach Lady Georgianna the games."

"Very well," Lady Colyford said. "But we will only play for buttons."

Lord Allerdale found them engrossed in a game of Faro some time later.

"Oh ho! I see I have entered a den of vice."

He watched only for a few moments before seating himself beside Georgianna. He picked up the meagre pile of buttons at her elbow and let them trickle through his fingers. "My mother is fleecing you shamelessly, Lady Georgianna. I cannot stand by and watch the decimation of your fortune."

He proceeded to whisper advice into her ear whenever she made an unwise move. Fortunately, he did not seem to have the same distracting effect on her as Mr Knight had and by the end of the evening, she was the clear victor.

Smiling, she divided her mountain of buttons into

two piles and pushed one towards him. "I think it only fair we share the spoils, sir."

He gave a rather forced laugh. "If they were golden guineas, I would be very tempted to accept your generosity, ma'am."

CHAPTER 13

Alexander leant against a tree with his eyes fixed firmly on the Tweddles' farmhouse. He was very grateful that the winds and rain that had battered the landscape for the last two nights had abated. If the storm had still raged and the moon had not been able to light her way, Molly Tweddle might not have kept her rendezvous and he found himself impatient to bring this business to a close.

He rubbed his hands together; there was a chill in the air that spoke of Autumn's approach. Time seemed to crawl by, and it was only when his head suddenly jerked forwards that he realised he had fallen asleep where he stood. His eyes darted towards the house. The dim light that had flickered behind the curtained window had been extinguished. Had he missed her or had this meeting existed in his imagination only? He glanced at the moon and muttered an oath. It must be well past midnight now.

He cast one last glance at the farmhouse and turned to go. He had taken no more than a step when he heard the faint click of a door being gently closed. He stilled and stepped back behind the tree. A shadowy figure in a long, dark cloak with the hood pulled up, hurried past him.

He followed at safe distance, his eyes straining to distinguish her from the other shadows. When she followed the stream up the hill, he felt certain that the shepherd's hut was her destination and slowed his pace. Neither of them carried a lamp but whereas she knew the terrain intimately, he did not. If he stumbled and fell, she would in all likelihood hear him.

He knew his hunch had been correct when he saw a light in the hut's small open window. He approached it slowly and sat on the damp grass beneath it.

"Wait a little longer, Tom. If the duke sends some money, we can leave here and start again somewhere else."

"Aye, so you keep tellin' me. But I've been waiting long enough, Moll. I've not even held my bairn in my arms and he's nigh on two month's old."

"If we go with nothing, what chance have we got?"

"Perhaps we shouldn't go at all. I've never been happy about deceivin' everyone."

"No more have I, but what other choice did we have? Pa still talks of what happened to great granfer as if it only happened yesterday!"

"Aye, mine too. It weren't nobody's fault he cracked his head on a stone and your pa still treats us as if were murderers."

"Well, there you go, then. If we stay, my family will disown me and I'll be forced to come and live with you. It don't bear thinking about. Your ma and pa would look at me every day as if I was a cockroach! And they'd crush me just as easily."

"Maybe at first, Moll. But once they got to know you, they'd be bound to love you, just like I do."

Judging by the silence that followed, Thomas was hoping his kisses would persuade Molly. After a few moments, a soft sigh drifted through the window.

"It wouldn't work, Tom. How do you think I'd feel every Sunday sitting opposite my own blood in church and them pretendin' I didn't exist?"

Alexander had heard enough and made his way back down the mountain. Whilst he was pleased that James had not proven himself dishonourable and that his father would not be gulled by the lovelorn couple, he found he felt rather sorry for them. He had seen families torn apart by war, it seemed a shame that these two families should be torn apart by love. By the time he had reached Lake Cottage, the beginnings of a plan had begun to form in his mind.

As he moved towards the barn, he heard someone humming. Although it was not very tuneful, he recognised the melody as that of a waltz. He strolled towards the garden and saw Miss Ravenchurch, dressed only in her nightshift, waltzing barefoot by the light of the moon in the arms of an imaginary partner. Concerned, he took a hasty step forward. The night was far from warm and the poor lady must be cold even if she did not yet realise it.

"Wait!"

He swivelled on his heel and saw Miss Felsham. She hurried up to him and said in hushed tones, "You must forgive me, sir, I have dressed all by guess and probably look a fright. Not that it matters at a time like this. I had left my window ajar and heard Agnes but a few moments ago. I am pleased that you are still up as I shall be very glad of your assistance, especially if she becomes agitated."

"You are welcome to it, ma'am. But why did you stop me?"

"I know that Lady Colyford does not agree with me, but I think she has reached the stage where it is better not to try to bring her back to reality too suddenly. It only upsets and confuses her. We must try to get her back to bed without disturbing her… her, oh, dream for want of a better word."

Alexander nodded decisively. "You may leave it to me, ma'am."

"What do you mean to do?" Miss Felsham said, a little apprehensively.

"I am about to become her long-lost beau," he said, grinning.

He walked as stealthily as a man of his size could towards Miss Ravenchurch. He soon realised he need not have taken the trouble for her eyes were closed and she seemed completely oblivious to his presence. He attempted to slot himself into the position of her imaginary partner, but she turned at the last moment and he found himself stranded with his arms held out. This happened a further two times and he realised how ridiculous he must look when he glanced up and saw Miss Felsham with her hand to her mouth as if she were trying to suppress a laugh.

He smiled, but as Miss Ravenchurch suddenly swivelled toward him, he moved quickly forwards and finally managed to grasp her. He was so tall and she so short, that he had to bend both his knees and his back to avoid lifting her completely off her feet. A definite chuckle reached his ears.

His neck soon began to ache, and his back protested as his old war wounds pulled at his skin. He suddenly swooped and lifted the little lady into his arms. Her eyes snapped open, and she gazed up at him in adoration.

"Mr Antsy, whatever are you doing?"

He had been asking himself that question for some moments but smiled and said, "I fear you have twisted your ankle, ma'am. I am merely removing you to a more comfortable place."

She sighed. "You are always so much the gentleman."

Miss Felsham turned and hurried into the house, leading him to Miss Ravenchurch's room. He laid her gently upon her bed and Miss Felsham pulled the covers over her. Miss Ravenchurch smiled and murmured something indiscernible before her eyes fluttered shut. Miss Felsham led the way from the room, locking the door behind them.

"Thank you, Mr Knight. You handled the situation very well."

"And afforded you some amusement, I think."

"I was not laughing at Miss Ravenchurch, you understand."

"Yes, I am fully aware my performance was the source of your mirth, ma'am."

She smiled at his haughty tone. "You do not fool me for an instant. You are one of the most even-tempered gentlemen it has ever been my pleasure to meet."

He looked down into her trusting eyes, his expression suddenly serious. "I am afraid I have fooled you, ma'am. I have fooled you all."

"Do you think so? We shall see. Come into the drawing room."

Miss Felsham listened to his story with polite interest. When he finished, she said, "Lady Colyford thought you must be Rushwick's son. Apparently, you are remarkably like your father."

He frowned. "But why did she not say anything? Is Lady Georgianna also aware of this?"

"It seems you did fool us, after all. Lady Colyford did not mention the matter as she thought you must be his *natural* son, which made it a little awkward as I am sure you can appreciate. As for Lady Georgianna, I doubt very much whether such a topic has ever been discussed between them. I have long been Lady Colyford's confidante, and so it was only natural that she should share her thoughts with me."

"I see," he said thoughtfully.

"I am sorry about your brother. I can quite see why you wished to be sure the baby was his, of course. May I ask what you intend to do now that you know the truth? It was very wrong of them to try and extort money from the duke, but they must be desperate."

"I am going to try and bring the families together. Small communities like this need to keep their young blood if they are to survive."

"That is very good of you, Mr… Lord Somerton. It will be quite a feat if you can accomplish it."

"It is the vicar who will do that, I hope. I shall pay him a visit first thing in the morning."

He arrived at the vicarage at an unseasonably early hour and had to use all of his charms to persuade Mrs Dibbons, the housekeeper, to permit him entry. He found the vicar enjoying a hearty breakfast.

"Mr Knight!" he said, getting hastily to his feet. "I hope there is nothing amiss at Lake Cottage?"

"No, sir. But my business is urgent so please forgive the early call. Please carry on with your meal. I can speak as you eat."

Mr Simpson soon lost his appetite and laid down his fork. By the time Alexander had come to the conclusion of his tale, he looked thunderstruck.

"I wish you had come to me with your doubts at the outset, sir," he said, flustered. "I cannot think it was necessary or right that you kept your true identity from me, that is unless you thought…" His cheeks flushed and his eyes widened as he realised his culpability in the matter. "I am mortified to have been the agent who made this false claim possible, Lord Somerton. I assure you I had no reason to doubt it."

"I believe you, sir. The only thing I suspected you of was perhaps having too trusting a nature. You had already proved yourself an able defender of your flock and I did not wish to have my investigation hindered by subjective loyalties. I hope you understand."

"I suppose I do," he conceded.

"I must thank you for persuading the family not to bandy my brother's name about as the father of the child."

As the full import of Alexander's words sank in, Mr Simpson became quite agitated.

"It is indeed fortunate, sir! What a fool I would have appeared when the truth finally came out, as it now must, but at least only a few will know of it. That

Molly should have spoken untruths to her spiritual preceptor is a very grave offence indeed. To have perjured her soul in such a way is most distressing. I shall pray for her."

Now that he understood he was not under suspicion and had resolved on a course of action, he seemed to rediscover his appetite. He again picked up his fork and scooped up a rapidly congealing mess of scrambled egg.

"I hope you will do more than that, Mr Simpson," Alexander said firmly.

The vicar hastily swallowed and waved his fork. "I shall, of course, visit the family this very day. There will be such a rumpus!"

Alexander calmly removed a piece of stray egg from his coat. "Of that, I have no doubt, but not one of your making, I hope. This is your chance to heal the rift between the families, sir. Think of the respect you would garner if you achieved it."

Mr Simpson looked much struck by this suggestion. He again put down his fork, pursed his lips, and steepled his fingers as he considered his guest's words. "It would be a triumph indeed if I could bring it about," he conceded. "But the enmity is of such long standing…"

"It may not be as difficult as you suppose. I have reason to believe that Sam Tweddle does not believe in holding grudges and it would be in Thomas Mossop's interests to build some bridges between the families. It seems to me that it is the elder generation that is the real problem. Gather both families here at your house, sir, and use your not inconsiderable oratory skills to persuade them. Do not lay the blame at Molly's door alone but make them see that they are all guilty. Point out that their children have been forced off the path of the righteous by their stubbornness. Preach forgiveness. And as a clincher, let them consider that it is not only Molly Tweddle's soul that is as risk, sir, but her person. Her fraudulent claim is a serious crime. I doubt she would enjoy a spell in prison or the pillory. You may inform them that my father will pursue the matter no further on the condition that they reconcile their differences."

A slow smile spread across the vicar's face. "If I throw in a bit of fire and brimstone for good measure, it might well work."

Alexander smiled. "That's the spirit. I almost wish I might be present at this momentous occasion."

"I hope you will be, sir. I might need your support."

Alexander shook his head. "I would only cramp your style, sir. Besides, I have some other business to attend to. You may send word to Lake Cottage of the outcome of your meeting. Now, I will leave you to finish your breakfast in peace. I can see myself out."

"Wait!"

Alexander turned and raised a questioning brow.

"It may well be that my words shall prove persuasive, but only if they can be heard in the first place. I can just imagine it now; I shall mention what Molly and Thomas have done and before I can lay the blame squarely on everyone, they will be hurling accusations at each other, and may even erupt into violence. Although I hope that they would not be so disrespectful as to conduct a brawl in my house or my presence, I would be much easier in my mind if you were here. I feel sure that with your history, you may have some experience of controlling angry mobs."

Alexander frowned. Although Mr Simpson may have exaggerated a little, there might well be some trouble at first, but he wished to be on his way to Brigham. It was time to have a conversation with Allerdale. He had already taken his leave of Miss Felsham having discovered that Miss Ravenchurch had no recollection of the previous evening's events and was quite herself this morning.

"Very well," he said. "But send for them now, if you will. By the time they can all be gathered together half the day will have passed. I am going to Brigham to have a word with Lord Allerdale and will now return much later than I intended. I had promised Lady Colyford that I would keep an eye on the ladies at Lake Cottage. Will you drop in on Miss Felsham and Miss Ravenchurch later to check all is well?"

"You may be sure, I will, sir. And I will send for the Tweddles and Mossops without delay, once I have finished my breakfast, that is."

CHAPTER 14

Georgianna was relieved to discover the sun was shining. The storm had raged for two days and she was more than ready for some exercise. Left to its own devices, her mind had a stubborn tendency to dwell on Mr Knight, so she had availed herself of Lord Brigham's library. After an extensive search, she had found two tomes about herbal remedies. She had not understood everything she had read but certainly felt more enlightened than she had been before.

Lord Allerdale had discovered her poring over the books, taking notes, and although he had teased her, there had been no malice in his quips. Citing extreme boredom, he had whisked her off to the billiards room and attempted to teach her to play. She had been hopeless, of course, but he had given her a generous handicap, allowing her three attempts to pot a ball to his one.

She had been a little anxious when Lady Brigham had discovered them as she was fully aware it was not a ladylike pastime, but she had merely laughed and said, "I also like to try new things, Lady Georgianna. I do not understand why our activities must always be so limited and uninteresting."

Lord Allerdale had looked at his mama with a lopsided grin, a wealth of affection in his eyes.

"It is true, Lady Georgianna. You would not believe the number of scrapes my father has had to rescue my mother from. I think my favourite is the time she lost a great deal of money to an unscrupulous gentleman. She subsequently discovered that he was a cheat and decided to adopt the disguise of a high-wayman and hold his carriage up rather than admit her losses to my father."

"Miles!" Lady Brigham protested. "You will make Lady Georgianna think I am not at all respectable."

He laughed. "If my father was not such a downy one, the whole world would know it, Mama."

"And did you succeed, Lady Brigham?" Georgianna asked, intrigued.

"No, she did not," Lord Allerdale said.

"I was extremely angry and determined to wreak my revenge upon him, and I am sure I would have if my detestable maid had not run to my lord once she knew what was in the wind! I had not expected that; I had thought she was the most reliable girl."

Lord Allerdale had thrown back his head and laughed. "And so she was, and you know it! You might have been killed! There wasn't a gentleman, then, who did not carry a pistol in his pocket when he was upon the road at night."

"And so Lord Brigham paid the debt and forgave you?" Georgianna asked.

A fond smile curved Lady Brigham's lips. "Not quite. He forgave me, certainly. He did not forgive the man who fleeced me. He is not fond of gambling, which I have never understood, for he is extremely good at all games of chance, but he sought him out and won back three times as much."

Lady Georgianna had begun to realise that Lord Brigham, who always appeared to be the epitome of respectability, had hidden depths.

"And let us not forget the curricle race—"

"Miles! We *will* forget the curricle race. I wish you would not fill Lady Georgianna's impressionable ears with my foolishness!"

"As you wish, Mama," he had said, bowing over her hand, before raising a quizzical brow to Georgianna.

"Do you drive?"

"No," she had admitted. "I ride, however."

"Would you like to learn?"

"Of course she would like to learn. And I can think of no one better to teach her. I am the first to admit that where my son is concerned, Lady Georgianna, I am fiercely partisan. However, even my lord will admit that he is a first-rate whip."

This comment had held some sway with Georgianna, for she had not failed to notice Lord Brigham's tendency to be as harsh with his son as his lady was lenient. "Then if my aunt does not object, I would certainly like to learn."

"You need have no worries on that score. Hester is very fond of Miles and knows that he would not go beyond the line with anyone who is respectable, and you are practically family, my dear."

"Mama, I had not thought of that before. I need no longer feel any qualms; it is perfectly respectable for me to teach my cousin to drive."

Georgianna had laughed. "Forgive me if I doubt your qualms, my lord. And calling me cousin is stretching the tie to the limit."

He had grinned. "When you know us a little better, *cousin*, you will know we, by that I mean my mother and I, always stretch everything to its limit! On the first fine day that presents itself, I shall certainly teach you to drive."

He had sounded so adamant, but Georgianna was not at all sure his promise would hold fast. She had returned one of the books she had borrowed to the library before she had retired last evening and had been halfway up the ladder to replace it, when she had heard voices. Lord Brigham's study abutted onto the room and she could not help but hear the tail end of a row.

"But my honour is at stake, sir!" Lord Allerdale had cried.

Lord Brigham's implacable tone had been far more measured but had carried, nevertheless.

"What little of it you have left. You must ask Devonan for more time and follow my advice, Allerdale. I would ask that you do not meet him here, however. He has upset your mother, and that I will not tolerate."

"How, sir?"

"He has had the audacity to send her a letter suggesting she use her influence to ensure that you do not lose your reputation as a gentleman. We had a most unpleasant interview. I forbade her to sell any of her jewellery or anything else to help you out of this scrape."

"Sir! I would—"

"Do not look so indignant, Miles, I know full well that you would not ask her to, but that does not mean she would not do it. She would move heaven and earth to protect her only son, as well you know. Two very rare and expensive vases were smashed in the course of this interview. I shall replace them, of course; by rights, I should also deduct that money from your very generous allowance, but if you do what I have asked, I shall not. Your mother will no doubt be feeling quite wretched about her loss of temper; it is some time since I have witnessed it."

"Devonan is a dog!" Lord Allerdale had growled. "I shall—"

"What you shall do, Miles, is just what I have instructed you to do. Devonan could not have upset Julia if you had not given him the ammunition. You will now make amends. On reflection, however, I think it best that I see him in your stead. I shall send for him in the morning; make yourself scarce, will you? I doubt very much Julia will be up before midday, for if she manages a wink of sleep, I shall be surprised. She realises that Devonan must be quite desperate to be acting in this way and her imagination is running riot; she is already halfway to persuading herself that he might carry out some dastardly deed on your person. As you know, I can be very persuasive, but I shall not ask him to wait longer than two weeks; your mother's nerves would not stand it."

It seemed that her aunt had been correct in her assessment of the trouble between them. Georgianna had by now replaced the book and come carefully back down the ladder. She beat a hasty retreat. No one knew better than she how tricky familial relationships could be; she would certainly not have liked anyone to have overheard her last conversation with her mother.

Deciding to hedge her bets, she donned a very fetching deep blue riding habit. If Lord Allerdale cried off, she would go for a ride. Lord Brigham had assured her he had mounts enough in his stable.

"Very smart," Lord Allerdale approved as she entered the breakfast parlour. "Are you ready for your driving lesson?"

"I am looking forward to it," she said, surprised to find him in such good temper.

"I hope you will have your groom up behind you," Lady Colyford said.

"I will if you think it necessary, ma'am."

"I do." She turned to Georgianna. "I have sent a note to Miss Hughes. I thought we might pay her a visit this afternoon."

"Good. There is more to her than meets the eye."

"So we would all have discovered if it were not for your quick actions—"

"Allerdale!" Lady Colyford snapped. "Do not be coarse!"

"Sorry," he murmured, with an unrepentant grin.

"I was referring to her insight into the human character, sir," Lady Georgianna said coolly. "Perhaps I should have enquired as to her opinion of you."

"Enquire away," he said. "We are old friends. My father has always liked Sir Gerard for, his bluster aside, he is very astute where farming is concerned. I might well come with you this afternoon."

"I will admit you have always been very kind to Hannah, Miles," Lady Colyford conceded. "Which is why I am surprised you would poke fun at her."

"Oh, it was only the presence of that little viper, Lady Priscilla, that upset her. I am sure she will be laughing merrily at the whole episode by now."

"Yes," Georgianna said, "she did laugh when we were in my room. Did you know she is to marry Mr Tucker?"

Lord Allerdale looked quite startled. After a moment he said, "No. I did not, but I am delighted. Sir Gerard took her to Town for a season a few years ago and she hated every moment of it. I always knew I would find her hiding away in the darkest corner of a ballroom. Hannah is not shy, but neither is she made for the cut and thrust of Town life. She and Tucker will suit each other admirably. Now, if you have quite finished, cousin, we shall be on our way."

Lord Allerdale handed her up into the curricle with a smile as charming as any that Mr Knight had given her, but rather than making her heart beat a little faster, it made her a little suspicious. She had spent a not inconsiderable amount of time in Lord Allerdale's company during the last few days and had seen him smile many times, but never in quite this manner. He had been friendly, certainly, and at times outrageous, but at no point had he tried to flirt with her. She had remembered her aunt's words and had tried neither to repel or attract him but had just been herself. She had been very happy with the result. She hoped he was not going to spoil things by suddenly turning romantic.

Her fears were allayed as he alternately laughed at her and instructed her. It did not matter how many times he told her to go easy on the reins or feel the horses' mouths, they proceeded down the drive in a far from smooth manner. When she saw the gates that marked the edge of the estate ahead, she handed the reins back to him.

"I do not trust myself to drive us on a public road, Lord Allerdale."

She thought she heard a sigh of relief from the groom behind them.

"You are very wise, cousin," Lord Allerdale said, keeping an admirably straight face. "I fear I must be a very poor tutor."

Georgianna laughed. "Nonsense. I clearly have no aptitude for this particular activity."

"A rare event, for you, I think. I heard the not inconsiderable list of accomplishments that that bore, Maudley, wrung from you the other evening. I did enjoy how you turned the tables on him."

"You are a shameless eavesdropper, sir."

"Perhaps," he admitted. "But I would prefer to listen to almost anything other than Lady Priscilla's conversation."

Once they had passed through the gates, he flicked his whip and set the horses to a brisk trot.

"This is far more comfortable," Georgianna said. "Where are you taking me? We must not be too long, for I will have to change before I visit Miss Hughes."

His jaw tensed and he turned away, his gaze suddenly becoming transfixed on the road. "To Cockermouth, ma'am. It is only a few miles distant. I thought I would kill two birds with one stone. Whilst we enjoy some refreshment at The Swan Inn, a most respectable establishment, my groom will carry out some trifling business for me."

She wondered if this trip had anything to do with the argument she had overheard last night. Perhaps he was going to send his groom to pawn something for him so he could pay his debt.

Lord Allerdale's manner became more constrained as they approached the town. She hoped he was not about to part with a family heirloom. Perhaps she should make a push to dissuade him; despite his mercurial temperament, she liked him and would help him from sinking himself further into disgrace if she could.

"Is anything worrying you?" she finally said. "You seem a little distracted."

He glanced down at her, an enigmatic look in his eyes.

"You are perceptive, ma'am. I may be mistaken, but I think one of my horses has developed a slight limp."

"I hadn't noticed nothing wrong," his groom said.

"But then you do not have such a good view, Tibbs. Check them over will you?"

They had just swept under the arch of the inn. He handed her down from the curricle and led her to a sunny parlour.

"I shall just go and order some refreshments."

Georgianna sat in the window seat and idly watched the people walking down the street. Lord

Allerdale soon returned, closed the door behind him, and gave her a rueful smile.

"This is the second time we have found ourselves at an inn together, but this time I think we understand each other a little better. Perhaps, I might even claim that we are friends?"

Georgianna smiled. "I hope so, sir."

He came forwards, swung a chair out from the table, and sat down. He crossed his legs and leant an arm on the table. Although his posture was relaxed, Georgianna sensed the tension in him.

"Lady Georgianna, do you like it at Brigham?"

"I am enjoying a very pleasant stay, Lord Allerdale."

"And you like my mother?"

Georgianna smiled. "How could I not? Lady Brigham has been extremely welcoming and is so lively and amusing that it would be a strange person indeed who could not like her."

"I believe your situation at home is not a happy one, Lady Georgianna."

Her brows rose at this rather abrupt statement.

"It may not surprise you to know that my mother is not always discreet. She has learned something of your story from my godmother." He frowned. "Mine also is not always happy, but that is a situation of my own making."

It seemed as if he were going to confide in her, after all. Hoping to make the situation easier for him, she said, "I am afraid you are not the only eavesdropper, although I did not mean to do it. I overheard a very little of your conversation with your father last night when I returned a book to the library. Only something about your honour, asking Devonan for more time, and following his advice. I assume you are in debt to Lord Devonan, but I do not understand why, if he is your friend, he is pressuring you in this way."

"I would not expect you to. He is an acquaintance rather than a friend, but even if he were in my inner circle, it would not matter; all gambling debts are debts of honour, ma'am, and must be paid immediately."

Her brow wrinkled. "But if this is so, why did you stake more than you could pay?"

He stood and began to pace. "I have been a fool for the last several months, ma'am. Something happened that upset me greatly——"

"The man in the lake?"

He threw himself back into his chair. "So you know about that?" His face darkened. "I was fond of Somerton. We had hauled each other out of some hair-raising situations in our time. But on this occasion, I failed him."

"What happened?"

"I hardly know," Lord Allerdale said curtly. "We had both decided to mend our ways and thought it wise that we stay away from Town for a while. I suggested I show him something of my own country. We had been fishing and I was rowing us back when he suddenly stood and stripped off his shirt. He said he would race me and dived into the water before I could advise him not to. My back was to the shore, and it was only when I reached it that I realised he was not there. I immediately swam out to find him, but the water in October is extremely cold and it was not long before I found myself in difficulties."

"It was an unfortunate accident," Lady Georgianna said, "but I cannot see what else you could have done."

"No. Perhaps not. My father thought I should have warned him earlier, but it never occurred to me that he would attempt such a thing." He shook his head as if to clear it. "We have digressed, where was I?"

"You were telling me how you have been a fool."

"Yes. I decided to live up to my father's opinion of me and have rarely come home since. I am very good at cards, my father ensured it, and generally win more than I lose. Devonan is not particularly skilled, and I do not understand how I lost so heavily to him. I am not such a fool that I allow myself to become inebriated when playing. But that evening, I somehow found my head swimming, perhaps I was ill, I don't know. Whatever the reason, I played poorly. It was not until the next day when he visited me and presented me with my vowels that I understood just how heavily I had lost. I came home and told my father the whole, but he refuses to advance me my allowance unless I do as he wishes."

"And that is?"

"To marry, ma'am. He believes the responsibility of my own family will sober me. He may be right. I must admit, I am weary of the existence I have been leading. There, I have told you the whole. I like and respect you; it has occurred to me that we could help each other. I believe your mother is as eager to see you wed. I am aware that I have not painted myself in a very good light, but I would attempt to mend my ways, ma'am."

Georgiana felt quite stunned. She had not expected a proposal. A wry smile twisted her lips. And what a proposal! She certainly could not accuse him of being romantic. He was offering her a marriage of convenience. Could it work? She liked him and he had close ties to her aunt. Any reputation he might have acquired for being wild and reckless would be easily overlooked by her parents; the heir to a marquess was not to be sniffed at. Lord Allerdale was regarding her with some urgency, she realised.

"Such a match would certainly please my parents, sir, but would it please me? I am glad that you have been so transparent in your motivations and appreciate your honesty, but although I do not doubt that you mean it when you say you intend to become more steady and mend your ways, I am not at all sure you will be able to do it. You are volatile, like your mother."

He leaned forwards eagerly, clearly relieved that she had not refused him outright.

"Yet you like her, as you like me, I believe. My mother has not got into any serious scrapes for many years now. We are not, I believe, unreformable."

"That may be so," Georgianna admitted. "But that is due to your father's influence, I think. I am not at all convinced that I would have any power over you, at all."

She did not doubt that Lord Allerdale was capable of love; he adored his mother and hated to upset her, but if any woman was to tame him, she would need to provoke the same degree of affection in him. Her character was so different from Lady Brigham's, she felt sure she was not that woman.

Perhaps sensing that he was losing this battle, he came to sit with her on the window seat and took her hands.

"I would do my best to make you happy."

Georgianna noted that her hands did not tremble in his, and when he raised one to his lips, she remained unmoved.

"But would your best be good enough?" she said reflectively. "I do not wish to be indelicate, but I will match your honesty. I am not at all sure I wish for a husband of your temperament; I believe I would deal better with an even-tempered man. And although we may have enjoyed each other's company over the last few days, I am not convinced there is any spark of attraction between us."

Lord Allerdale's dark brows winged up and a rather predatory glint came into his eyes. He suddenly pulled her to him and kissed her. Georgianna felt a spurt of annoyance rather than any alarm. She sat very still, neither struggling nor encouraging him. After a moment, he released her and gave a dry laugh.

"Perhaps you are right. But it is not necessary, you know. You need only provide me with an heir or two and I will leave you alone."

He could not have said anything to repulse Georgianna more. She now understood why he had appeared so startled when she had mentioned Miss Hughes' engagement to Mr Tucker. How convenient that connection would have been for him; she was an old friend who did not enjoy Town, so Lord Allerdale could have easily kept a mistress without her having any inkling of it. How pleased she was that Miss Hughes was already taken; she would be much happier with Mr Tucker, she felt sure. Georgianna stood and moved quickly to the chair he had vacated. When she spoke, her voice was cold but calm.

"How dare you kiss me? My words were not a challenge but a factual observation. As for the sort of marriage you describe, it would not please me at all, sir. I must refuse your offer."

The servant girl arrived at last, with two small glasses of wine and a plate of pastries. Lord Allerdale tossed his off in one swift movement and sat frowning, staring at the floor.

"I find I have no appetite," Georgianna said, "and would now like to return to my aunt."

When he raised his eyes, she saw the wild glitter that she had observed as he left the inn after their first meeting. It no longer frightened her, however. She did not believe she was in any real danger from him. His temper was merely up; he did not like to be crossed. However, she breathed a little easier when he stood and bowed.

"Very well, ma'am. I will go and tell Tibbs to prepare the horses."

CHAPTER 15

Lord Allerdale was gone for some time. Georgianna took a sip of her wine and nibbled at a pastry. She hoped he would regain his good humour by the time he returned or their journey back to Brigham would be an uncomfortable one. She stood as the door opened. Lord Allerdale strode in and offered her a rather flamboyant bow.

"Your carriage awaits, Lady Georgianna. I am afraid my horse is indeed lame and there is not a matching pair to be had. The only vehicle to hire is a post chaise and four, which will at least ensure a speedy conclusion to our journey."

Georgianna felt only relief at this news, for there was a rather reckless air about her escort. He handed her up into the carriage and followed her in, pulling the door closed behind him. As they moved off, she began to feel a little uneasy; it was not at all the thing to be alone with a gentleman in a closed carriage.

"Where is Tibbs?" she said.

"I do not trust anyone else to attend to my horses, ma'am."

She could well believe this; her father was just the same with his favourites. After a few moments, he turned to her and said conversationally, "Will you make your come out next season?"

Georgianna relaxed; it seemed he was not going to be awkward, after all. "I do not know my mother's plans. Perhaps."

He proceeded to draw for her a colourful picture of the many and varied amusements that she could expect to enjoy. Despite his previous outrageous behaviour, she found herself laughing as he enlivened his descriptions with amusing, if slightly malicious, anecdotes of the characters she was likely to meet. They passed a pleasant half hour in this way.

When he at last came to the end of his recital, Georgianna turned, still smiling, to look out of the window. Her brow furrowed. They had been travelling at a smart pace and she had expected to recognise the countryside around Brigham by now. Not only was this not the case, but she saw a signpost informing her that she was on the Carlisle road.

"There has been some mistake, sir. We are going in the wrong direction."

"Not at all, Lady Georgianna. The postilions are following my instructions perfectly," Lord Allerdale said, the glitter back in his eyes. "I had hoped you would not realise our change of plan just yet, but it was a forlorn hope, I suppose. You are an extremely observant young lady."

"I am also an extremely annoyed one, just at

present. You know I have another engagement today. Where are you taking me?"

"Gretna Green," he stated baldly.

Georgianna felt a cold rage course through her veins. "Are you quite, quite mad?" she exclaimed. "Give the postillions some new instructions, at once."

"No," he said softly. "You will marry me. My honour will be restored and your future secured."

"Oh," Georgianna gasped. "Do not pretend you are concerned with my future; it is your own that you are trying to protect. You would not have asked me if you had not learned of Miss Hughes' engagement."

"But I did learn of it," he said. "And I must thank you for ensuring that I did not waste my time. Time, you see, is of the essence."

"Do not be such a fool," she snapped. "You are like a spoilt child who must always have his way. You will not have it with me, however. I believe both people must give their consent to be wed, even in Scotland, and I shall certainly not give it."

Lord Allerdale's eyes flashed but his voice remained calm. "You may change your mind when you have spent the night at Carlisle."

"I would sooner be ruined than married to you, sir, any reservations I may have had before having now been increased tenfold. You know nothing of honour and are not fit to be anyone's husband."

When her scathing condemnation of his character and morals failed to make any mark on him, she changed tack.

"Come," she said in gentler tones. "You are in a temper and acting wildly. Think of the pain you will cause Lady Brigham."

"I am thinking of her, I assure you. She will be delighted to have you as a daughter-in-law and think the episode entirely romantic. Whatever you say to her, she will not be able to bring herself to believe that you could not grow to love me."

Unfortunately, Georgianna could well believe these claims.

"Then think of how much further you will sink in your father's estimation," she said, a little desperately.

"Perhaps, in the short-term," he conceded. "But once he sees that I intend to treat you well, and I assure you I do, he will forgive me."

Georgianna finally accepted the futility of arguing with him in his present mood. She felt sure that his determination to wed her was driven more by his desire to alleviate his mother's worries, and perhaps even to prevent her from committing some folly, than his concern that his reputation would be besmirched by Lord Devonan's threat to expose him as a man who did not pay his debts. She felt sure that once his temper had burned itself out, he would regret his impulsive actions. She only hoped that she was not quite ruined before that happened. She certainly would not rely on it, however, she would just have to bend her mind to the problem of how to escape his clutches.

She eyed his greatcoat speculatively several times, wondering if he kept a pistol in his pocket; but even if he did and she had an opportunity to steal it, she doubted very much he would believe she had the courage to use it. She doubted it herself.

When they reached Carlisle, three hours later, she had still formed no coherent plan. Any idea of raising a hue and cry and appealing to someone to help her was dashed as Lord Allerdale took her arm in a firm grip as soon as she had alighted from the carriage and bundled her into the inn. She grimaced. The idea of creating such a scene made her shudder, and she was sure that his fiendish mind would have no trouble concocting a story that would leave her looking extremely foolish. She would need to be more subtle.

The inn was large and busy, the only private parlour still to be had faced on to the stable yard. It was reached by a flight of eight stairs, was extremely small, and boasted no fireplace. She suspected that it had probably once been used as a storeroom.

Lord Allerdale bowed to her and removed the key from the door.

"I shall give you some time alone to consider your position, Lady Georgianna. It is not far to the border from here; we could be married today and be home by nightfall if you should change your mind. It would at least protect you from the scandal of having spent the night in my company."

He closed the door and she heard the grate of the key in the lock.

Georgianna hurried to the window and tried to push it up. It rose an inch or two but then jammed. Glancing down into the yard, she realised that she could not easily have escaped through it; she would probably break her ankle if she tried to drop down onto the cobbles from this height. She spent a few fruitless minutes pacing back and forth, hoping he did not start drinking or the chances of him coming to his senses would go from slim to none.

A small cry escaped her as her foot struck a chest

that was set against the wall. She sat on it, gritted her teeth, and grasped her injured limb. A strangled sob escaped her. Mr Knight had promised to slay any dragons that threatened her, and at that moment, she wished very much that he was here and would run Lord Allerdale through with his sword. He was not here, however, and he had no sword that she knew of, which was perhaps just as well; in a duel, by pistol or sword, his size might count against him. She would just have to slay this particular dragon herself.

When the pain in her toes had subsided to a dull throb, she stood and looked down accusingly at the plain, wooden chest. Bending suddenly, she opened it. It was filled with a rather random selection of objects from tarnished candlesticks to spare tankards and cutlery. She knelt, an arrested expression in her eyes. Reaching into the chest, her fingers curled around a round knob made of iron. She pulled it and the long length of a poker was revealed. She stood and moved over to the door, testing the weight of the handle in the palm of her hand. It was not at all subtle but might just work.

The sound of an unhurried tread on the stairs reached her ears and she flattened herself against the wall. She heard the scratch of the key being inserted into the lock and watched the handle turn. The door opened and Lord Allerdale stepped into the room. He took two hasty steps forwards and stopped; his eyes fixed on the window. He gave a low laugh.

"It seems I underestimated you, L—"

She raised the poker and struck him. He swayed for a moment and then crumpled to the floor. Feeling quite sick, Georgianna knelt beside him and laid her weapon down. She assured herself that he was still breathing and then reached into the pocket of his greatcoat. She did not find a pistol but a money pouch. She stood, frowned down at his pale face for a moment, and then fled.

She enquired in the yard if there was a horse she could hire and felt a giddy rush of relief when she discovered there was. Although it took the stable boy only minutes to make the horse ready, she tapped her foot impatiently and could not help glancing nervously up at the parlour window. It was only when she was cantering away from the inn that her heart stopped pounding in her chest.

For the first few miles, she found herself glancing anxiously over her shoulder every time she heard a carriage behind her, but she gradually relaxed. She doubted very much Lord Allerdale would be in any fit state to pursue her for some time. Even so, she would have liked to have left the road, but she did not know the country and feared she would get hopelessly lost.

She had been riding for perhaps an hour when she saw a signpost for the village of Thursby. Ominous clouds troubled the sky, and she was tired and in desperate need of some refreshment. She turned onto the lane and soon came to the village. The Ship Inn faced onto the village green and looked reputable. She was relieved to discover that it was also extremely quiet.

The landlord gave her a thoughtful glance when she requested a private parlour.

"Are you all alone, ma'am? It seems a trifle irregular."

She considered him coolly for a moment. He had

an honest face. Should she confide in him? She decided against it; the fewer people who knew of this disgraceful episode, the better. If her father ever caught wind of it, he would insist she marry Lord Allerdale.

She raised a haughty eyebrow. "A series of unfortunate events, which I have no intention of sharing with you, have led me to your inn, sir. I am chilled, thirsty, and tired. Escort me to a private parlour and bring me some tea and bread and butter immediately."

Seemingly impressed by her confident manner, he bowed and showed her to a room far more comfortable than the one she had so recently escaped from. He brought in the tray himself and made up the fire, shooting her an inquisitive glance as he got to his feet.

"Are you going far, ma'am?"

"To Cockermouth," she said. "I had not realised quite how far it was."

"You sure you're not going t'other way, ma'am?" he said, his eyes kindly.

"Have I not just said so? Is there a stagecoach that passes this way?"

"Not many stop here now, ma'am." He shook his head sadly. "Used to be a different story in my father's day."

Her heart sank.

"But as it happens, your luck is in. The Whitehaven coach will stop here in about an hour, and that stops at Cockermouth right enough."

A relieved smile curved her lips. "Do you think I will be able to get a seat on it?"

"Shouldn't be no problem, ma'am. As long as you've got the fare. I'll let you know when it arrives."

"Thank you. And have you someone who could return the horse I hired in Carlisle?"

"That can easily be arranged, miss."

She took the tray over to the fire, set it on a small table, and sank gratefully into one of the comfortable armchairs that sat beside the cheerful blaze. Once she had eaten the small repast, she leaned her head back and closed her eyes. The excitement of the day caught up with her and she fell into a light sleep. She awoke when her head fell awkwardly to one side. She opened sleepy eyes and blinked hastily, wondering if she was still dreaming. When the vision before her did not fade away, she briefly closed them again and gave a long, low sigh.

Lord Allerdale sat completely at his ease in the other chair, a blood-stained bandage wrapped around his head. He grinned ruefully at her, a mixture of amusement and respect in his eyes.

"I felicitate you, cousin. You are a remarkable woman. Not once this day, have you treated me to hysterics."

"They would have availed me nothing and wasted a great deal of energy," she said dryly.

"Very true," he acknowledged. "You are also very resourceful. Your method of relieving yourself of my presence was a little crude, but very effective. Did you think you had murdered me?"

"I checked you were still breathing before I left."

"How very conscientious of you. I really did not deserve such consideration."

"No, you did not. How did you find me?"

"Logic," he said. "A hired horse can only go so far in an hour."

She eyed him warily. "What do you intend to do now?"

He smiled. "It seems that in knocking me senseless, you restored my sanity, cousin. I am going to take you back to Brigham. You would make the devil of a wife if you took to hitting me over the head every time I lost my temper."

She looked sceptical. "Do you expect me to believe you?"

"Yes," he said. "My actions today may have been execrable, but I think you will discover if you cast your mind over all our conversations today, that I have not once lied to you."

"I think you are forgetting the matter of the lame horse, sir."

"Yes, I had forgotten that. But it is not surprising that it should have slipped my mind. It is a miracle that I have any wits left at all." He reached into his coat, withdrew a small pistol, and offered it to her.

"Take this as surety of my good intentions. I suppose I should be grateful that you only pilfered one of my pockets, or you might have been tempted to finish me off!"

She took the pistol and pointed it at him.

"What makes you think I will not do so now?"

The landlord strode into the room. "I'm sorry, miss, I was down in the cellars. I would not have allowed you to be—" His eyes widened. "Now you put that down, miss. When I saw the yellow bounder outside, I realised my suspicions were correct. You were headed for Gretna Green no doubt but changed your mind. It won't be the first time it's happened. A few days locked up in a coach with their intended has brought more than one female to their senses. Of course, by then, it's usually too late."

"Well it is not too late for me," she said. "And I did not go at all willingly, I assure you."

"Even so, ma'am, I'd ask as you don't go putting a bullet in anyone in my establishment."

She suddenly laughed and handed Lord Allerdale his pistol. "I believe you, now take me home, you disgraceful creature."

"Now, miss, don't be too hasty," the landlord said. "You'd be better to get on the stagecoach. How do you know you can trust him?"

Lord Allerdale rose. "It is not the lady who has come to her senses, sir, but me. She appears so genteel, doesn't she? But observe the bandage around my head, not only has she held me at gunpoint, but she has also knocked me out with a poker. I have decided we would not suit."

The landlord looked quite shocked. "And so you might, sir."

CHAPTER 16

The Mossops tried to leave once they realised the Tweddles were also present at the vicarage, but Alexander prevented them by the simple expedient of shutting the door behind them and leaning against it. Impressed by his size and slightly menacing manner they reluctantly took their seats. Mr Simpson played his part to admiration, every inch the disappointed custodian of his erring flock.

When he named Thomas Mossop as the father of Molly's child there was an uproar. Forgetting for a moment that he did not hold grudges, Sam Tweddle lunged at Thomas and there would have been a mill if Alexander had not stepped in and banged their heads together. Before they could regain their feet, he brandished a pistol at them and snapped out an order for them to sit down and hold their peace.

The vicar took advantage of the stunned silence that followed this manoeuvre, to roar out a verse from Revelations.

"But the fearful, and unbelieving, and the abominable,

and murderers, and whoremongers, and sorcerers, and idolaters, and all liars, shall have their part in the lake which burneth with fire and brimstone: which is the second death."

That certainly caught their attention. He expounded on the folly of human nature and the evils of parents poisoning their children with their own sins. He laid the blame equally on all of them until Mr Mossop and Mr Tweddle sent each other sideways glances and shifted in their seats.

"If we say that we have no sin, we deceive ourselves, and the truth is not in us. If we confess our sins, he is faithful and just to forgive us our sins, and to cleanse us from all unrighteousness. If we say that we have not sinned, we make him a liar, and his word is not in us."

When he pointed out the danger to Molly in this life as well as the next, she burst into tears and jumped to her feet.

"But I didn't mean no harm. I couldn't think what else to do."

"Then you had better hope my words have been heard and taken to heart, Molly. There is one in this room, other than God, who can offer you forgiveness. But he will only do so if there is a genuine reconciliation between both families."

All eyes turned towards Alexander. Mr Tweddle got to his feet, a slightly belligerent look in his eye.

"And just who might you be, sir? I can't say I'm best pleased at having all our dirty linen hung out to dry in front of a stranger."

"Perhaps not, Mr Tweddle, but I believe I have every right to be here. I am Alexander Knight, Marquess of Somerton, heir to the Duke of Rushwick, and brother to the man Molly claimed to be the father of her child."

An audible gasp went around the room.

"I'm sorry for your loss, sir," Mr Tweddle said. "And I'm sorry for the rest of it, an' all. You don't look much like a marquess, I would have put you down as a soldier the way you handle yourself and bark out orders."

"I was Major Knight in a former life."

"I knew it!" he said, pleased at this proof of his native shrewdness. "I'd be very grateful to you, sir, if you would forgive my Molly. She's a good girl really, and as Mr Simpson has pointed out, we are all to blame."

Mr Mossop stood up.

"I would also ask you show Molly some mercy, sir. I doubt my boy would have gone along with her plan if she hadn't talked him into it, but—"

Mr Tweddle rounded on him. "If it isn't just like you, Fred Mossop, to—"

"Enough!" Alexander's voice cracked out. "You have heard my terms. If you cannot abide by them then I will be forced to take matters further."

Both men observed the steel in his eyes and subsided. Mr Tweddle nodded and stepped up to his nemesis. He held out his hand.

"I'll shake on it if you will."

Mr Mossop stared down at the swollen knuckled hand for a moment and then took it in his own. Thomas and Sam soon followed their example. Molly threw herself into Thomas' arms and burst into noisy sobs upon his chest.

Mr Tweddle looked on indulgently. "I hope you'll see fit to marry them 'afore long, Mr Simpson."

The vicar was beaming. "I insist upon it," he said. "Just as soon as the banns can be read."

"We can't never thank you enough, sir," Mr Tweddle said to Alexander.

"Just see to it that you stick to your side of the bargain," he said. "Good day."

He turned on his heel and marched from the room, pleased with the outcome of the meeting but impatient to be on his way.

Alexander did not reach Brigham until mid-afternoon. He felt a spurt of annoyance when he discovered Allerdale was not at home but gave his card to the very correct butler and asked that it be taken to Lord Brigham. The butler glanced down at it and then back at Alexander a little more respectfully.

"Certainly, sir. If you will just come this way."

He left him in the library. Alexander took a turn about the room, pausing at a table with a book on it. *Culpeper's English Physician: And Complete Herbal.* He rested his fingertips upon it for a moment, certain that Lady Georgianna's fingers had also lain there not very long ago. He had missed her, he realised. A wry grin twisted his lips. His determination to come here had not been solely due to his wish to talk with Allerdale; it had not even been his prime driver. He had not understood that until this moment.

He had seen many men who were not yet hardened to warfare despair over the loss of a friend, and Allerdale showed all the symptoms. His disquiet where that gentleman was concerned had changed; he no longer suspected him of any wrongdoing where his brother was concerned, but neither did he trust him to toe the line with Lady Georgianna.

A man who was not himself and naturally wild, could not be relied upon. Even if he had been less than complimentary about her after their first meeting, Alexander could not believe that Allerdale had spent three days in Lady Georgianna's company without succumbing to her allure. He imagined Allerdale would see her as a challenge. He only hoped that he had not succeeded in winning her over with a show of charm. Alexander had promised to slay any and all dragons that threatened her and had found the last few days a sore trial. She had gone straight into the dragon's lair and he had been powerless to prevent her.

He noticed a notebook lying neatly next to Culpeper's guide. He was not sure of the etiquette of notebooks. If it had been a diary, he hoped that he would have had the strength to resist opening it, but if it was, as he suspected, merely a list of notes concerning herbal remedies, there could surely be no harm? He quickly opened it, merely wishing to see her handwriting. He smiled, her letters were precise, neat, and efficient. He would have expected nothing less.

"If you will come this way, sir?"

Alexander closed the notebook, glad that his back was to the door and so the butler could not know he had been prying. He followed him to Lord Brigham's study.

"A bottle of claret, please, Lancet," the marquess said.

"Certainly, sir."

Before he left the room, the butler went to a small

table set between two armchairs and removed two glasses and a packs of cards.

Lord Brigham sent an assessing glance at his uninvited guest.

"You are the image of your father, Lord Somerton." He waved to an armchair. "Please, make yourself comfortable."

Alexander seated himself in the chair indicated and crossed his legs.

"You must wonder why I have paid you this unexpected visit, sir," he said.

"Not at all," Lord Brigham said softly. "It is my son you wished to visit with, I believe. I think I can hazard a guess as to why."

Alexander merely raised a brow.

"What rank did you rise to?" Lord Brigham asked after a moment.

"Major, sir."

"I'm not surprised," Lord Brigham said. "You have a certain presence. Even if your brother had not mentioned your profession, I would have known it; the cut of your coat speaks of Scott's tailoring. I imagine you wish to discover for yourself all the circumstances of your brother's unfortunate death. I must say that I was surprised your father did not come himself when it happened."

"I believe it would have been too painful for him, and he is not as fit as he once was. It is a long way for an old man to travel."

"Very true," Lord Brigham conceded. "I can and will furnish you with an account of what occurred."

Alexander listened in silence to Lord Brigham's

concise, objective description of the event. It was as he'd suspected, an unfortunate accident.

"You may believe me when I tell you that these are all the facts Allerdale knows. Whatever unpleasant situations he finds himself in, he always confides in me." Lord Brigham frowned. "I did not understand just how deeply your brother's death had affected him at first, and I am afraid I dealt rather harshly with him."

"In my experience, sir, it would not matter how you dealt with him. If a man feels guilt that he is alive and his friend is not, it tends to eat away at him no matter how many times someone tells him there was nothing he could have done."

Lord Brigham winced. "But I told him no such thing; I told him he should have warned your brother not to go in the water. Of course, it never occurred to Allerdale that anyone would do so in October."

Alexander had come to Brigham in search of reassurance but instead found himself giving it.

"And why would he? My brother was often impulsive, sir, but even I would not have expected him to do such a thing." He smiled wryly. "Father-son relationships are strewn with difficulties, are they not? I have had some harsh words directed at me in my time, and I went directly against my father's wishes when I signed up, but I have never doubted his regard. A man must face his demons and conquer them on his own. Perhaps, sir, it might help Allerdale to know that I do not hold him responsible for James' death."

Lord Brigham looked at Alexander with some respect.

"I judge you to be a little younger than Allerdale,

but your experiences abroad have taught you wisdom, Lord Somerton."

Alexander smiled. "Perhaps, a little."

"Let me introduce you to my wife. She liked your brother and will wish to meet you. We also have our cousin, Lady Colyford, visiting at the moment, and her niece Lady Georgianna Voss."

"I am aware, sir. I have been staying in the barn at Lake Cottage."

Lord Brigham looked amused. "I am sure you had a very good reason for staying in such rough lodgings. I do hope you intend to share it with me."

"I will be happy to do so, sir, but as I shall also have to explain it all to Lady Colyford, would you mind very much if I wait until we join the ladies?"

He looked surprised. "She does not know then?"

"I am afraid I have been guilty of practising a little deception. I have been travelling incognito."

"I must admit to being more than a little intrigued. However, I doubt very much if you deceived Hester; she could not fail to have noticed your resemblance to Rushwick. I believe he was one of her beaux at one time."

Alexander could easily imagine that his father would have been attracted to Lady Colyford when she was a young lady but found it interesting that she had claimed not to remember him.

"According to Miss Felsham, she assumed I was his natural child."

"Ah, I see. Well your father did have quite the reputation at one time, but I would be very surprised to discover he had a natural child of your age. He was a changed man once he married and finally settled down. I have observed that the married state often sobers a man."

Lady Colyford glanced quickly up as they entered the drawing room.

"Mr Knight!" she exclaimed, rising to her feet. "Has something happened at Lake Cottage?"

"Nothing to concern you, ma'am," he said.

Lady Brigham rose and smiled at him.

"My love," her lord said, "this is Lord Somerton, Rushwick's son come to visit us."

"Poor James' brother?" she said.

"Yes, ma'am."

She rushed forwards and took his hands. "I am so sorry about what happened to him. He was a great friend of my son's and we liked him very much." She turned to Hester. "But why did you call him Mr Knight?"

Alexander went to Lady Colyford and took her hand. "I have not enjoyed deceiving you, ma'am. But I thought it necessary."

"I do hope you intend to explain," she said with some asperity. "It was no way to repay my hospitality."

Lord Brigham laughed. "Quite so, Hester, especially when you allowed him to sleep in the barn!"

Lady Brigham's eyes widened. "The barn, Hester? You allowed the son of a duke to sleep in your barn?"

Lady Colyford's lips suddenly twitched. "As well as move some large boulders from my garden and chop the wood."

"Hester!" Lady Brigham cried. "You are quite outrageous!"

Alexander smiled. "It was my pleasure, ma'am."

Lady Brigham bade him sit down. "Now, you must

explain it all. I am bursting with curiosity. Why were you travelling incognito? Is there a lady involved, perhaps? It sounds very romantic."

"There was a romance involved," he said.

Lady Brigham clapped her hands. "I knew it. Tell all!"

"But it was not my own."

Lady Colyford gave him a knowing smile. "Are you quite sure of that?"

Rather than answer this question, Alexander launched into his tale.

"Well," Lady Colyford said when he had finished. "I must say, I think you did very well, Lord Somerton. It is a happy outcome indeed. And Mr Simpson has certainly risen in my esteem."

"He performed his part very well, ma'am."

Naturally curious, Lady Brigham said, "What would you have done if the child had been your brother's?"

"My father would have insisted he be brought up at Rushwick."

"I am pleased to hear it," Lady Colyford said brusquely.

The butler came into the room and presented Lord Brigham with a card.

"Thank you, Lancet. Please bring Lord Westbury here."

Lady Colyford groaned. "He would choose this, of all moments, to put in an appearance."

Alexander looked at her closely, wondering why this moment, in particular, was not convenient.

Lord Westbury just then entered the room. He was tall and dark like his daughter, but his eyes were the same light blue as his sister's. Once he had made his bow to everyone, he frowned at Lady Colyford.

"I would like a word in private with you, sister. I have been some hours upon the road and was most displeased to find you from home."

Lady Colyford's chin jutted forwards and her eyes narrowed. "As you had not informed me of your impending arrival, you can hardly blame me for that. And I cannot think of anything you might wish to say to me that cannot be said in front of my friends."

A dull colour infused Lord Westbury's cheeks.

"Sit down, Westbury," Lord Brigham said firmly. "I shall send for a glass of wine. You will, of course, spend the night, and so will have ample opportunity to speak with Hester alone."

"Thank you, Brigham, one would be most welcome." He turned again to Lady Colyford. "Where is my daughter, ma'am?"

Lady Brigham said brightly, "I must tell you how much I like your daughter, Lord Westbury. She is a charming girl. Her manners are all they should be."

"I am pleased to hear you say so, ma'am. I would ask you to send for her; it is some time since I have seen Lady Georgianna."

"If you have seen her above five times in the last year, I will own myself astonished," Lady Colyford said dryly.

"I am afraid you will have to wait just a little longer, sir," Lady Brigham said. "My son has taken her for a driving lesson in his curricle."

Lord Westbury frowned. "Allerdale has taken her out alone?"

"No," his sister said. "I insisted he take his groom, of course."

"I should think so," Lord Westbury said. "How long have they been gone?"

"Oh, it is some time now," Lady Brigham admitted. "But young people lose track of time so easily, do they not?"

"How long precisely, ma'am?" Lord Westbury said sternly.

"Oh, sometime this morning, I believe," she said airily.

"Since breakfast." Lady Colyford said. "It must have been about half past ten. I am most put out, for we had an engagement this afternoon."

"Why did you not inform me of this?" Lord Brigham asked his lady.

"You have been shut up in your study with Lord Devonan all day, my lord. And you had informed Lancet that on no account were you to be disturbed. Hester has been fretting these two hours, but I told her that no harm can come to Lady Georgianna when she is with Miles."

"I cannot share your optimism, ma'am," Alexander said sharply. "What if they have suffered some accident? A search must be organised, at once."

"At last, the voice of reason," Lord Westbury said.

Lord Brigham stood. "I shall arrange it. Sit down, Lord Somerton, you do not know the country. I will send out the grooms and stable lads, who know it very well. I doubt anything serious has befallen them or Allerdale's groom would have informed us of it. They are probably quite comfortable in a local inn whilst they wait for some trifling repair to the curricle to be attended to."

Alexander would far rather have joined the search, but he could not fault Lord Brigham's reasoning.

"I shall arrange for some refreshments," Lady Brigham said, rushing after her husband.

A rather awkward silence fell upon the room. Alexander felt the tension between Lord Westbury and Lady Colyford. He strolled to the far end of the room and stood gazing out of the window.

Lord Westbury sent his sister a look from under beetling brows.

"Who is that strange woman you have living with you, Hester?" he finally said.

"Are you referring to my companion, Miss Ravenchurch?" she said coolly.

"Dash it, Hester. You can't have that woman as your companion, she is clearly queer in her attic. Seemed to think I had come to take her for a drive around the park."

"That woman, is a distant cousin of ours, Westbury. And she may sometimes become a little confused, but she is harmless."

Lord Westbury's face fell. "She can't be," he protested. "We've never had a lunatic in the family. You must put her away, Hester. We can't have it become general knowledge."

"I, unlike you, brother, am not one to turn an impoverished relation from my door."

"Now that is hardly fair. It was Serena who insisted that you leave."

"Of that, I have no doubt. As to your assertion that we have never had a lunatic in the family, I beg leave to differ," Lady Colyford said in a hard voice. "Are you aware that Serena told Georgianna that she hated her?"

Alexander's brows rose, and he sent a sideways glance in Lord Westbury's direction. He looked quite stunned.

"You must be mistaken, Hester. Why would she hate her own daughter?"

They seemed to have completely forgotten Alexander's presence. He ought to quietly leave the room, of course, but he wished very much to hear the answer.

"I assure you I am not. She told Georgianna, that it was because she was a girl, and so, in her words, has had to endure your maulings—"

"That is enough!" Lord Westbury growled.

"But it wasn't enough for Serena," Lady Colyford said scathingly. "She did not hesitate to inform Georgianna that you were in Town with your mistress! Not something, I think you will agree, that any girl just out of the schoolroom should hear. I imagine you were furious when you heard she had sent her to me. She did it to punish Georgianna, of course, thinking I was living in a hovel. She often punishes Georgianna, by the way. She regularly questions the girl's personal maid so she can find some excuse to do so. Were you aware of it?"

Alexander's fists clenched. He and Lady Georgianna had never talked of their families. He had not asked because it would only have invited enquiries about his own and he had not wished to lie to her. Now he understood why she had also avoided the subject.

"No, I was not," Lord Westbury said in a tight voice. "What have I to do with the schoolroom?"

"You have clearly had very little to do with it, but it is past time you took an interest, Westbury. Are you aware that Rupert is running wild? That he caused his nurse to fall down the stairs?"

"But Serena laid the blame for that at Georgianna's door."

"Of course, she did. I expect you have come to take her back to Avondale, but I would ask you to consider all that I have said before you do. She is far happier with me, I assure you."

Alexander grimaced. He hoped Lady Georgianna would never have to go back to her home. It sounded as if her life had been a living hell.

Lady Brigham had been gone at least half an hour, but now she came tripping into the room, a delighted smile on her face.

"Is there some news, ma'am?" Alexander asked.

"No, not as yet. At least, not news about Lady Georgianna. I am still convinced it will be just as my lord said. Something stupid like a broken wheel will have delayed them."

"And what about the refreshments?" Lady Colyford asked.

"Oh, I had completely forgotten."

"Do not concern yourself," Lady Colyford said. "I do not think I could stomach anything just at the moment."

"No, well perhaps it is as well then, that I have asked cook to put dinner back an hour."

CHAPTER 17

I t was nearing half past five when Lord Brigham strode into the drawing room, a frown between his eyes.

"Everyone has reported back and there has been no sighting of them. All the wheelwrights and blacksmiths within a reasonable distance have been checked, as have the inns. I do not pretend to understand it. Lady Colyford, you are the only one who breakfasted with them. What was discussed?"

"Very little," she said. "Allerdale asked Georgianna if she was ready for her driving lesson. I insisted he take his groom. We talked of visiting Miss Hughes, and Miles said he might accompany us. Georgianna mentioned that Miss Hughes was to marry Mr Tucker. I do recall that Miles seemed a little surprised at this news, and then they left."

Lord Brigham's frown deepened. Lancet just then announced Sir Gerard and his daughter. Lord Brigham introduced them to Lord Westbury and Alexander.

"Very pleased to make your acquaintance, I am sure," Sir Gerard said, although he sent a hard glance in Lord Westbury's direction.

Alexander noted that Miss Hughes looked rather pale.

"I am sorry to disturb you at so late an hour; I am well aware that you generally dine at six." He gave Lord Brigham a meaningful look. "I am afraid I bring tidings which may not be welcome, sir."

Lady Colyford stood, crossed the room, and put her hand on his arm. "Sir Gerard? Is it concerning Georgianna? Do not tell me she is hurt!"

He patted her hand. "Not as far as I am aware, my dear," he said gravely.

"Then, is it Miles?" Lady Brigham asked, her voice trembling.

Sir Gerard's glance took in the assembled company.

"You may speak freely," Lord Brigham said.

Sir Gerard nodded. "Very well. I was worried when Hester and Lady Georgianna did not visit this afternoon."

"I am sorry," Lady Colyford said. "I should have sent a note, but I have been a little distracted."

"I quite understand, Hester." He turned to Lord Brigham. "Your stable lad, Jem, came over, asking if Allerdale and Lady Georgianna had been to visit. I questioned him, of course, and he admitted that they have been missing since this morning. When he had gone, I recalled that Hannah had been surprisingly quiet all day."

All eyes turned to Hannah. Her face turned an

unbecoming shade of red and unshed tears trembled in her eyes.

"Hannah!" Lady Brigham cried. "If you know something you must tell us at once."

"Go on, Hannah," Sir Gerard said sternly.

She dashed a hand over her eyes. "Papa and I went into Cockermouth this morning. Whilst Father conducted his business, I went with my maid to purchase some gloves. We went for a walk down by the river afterwards. On our way back, we passed The Swan Inn. And I saw, I saw…" Her voice wavered and she gulped.

"What is it you saw?" Lord Brigham said gently.

"I saw Lady Georgianna and Lord Allerdale, sitting together in the window. He had her hands in his, and then he kissed her."

Alexander felt a cold chill run down his spine. "What did Lady Georgianna do next?" he demanded.

The harshness in his voice broke Hannah's composure. "I do not know, I hurried past," she said on a sob.

"The cad!" Lord Westbury snapped.

"He is not a cad!" Lady Brigham protested. "If she allowed him to kiss her, then you cannot blame my son. She is a very beautiful girl, what man who has red blood running in his veins would not wish to kiss her?"

"A man of rank might wish to kiss a lady of quality," Lord Westbury said between gritted teeth, "but he does not do so unless he is prepared to wed her."

"And what makes you think he is not prepared to do so?" Lady Brigham said. "They have become very great friends over the last few days."

"Then why have they not returned here?" Lord Westbury snapped.

"I'm sorry," Hannah sobbed. "I didn't say anything to Papa because I assumed that Miles had proposed to her, or at least I hoped he had. I am not one for gossip and like them both. I did not wish to put them in an awkward position if I was mistaken. But when I discovered they were missing, I told Papa the whole."

"This is dreadful." Lady Colyford said, her face ashen. "I have reason to believe that Lady Georgianna would not welcome his kisses."

"How can you know such a thing?" Lady Brigham protested. "Why should she not wish him to kiss her?"

"Because I believe her heart to already be taken," she said in a hollow voice.

Hope and despair fought for prime position in Alexander's breast. He ruthlessly subdued both.

"Whether she has developed a tendre for anyone else is now immaterial, Hester," Lord Westbury said. "Allerdale must marry her."

"I believe that is his intention," Lord Brigham said in a flat voice. "Whether she likes it or not."

The sound of shattering glass made all heads turn towards Alexander. He opened his hand and let the remains of his wine glass fall to the floor. Rivulets of blood poured down the palm of his hand and began to stain his coat sleeve. He calmly pulled out a handkerchief and wrapped it around his hand.

"You had better let me look at that," Lady Hester said, coming towards him.

"You need not trouble yourself," he said calmly, only the muscle twitching in his jaw hinting at the enormous self-control he was exerting. "Continue, if you please, Lord Brigham."

"I am afraid it is my fault. I decided it was time to put a stop to Allerdale's wild ways before he killed himself or somebody else. He lost heavily at cards to Lord Devonan and I refused to pay his debt unless he married. I believed it would give his life another direction, some meaning, perhaps, and steady him. Only yesterday, I told him he must find a wife within two weeks. I did not wish him to do it in this manner, however."

"But, my lord," Lady Brigham said. "Why two weeks?"

"Because I had some power over him, and he upset you!" Lord Brigham said sharply. "I knew you would not be easy until this matter was resolved. I did not expect him to marry within that time, only find a lady willing to accept his offer of marriage. It occurred to me when Hester mentioned his surprise that Hannah was engaged to marry Mr Tucker, that he had probably decided to offer for her."

"I mean no offence," Lady Brigham said, "but they would certainly not have suited."

Hannah shook her head. "No, we would not have. There was a time when I thought myself a little in love with him, but now I love Mr Tucker, I know it was nothing but infatuation."

Lord Brigham sighed. "He obviously decided to try his luck with Lady Georgianna, as I hoped he would. But as they have not returned, I can only assume she refused him."

"Do you mean to tell me, sir," Alexander said icily.

"That Allerdale intends to ruin her so she will have no choice but to marry him?"

"I keep telling you, she already has no choice but to marry him," Lord Westbury said, exasperated.

Lord Brigham's eyes did not leave Alexander's. "He would not force himself upon her, of that I am certain. But has it occurred to you that Gretna Green is only a few hours away? If he could persuade her that she is already ruined, as Lord Westbury clearly believes, she might be persuaded to marry him over the anvil."

Alexander stood and strode towards the door.

"Then it is to Gretna Green that I shall go."

Lady Brigham saw something in his face that alarmed her.

"Stop him, my lord! He will murder Miles, I think."

Lord Westbury's brows rose, and he looked over at his sister, his lips opening as if he would speak. She gave him a very direct look and he remained silent.

The crunch of wheels on gravel was audible in the silence that had descended at these words. Alexander paused, turned on his heel, and strode to the window.

"A post chaise and four," he bit out.

"I quite understand your very natural desire to tear my son limb from limb," Lord Brigham said. "But I would ask that you at least wait until we have all the facts before us."

"Brigham!" his lady cried.

"Be quiet, Julia," he said coolly.

A few moments later, the objects of everyone's speculation came into the room. Alexander's taut muscles relaxed slightly as his eyes took in the bandage around Allerdale's head and the calm composure of Lady Georgianna. Her eyes widened a little as they came to rest upon him, and then filled with dismay as she saw her father.

Lady Brigham flew across the room. "Miles! You are hurt! Was it an accident after all?"

"No, Mama," he said gently.

Her brow wrinkled. "But then, are you wed?"

He shook his head.

"Then you certainly must be," Lord Westbury said, rising to his feet.

"No, Papa," Georgianna said. "I am home before nightfall and so it cannot be thought necessary."

"Georgianna!" he said sternly, "Miss Hughes witnessed you kissing Allerdale at The Swan Inn!"

"No," Georgianna said firmly. "She did not. She saw Lord Allerdale kissing me, it is not at all the same thing. And it was the briefest of embraces."

"But your reputation!" he said.

"As I have not bandied my name about anywhere on the road, the only people who know of today's ridiculous episode, are those present in this room. I cannot think that anyone here would be malicious enough to spread word of it."

Lady Georgianna's insouciance did much to deflate the tension that had gripped the room for some hours. A chorus of assurances that, of course, they would not, poured forth.

Lord Westbury felt the ground slipping from beneath his feet. He turned to Lord Allerdale. "There is no point trying to reason with women! But you, sir, must realise that your honour demands you marry Georgianna!"

"I would be happy to do so," he said calmly. "But she will not have me. My head bears witness to it."

Alexander's lips began to twitch.

Lady Brigham looked at Georgianna with dawning respect. "You did this?"

"Yes, ma'am. I like your son well enough but could not contemplate being married to someone of such uncertain temper."

"Perfectly understandable, I am sure," Lord Brigham said. "May I ask what you used to incapacitate him?"

"A poker, sir."

Lady Brigham gasped. "But you could have killed him!"

Lord Allerdale gave a dry laugh. "Be grateful that she did not discover my pistol, ma'am."

"My compliments, Lady Georgianna. It seems you are a very resourceful young lady," Lord Brigham said, the hint of a smile upon his lips. "I must assume that Allerdale's lamentable temper had run its course by the time he regained consciousness. You did knock him out?"

"I did, sir. I cannot say with any degree of accuracy if his temper was immediately ameliorated, however, for I fled the scene. After I had made sure he was breathing, you understand."

Lord Brigham's eyes began to dance, but his voice was perfectly steady as he said, "I am extremely obliged to you. Yet you arrive here together, and relations between you appear to be quite amicable."

"When he is not being tiresome, Lord Allerdale is very good company."

"It is very magnanimous of you to say so," Lord

Brigham said. "Forgive my curiosity, but what were your actions immediately after you hit him over the head with a poker?"

"I stole his purse, sir, for you must know I had no money with me. I hired a horse and rode to an inn. I intended to get on the Whitehaven stagecoach, but Lord Allerdale found me there before it arrived."

He lifted a brow. "And you trusted him to bring you back to Brigham?"

"Yes, because he was no longer in a temper, and he gave me his pistol."

Lady Brigham gasped. "But, Miles, how did you know Lady Georgianna would not shoot you? She must have been very angry by then."

Allerdale smiled. "She was weary and certainly wary, but not angry. It was the landlord who came to my rescue. He discovered her pointing it at me and pleaded with her not to put on a bullet in me whilst we were in his establishment."

Lady Brigham gulped. "She was going to shoot you then?"

Georgianna rolled her eyes. "Lord Allerdale knows full well I was not. I gave the pistol back to him."

Lord Westbury was regarding his daughter with a fascinated eye, apparently unable to move or speak.

Lord Brigham was not so incapacitated. He bowed to Georgianna.

"Although I fully understand your reluctance to marry my son, I cannot help but wish that you would."

"It is a lost cause, I'm afraid," Lord Allerdale said. "It will have to be Lady Priscilla."

"No, I refuse to have her as a daughter-in-law!"

Lady Brigham said firmly. She laid a hand on her husband's arm. "Have I your permission to speak?"

"Yes, my love."

She turned to Allerdale her face animated. "There is no longer any need for you to marry anyone just yet, Miles. Your father was locked away in his study for some hours with Lord Devonan and has won back everything you lost."

Allerdale frowned.

"Are you not pleased, my son?" she said, bewildered.

Allerdale turned to his father and said, "I will pay you back, sir, however long it takes me."

"Very proper," Lord Brigham said. "But once I had played a few hands with Devonan, I realised that the only way he could possibly have beaten you, as you say you were not drunk – and I have never known you to lie to me yet – was to have cheated or drugged you. Considering the symptoms you described to me, I would favour the latter. Once I had realised that, I felt no compunction at bleeding him dry. If you truly wish to repay me, you will turn over a new leaf and take more interest in the minutiae of running our estates."

Allerdale bowed. "As you wish."

Lord Westbury suddenly found his voice. "I am still not satisfied—"

"Papa," Georgianna said, going up to him and taking one of his hands in both of hers. She looked him in the eye and said gently, "I do not know you very well, but I do not think you would wish me to be trapped in an unhappy marriage."

He looked a little bewildered. "No, of course not, but—"

"And I cannot help but think you would find Lord Allerdale an uncomfortable son-in-law. You would never be sure from one week to the next if he was going to create some sort of scandal."

"Well, yes, I suppose you are right, however—"

"Papa, please let the subject drop. No harm has come to me. And if you have come to take me back to Avondale, I beg you will not. At least, not quite yet. I have been so unhappy for such a long time, you see, and was not even fully aware of it until I came to stay with Aunt Hester. She has shown me more kindness and understanding than I have ever known."

Lord Westbury who had also been a stranger to kindness in his own home, felt strangely moved. He absently patted the hands that still enclosed one of his and said more gently than was his wont, "I am pleased to hear it, child. We will talk more tomorrow when the dust has settled a little."

Lady Brigham sniffed and raised a handkerchief to her eyes, Lady Colyford sighed, Alexander resisted the temptation to sweep Lady Georgianna into his arms and declare that he would never allow her to be unhappy again, and Sir Gerard took his daughter's arm and said with bluff good humour, "All a tempest in a teapot, after all, eh? We will be off now and leave you to your dinner."

"You certainly will not," Lord Brigham said. "You will, of course, stay."

"But we're not dressed for it," Sir Gerard protested.

"None of us are dressed for it," Lady Brigham said. "And dinner will be quite ruined if cook has to wait for us all to make ourselves presentable. Lady

Georgianna may wish to change into something more comfortable, but apart from that we will wait only for me to bathe Miles' head and wrap a clean bandage around it and Hester to attend to Lord Somerton's hand before we sit down."

Alexander met Georgianna's surprised gaze with one of apology.

"Somerton?" Lord Allerdale said, the colour draining from his face. "You are James' brother?"

"Yes," Alexander said, aware of a pang of sympathy for the man he had so recently wished to annihilate. "We will speak later, Allerdale, after dinner."

CHAPTER 18

With Grantley's help, Georgianna was
ready in less than twenty minutes. She
was glad that her aunt came to her
before she went downstairs. She had had no time to
dwell on the discovery that Mr Knight was in reality
Lord Somerton and heir to a dukedom but was aware
of a vague feeling of disquiet.

She had instinctively trusted Mr Knight; his relative lack of status had enabled her to view him as
neither a threat nor an opportunity. She had been
more herself in his company than she had been with
any other gentleman. But he had not been Mr Knight
at all. He had been playing a part, a part which she
did not as yet understand.

"I realised you might be a little confused, my
dear," Lady Colyford said. "I thought I had better
explain before we go downstairs."

Georgianna listened intently as her aunt outlined
the reasons for his deception and the result of it.

"It is a very satisfactory outcome," she admitted,

but still could not help feeling a little betrayed somehow.

As they began to make their way down the stairs, she said, "How did Mr... Lord Somerton hurt his hand?"

Lady Colyford said casually, "When Lord Brigham said he feared Allerdale intended to marry you whether you liked it or not, Lord Somerton's grip tightened on the glass he was holding, and it smashed."

Georgianna winced.

"He seemed most put out about the whole business," her aunt continued, "and was on the point of setting out for Gretna Green, with murder in his eyes, when your carriage pulled up outside."

Georgianna felt some of her weariness fall from her. Perhaps he was still her Mr Knight. It was his name, after all, if not his title. "Is the wound very bad?"

"No," her aunt assured her. "There was one deep cut, the rest were superficial. I have cleaned the wounds, sprinkled on some basilicum powder, and bound his hand up again."

"I wonder if Lady Brigham has any juice of loosestrife or cleavers in the house? They are both useful for cleaning and healing wounds."

"Then you must copy the methods into my book when we return to Lake Cottage."

Georgianna smiled but was not at all sure she would be returning there for any length of time.

Lady Brigham made a concerted effort to charm and entertain Lord Westbury at dinner, and her efforts were not wasted. Georgianna heard him laugh on several occasions. It was a deep, rich sound and one she had not heard him make before, she realised. That struck her as very sad. How different both her parents' lives might have been if they had not married for duty alone.

Georgianna divided her time equally between Lord Brigham and Miss Hughes, only once giving in to the temptation to glance across the table at Lord Somerton. His head was turned towards her aunt and she allowed her eyes to dwell on his strong profile for a moment before they dropped to his bandaged hand. That she could inspire such strong emotions in him both surprised and touched her.

When the ladies returned to the drawing room, Hannah took Georgianna's arm and led her to a sofa set a little apart from the main group of chairs.

"I hope you won't hold it against me, that I had to tell everyone what I saw, Lady Georgianna. It put you in a very awkward position with your papa. I wouldn't have breathed a word if you hadn't been missing all day."

"You did the right thing, Miss Hughes," Georgianna assured her. "I only hope it did not cause any unpleasantness between you and Sir Gerard."

"I was in his black books," she admitted. "Especially with you being Lady Colyford's niece. He was very concerned about the upset and trouble it might bring down on her. I must say, I was very relieved that Lord Westbury said nothing at all against her, for Papa would not have stood for it and there would have been a terrible scene."

"Is their friendship of very long standing?" Georgianna asked.

"We met Lady Colyford when she first came here five years ago. She stayed with Lady Brigham until some repairs could be made to Lake Cottage. Your aunt was quite rude to Papa, or at least *I* thought she was, but she made him roar with laugher. I had not heard him laugh like that since Mama had died, two years before. I wish she would take him seriously; I shall worry when I am not there to look after him."

"I was under the impression that Mr Tucker lived nearby."

"He does," Hannah said. "And I will visit Papa, often. But he always dismisses the servants once we have had dinner if we are not entertaining – he says he can't see why they should not enjoy their evening too when there is only us in the house – and who will wake him up when he falls asleep in his study late at night, nag him not to have another glass of wine, or remind him that lobster brings him out in blotches?"

"I see," Georgianna said thoughtfully, suddenly remembering something Miss Felsham had said to her.

Your aunt has a very kind heart and takes her obligations very seriously. But obligations can sometimes prevent a person from seeking their own happiness.

Had Aunt Hester's obligations to the various members of her household prevented her from deepening her friendship with Sir Gerard? Had she become another obligation?

Once the ladies had left the dining room, Lord Brigham said, "Allerdale, take Lord Somerton into the library and show him my painting of The Battle of Salamanca. I am sure he will wish to see it."

Alexander followed him there, noticing the tense set of Allerdale's shoulders.

"You need not show me the painting," he said curtly, closing the door behind them. "I was there, after all. No artist's depiction of any battle ever captures the acrid smell of gunpowder, the shrill screams that rise above the din of the artillery as men have arms or legs torn off by cannonballs, or the stench of death and fear that permeates the air."

Allerdale turned to him and offered a rather grim smile. "I suppose not. Are you trying to unnerve me? It is not necessary, I assure you. Tell me, have you killed many men?"

"Too many to count," Alexander said. "But never before have I experienced the almost overwhelming desire to kill a man who is not my enemy in battle, in cold blood."

Allerdale glanced at Alexander's hand. "Not in cold blood, I think. I can say nothing at all in my defence, but if I had known I was coming between two people very much in love, I might not have done it."

Alexander quirked a brow. "Might not?"

Allerdale frowned. "I will not lie to you, Somerton. I *hope* that I would not have done it, but I cannot be at all sure."

A faint smile lightened Alexander's countenance. "Sit down, Allerdale. I will pour us a drink."

"I think that should have been my line," Allerdale said dryly. "You have not lost the habit of command, I see."

"Sit down before you fall down," Alexander said firmly. "That head is bothering you more than you will admit. It is probably banging like a drum, something you should be grateful for."

"And why is that?"

"Because it is the only thing that has prevented me from planting you a facer."

Allerdale gave a ragged laugh. "Think of your hand, Somerton."

"The enjoyment it would have given me, would have far outweighed the discomfort, I assure you."

He poured two glasses of brandy and handed one to Allerdale before seating himself in the chair opposite. He stretched out his long legs and crossed them at the ankles, very much at his ease.

"I have not only killed a lot of men, Allerdale, I have also seen many friends die," he said softly. "It is never an easy thing to witness, but the first time is the worst."

"I did not see James die," Allerdale said, taking a hefty swig of his brandy. "If I had just looked over my shoulder, I might have seen he was in trouble and been able to save him. I swam out into the lake but did not know precisely where to look. He was there one moment, so full of life, and the next gone."

"You were a fool to do so," Alexander said. "It could very well have been two lives lost that day. I have swum out into the lake many times now and can tell you that even further out, there are places where rocks lurk not many feet below the surface. It is more than likely that he hit his head when he dived in and knew nothing more about it."

"I hope you are right," Allerdale said. "We had

rescued each other from so many tricky situations when we were kicking up a lark, it seemed so unreal, so pointless, that he died doing something so innocuous."

"The same thought had crossed my mind," Alexander said. "Share with me some of these larks that could have landed you both in trouble, however disgraceful. I have seen my brother only a handful of times in the last six years. I would like to be able to envisage his life during that time."

When only the marquess, Lord Westbury, and Sir Gerard joined them, Lady Brigham went over to her lord and said a little anxiously, "Where are Miles and Lord Somerton?"

"In the library, my dear."

"How could you leave them alone?" she said. "Lord Somerton is a mountain and Miles is injured! How do you know he will not harm him? I will go to them."

"No, you will not," Lord Brigham said softly. "You will have to trust my judgement, Julia. Somerton will not do Miles any harm and may even do him some good."

He led her over to a quiet corner to explain his reasoning, and Lady Colyford took advantage of her brother's unusually mellow mood, to give him some sisterly advice on how to deal with his daughter.

Sir Gerard smiled at Hannah and Georgianna. "Making friends, eh? I'm glad to see it, but I am afraid we must be on our way."

"Perhaps you will call in tomorrow?" Georgianna said. "There are a few things I would like to talk over with Miss Hughes."

Lord Brigham glanced up, "And I still haven't had a chance to discuss the milk yield of your longhorns."

"Cows," Hannah whispered to Georgianna.

"I had intended for us to return to Lake Cottage, tomorrow," Lady Colyford said. "I do not like to leave Miss Felsham and Miss Ravenchurch alone for too long."

"Nonsense," Lord Westbury said. "Miss Felsham seems a very sensible sort of woman."

"Well said," Sir Gerard seconded him.

"You are all welcome to stay as long as you wish," Lord Brigham said. "There should not be any awkwardness for I intend to send Allerdale off to our estate in Yorkshire tomorrow. It is the perfect size for him to manage and I have a very good steward there who shall keep him busy."

Georgianna glanced at her father, expecting him to protest.

He merely smiled and said, "Very wise, Brigham. We may well trespass on your hospitality for a day or two more."

Lord Westbury was feeling unusually relaxed. He was not averse to congenial female company and had found Lady Brigham's combination of deference and mischief quite captivating. He had also benefited from a very good dinner, a superior wine, and some very palatable brandy. The hint that his sister had just dropped in his ear had rounded off a very good evening.

"Come to dinner at the hall, tomorrow evening,

everyone is welcome," Sir Gerard said. "It is time I repaid some of your hospitality, Brigham."

As they left the room, Lord Westbury took the place now vacant beside Georgianna. He looked at her for some moments without speaking. She returned his gaze and then smiled tentatively.

"Papa?"

His lips twisted. "I wonder how many times I have heard you utter that word?"

"Not many," she admitted without rancour.

He lifted his hand as if he would touch her cheek, but let it fall at the last moment.

"You have turned into a beautiful young lady whilst my back was turned."

"Thank you, Papa."

He cleared his throat. "Georgianna, you said earlier that you did not know me very well, and to my shame, I have realised this day that I do not know you at all."

"That can be rectified," she said calmly.

He shook his head and chuckled softly. "Your self-possession does you credit, and you were certainly in need of it today. Most ladies in your position would have had the vapours."

"I believe I do not suffer from an excess of sensibility."

"But neither are you unfeeling, I think."

"No," she agreed.

"Your future husband will be glad of both circumstances."

"My future husband?" she said warily.

He smiled wryly. "Do not worry, child, I am not about to insist that you marry Allerdale or anybody else you do not favour for that matter; you would undoubtedly find a way to dispose of the unfortunate gentleman."

Georgianna laughed. "Perhaps, sir."

"But would I be correct in thinking that there is a certain gentleman of your acquaintance who is not distasteful to you?"

Georgianna's eyes dropped to the hands that were folded neatly on her lap, but the pink tinge that brightened her cheeks spoke for her.

"Judging by his actions this afternoon, Lord Somerton is certainly not indifferent to you, Georgianna."

"I do like him, Papa," she finally said. "There is *something* between us, although we have not spoken of it. But I do not know him well enough to be sure that we would suit."

Lord Westbury smiled. "That too can be rectified, Georgianna."

CHAPTER 19

The sound of a light footstep brought Alexander from deep sleep to wakefulness in an instant. His eyes snapped open and he shot upright.

"Still sleep with one eye open then, sir?" his valet said, a note of approval in his voice.

"Johns! Is it my father?"

"Easy there, now, milord. There's no need to be alarmed. There's nothing wrong with His Grace that a few days staying still won't cure."

"He's here?"

"I told him you wouldn't like it none, and he called me an impudent dog for my trouble."

Alexander laughed. "And a host of other things, I imagine. Is he very knocked up?"

"He was a little fatigued yesterday," the valet admitted. "We should have stopped at Kendal, but he insisted we push on to Buttermere. We spent the night at the vicarage and he's much recovered this morning. We arrived an hour ago."

"What time is it?"

"Past ten, sir. Heavy night was it?"

Alexander threw back his covers and strode over to his washstand.

"I do have a bit of a thick head," he admitted, bending down and tipping the water that was in the large jug beside it over his head.

Johns had picked up the coat Alexander had draped over a chair the night before and was examining the sleeve. He glanced over at Alexander's bandaged hand.

"Want me to take a look at that, sir?"

"It is nothing," he said. "I cut it on a broken glass."

"Is that so? Seems mighty careless of you, milord."

"Will you be able to get the stain out of my coat?"

Johns gave a dry laugh. "It won't be the first time, will it, sir? It's just as well I've brought you half a dozen others, and we picked up your things from that place you were staying in."

"Good man!" Alexander said. "That's the problem with being so large; I can't borrow as much as a clean shirt if I need one."

"Aye, it keeps me awake at night wondering how I'm going to make you look elegant," sighed Johns.

Alexander grinned. "I'll settle for clean and tidy."

"Oh, I think we can do a little better than that, sir."

Alexander hurried downstairs some twenty minutes later, in a Corbeau coloured coat, his cravat adorned by an amber tiepin, and boots that had been polished to a bright shine. He paused for a moment at the bottom of the stairs, unsure whether to try the drawing room or Lord Brigham's study.

The butler came to his rescue. "Your father is in the breakfast room, I believe. I shall show you the way."

But when he entered the room only Lord West-bury and Lady Georgianna were present. She smiled as he bowed, but there was a strained look about her eyes.

"Good morning, Lord Somerton," the earl said. "Help yourself to some breakfast. I recommend the kidneys; they are particularly good."

"Good morning, sir. I was looking for my father."

"The duke has taken a walk in the gardens with my sister," he said.

"I shall see if I can discover…" he paused as he received an imploring look from Lady Georgianna. "No, perhaps I will breakfast first."

"I should think so," Lord Westbury said. "There is a great deal of you to maintain."

Alexander helped himself to a generous portion of ham and eggs.

"That's the ticket," Lord Westbury said, dabbing his napkin to his lips before rising to his feet. "I must just have a word with Brigham, he should have seen that rascal of a son off by now."

"Coffee or ale, sir?" enquired a hovering footman.

"Coffee, please."

"I will just fetch a fresh pot, sir," the man said.

The moment he left the room, Alexander said, "What is troubling you, ma'am?"

"I am not troubled, precisely," Georgianna said. "It is just that I believe my aunt will benefit from some private conversation with your father. Please, do not ask me anything more, for it is not my story to tell."

"As you wish. Did he appear to be in good health?"

"His back was aching a little," Georgianna said. "He said a walk would set it to rights. How is your hand?"

It was on the tip of his tongue to tell her it was not troubling him at all when the footman returned with a steaming pot of coffee. Whilst he poured out a cup, Alexander remembered her notebook.

"It is a trifle sore," he said. "Perhaps I should ask your aunt to look at it again."

"I would be happy to tend it, sir."

"Thank you. Perhaps after I have seen my father."

Lady Brigham came into the room.

"Chocolate, please, Henry," she said, sitting down and reaching for a honey cake. "I am not at all happy that Miles has been sent away so soon. I am sure it was all very uncomfortable for you, Georgianna, but he was the one who was injured, after all."

It seemed the footman had more discretion than his mistress, for he discreetly withdrew.

"He need not have gone on my account," Georgianna said.

"I will admit you were very gracious, dear," Lady Brigham conceded. "But it seems very hard that my lord should banish his son from the house whilst throwing open its doors to every person who crosses the threshold."

Realising that no amount of reasoning would bring Lady Brigham to a realisation of just quite how dishonourable her son's actions had been, Alexander said, "I think you will find, ma'am, that Allerdale wished to go. He will feel much happier once he has repaid his father for extracting him from his recent embarrassments."

"All this talk of repayment is nonsense; it was not even his fault that Devonan—"

Alexander's patience was wearing thin. He may have reached some sort of understanding with Allerdale last evening, but he had certainly not forgiven him for eloping with Georgianna or stealing the kiss that should have been his.

"Ma'am," he said, in the stern tone that more than one subordinate in his regiment had come to dread. "Allerdale's latest adventure was the worst of a series of foolish, not to mention, dangerous escapades that could have resulted in his demise."

Lady Brigham's eyes widened, shock, respect, and then fear chasing themselves across them. It seemed this, at least, she could understand.

"Lord Brigham has shown a great deal of wisdom in sending Allerdale into Yorkshire to manage his estate. Surprising as it may seem, a man who cannot easily be led, sometimes makes an excellent leader. The responsibility now thrust upon him, might just be the making of him."

"Let us hope so," Lord Brigham said softly.

All eyes swivelled to where he stood in the doorway, the suspicion of a smile in his eyes.

"Lord Somerton, I expect you are eager to see your father. You will find him in the library."

"Thank you, sir," he said, rising immediately and striding towards the door.

"And your aunt, Lady Georgianna, has gone up to her room. She looked a little distressed."

Lady Brigham jumped up. "I shall go to her."

"Do not trouble yourself, ma'am," Georgianna said firmly. "I shall go to her."

"Good girl," Lord Brigham said, his eyes turning to his wife, who still looked shaken and a little tearful. "I would be honoured, my lady, if you would take a turn about the rose garden with me."

Georgianna had fully understood how her aunt had immediately recognised Lord Somerton as the duke's son as soon as that gentleman had come into the room. Her eyes had turned swiftly towards her aunt. Lady Colyford had stiffened and turned a little pale but had returned his greeting with perfect politeness before rising from the table, declaring that she had promised to cut some flowers and must do so before the day became too warm. The duke had outmanoeuvred her, however.

"I shall come with you, Lady Colyford," he had said. "My back is aching, and I find I cannot face sitting down again just yet."

The footman had opened the door for them and gone in search of a basket.

"I believe he was one of several young men Hester had in her train when she made her come out," Lord Westbury had said to Georgianna. "I must say I am glad that she had the sense not to succumb to his charms, for he was as ramshackle as Allerdale in his youth by all accounts. Became a changed man after he married, so I can quite understand why Lord Brigham wishes Allerdale to wed, but on reflection, I am very pleased that you were not saddled with him. The less said about that the better, eh? Somerton seems of an entirely different calibre I am pleased to say."

Georgianna had been surprised to discover that her father valued character over rank. She was finding him much less forbidding and starched up than when he was at Avondale.

She had wondered if she should find some excuse to go after her aunt and the duke but had decided against it. It had occurred to her that if she did marry Lord Somerton, she would very much like her aunt to remain part of her life and it would be far less awkward if they made their peace.

She found Lady Colyford sitting in a chair, a letter hanging loosely from the hand dangling by her side, and a blank look in her eyes. She did not glance up as Georgianna entered her chamber and seemed unaware of her presence. Georgianna knelt at her side, removed the letter from her aunt's grasp, and clasped her hand in her own.

"Aunt Hester?" she said gently.

Awareness slowly seeped back into Lady Coly-ford's eyes.

"Georgianna," she said softly. "Oh, Georgianna."

As silent tears began to fall down Lady Colyford's cheeks, Georgianna rose, perched on the arm of the chair, and wound her arms about her aunt's shoulders. They stayed like that for some time. Eventually, Lady Colyford patted her arm.

"I am quite recovered now, child," she said softly.

Georgianna pulled the other chair in the room closer to her aunt's and sat down.

"I should not have left you alone with him. I am sorry."

"You did well, child. We had a very interesting and enlightening talk. I was crying over lost opportunities, which is a singularly foolish thing to do; one should always look to the future not the past. Everything I thought I knew has been turned on its head. You may imagine my indignation when Sebastian told me he had forgiven me long ago and hoped we could be friends."

"Forgiven *you*? Whatever for?"

Lady Colyford sighed. "He bolted for Paris because when he returned home after the masquerade, he received news that his father was dangerously ill from a fever. He set out at once. He remained there until the duke was well enough for him to bring him home."

"But why did he not send you word?"

"He claims he did, although he did not think of it until he had been in Paris for some days. It was not at all the thing for a lady to receive a letter from a gentleman who was not a member of her family, so perhaps my father destroyed it. No, he would have opened it had he received it. I think it far more likely that it got lost somehow."

"Then he did mean to marry you?"

"Yes," her aunt murmured. "But by the time he returned and had delivered his father to Rushwick Park, I was already wed. The fool thought he had been mistaken in me, that I had been too fickle to wait for him."

Georgianna considered this for a moment.

"It is understandable," she finally allowed. "You had only known each other for a short time and then only met at society functions."

Lady Colyford gave a ragged laugh. "Very true."

"Did you never meet afterwards?"

"Colyford and I did not often go to Town; it is a very expensive business. On the rare occasions we were in the same room, we avoided each other. It occasioned no remark; despite his title, many high sticklers did not approve of him."

Georgianna remembered the look of pique in Lord Allerdale's eyes when she had remained unmoved by his kiss.

"I expect the duke was very angry and revelled in living up to his reputation after you betrayed him."

"Georgianna! I did not betray him."

"When he thought you had betrayed him then."

Lady Colyford smiled. "Very true." She suddenly laughed. "You horrid child. I am telling you a tale of tragedy, high drama, and heartache; you should be wringing your hands, clutching your breast, and decrying cruel fate."

Georgianna raised a brow. "I think you have been reading too many of Miss Felsham's novels."

Lady Colyford sobered. "Miss Felsham has delivered the second shock of the day. Read the letter she sent with Rushwick."

Georgianna retrieved it from where she had placed it on the floor.

Dearest Hester,

By the time you read this, Miss Ravenchurch and I will be on our way to my home. Her symptoms are worsening, and she will soon need watching every moment of the day. As you know, I have a considerable amount of experience in looking after someone in her condition, as do my staff.

I am fully aware that my actions may appear a little high-handed, but I hope you know that I believe I am acting in all our best interests. I have left my affairs alone for far too long, as have you, I think.

It has been a lovely idyll, my dear, but it is time we both took our place in society again. I will miss you, Hester, but I will not miss the icicles that sometimes form on the inside of my window in winter or the way the cold makes my bones ache.

I am fully aware that I am an interfering old woman, but I have asked the duke to speak with you about what happened all those years ago for your own peace of mind. I said no more than that and would ask that you listen to him. That scar has never quite healed, has it?

I would also ask that you seek the happiness that could be yours if you could overcome your stubborn belief that your independence is of greater importance. It will become a hollow prize, in time.

Your dearest friend,
Leticia Felsham

<u>PS</u> Encourage Georgianna to trust her feelings; her head too often rules her heart. She and Lord Somerton should suit admirably; both of them are wiser than their years should allow.

Georgianna read the last passage over several times before raising her head.

"I think it for the best," she finally said.

"But poor Leticia has already sacrificed so much of her life to her father. Why should she spend the rest of it looking after my relative?"

"She said to me that she liked to be needed and that you did not need her anymore. Besides, if her staff are used to such cases, she will not have to always be with Miss Ravenchurch."

"But what am I to do?" Lady Brigham said. "I cannot live at Lake Cottage alone."

"I assume you will either employ another companion or follow Miss Felsham's advice. Now, I promised I would take a look at Lord Somerton's hand. I shall go and ask the housekeeper what she has in her stillroom."

"And will you also follow Miss Felsham's advice, Georgianna?"

Georgianna paused with her hand on the door-knob. "We do not even know that Lord Somerton intends to offer for me, Aunt. It is all conjecture."

Lady Colyford smiled. "Perhaps you are not so wise, after all."

"I never claimed that I was. My father is going to invite Lord Somerton for a visit to Avondale. Then, we shall see," Georgianna said looking over her shoulder.

Her aunt pulled a face.

"He must meet my mother, after all," Georgianna said and went out of the room.

Mrs Ferrars, the housekeeper at Brigham, informed Georgianna that it was the roots of comfrey that she required, and immediately sent off one of the kitchen maids to gather some.

"Some say to lay the roots over the affected area, but it is not necessary. If you bruise them, they will produce a thick, sticky juice. Spread it over the wound and bind it up again. It works wonders."

Georgianna followed these instructions and armed with her potion, some boiled water, and a fresh bandage, went in search of Lord Somerton.

CHAPTER 20

"You should not have come all this way, sir,"
Alexander said as he strode into the library.

The duke gave him a rather weary smile.
"I've told myself the same thing many times over the
last two days, my boy. Couldn't shake the feeling that
you might get into some mischief."

"James may have looked more like my mother
than I, sir, but I believe it is I who have inherited her
even temper."

Rushwick chuckled, his eyes dropping to his son's
hand.

"You've heard about Allerdale's latest idiocy,
then," Alexander said.

"Brigham was refreshingly frank. And extremely
thankful that you, at least, could control your temper. I
hope you did yourself no serious injury?"

"No. A mere scratch, I hardly notice it. I cannot in
all honesty think that I would have kept my temper if
it were not for the quite comical end to the abduction.
He came into the drawing room with his head

wrapped in a bandage that kept threatening to slip over one eye, and a rather sheepish look on his face. But it was Lady Georgianna's composure that saved him. She has a remarkably cool head."

"So it appears," the duke said. "As this abduction roused in you such ire, may I assume you are in love with the girl?"

"Yes, sir."

"Then why have you not yet offered for her?"

A wry smile twisted Alexander's lips. "I would most certainly have done so if Westbury had held to his view that Allerdale should marry her. I am glad that he did not force my hand, however. I am not at all sure of her feelings, and I do not think she is either. She is very young after all, although it is sometimes quite easy to forget it. She is not one to make rash decisions, sir, and I would not wish to take a false step."

"Then you must get to know her better."

"I intend to, sir."

The duke frowned. "She looks very like her aunt, but Hester was far more impulsive in her youth."

"Yes, there is a tale there somewhere, I suspect."

"If you intend to wed her niece, you had better know it."

"No wonder Lady Colyford looked at me as if she had seen a ghost when we first met," he said when the duke had enlightened him as to the nature of their relationship.

"I am surprised she did not immediately send you on your way."

"She thought I was your natural child, sir, and had some sympathy for me, I believe."

Rushwick gave a crack of laughter. "Had no very great opinion of me, did she? I can hardly blame her, I suppose, now I know the truth, but I assure you that after I married your mother, I was a pattern card of respectability."

"I know it, sir."

"Yes, well, don't drag your courtship of Lady Georgianna out too long, will you? You don't want anyone else stealing your thunder."

They glanced up as a light knock fell upon the door. Georgianna came in and curtsied. "I am sorry to interrupt you, but as Lord Somerton informed me that his hand is quite sore, I feel I should tend to it sooner than later."

Rushwick raised an ironic brow at his son, reached for his cane, and stood. "Thank you, Lady Georgianna. We have caught up on all our news, and I shall now go and lie down for a short while."

She set her things on the occasional table by Lord Somerton's chair and went to fetch another.

"Allow me," he said, rising swiftly and bringing one to her.

"Thank you," she murmured, seating herself and reaching for his hand.

She quickly unwound his bandage and examined it closely. Alexander glanced down at her bent head, his eyes dwelling on the delicate nape of her neck. He was aware of the urge to place the lightest of kisses there.

"You were fortunate not to have done more damage," Georgianna said softly, gently dabbing at the deepest cut.

"I was imagining my hand was around Allerdale's

neck," he admitted. "I had promised to slay all dragons that threatened you remember."

She glanced up and smiled. "I did think of that, for a moment, when I was locked in the parlour at the inn in Carlisle. But I think, perhaps, that it was better that I rescued myself."

"Undoubtedly," he agreed, pleased that she had thought of him.

She dipped her finger into the salve she had prepared and began to smooth it onto his hand. The slight sting he experienced was more than compensated for by the warm, pleasurable sensation that spread across his palm.

She began to wind the clean bandage about his hand. "You must have been very angry indeed to have crushed a glass with your bare hand."

Alexander drew in a long, deep breath. It appeared Lady Georgianna was giving him an opening; he had not expected that.

"I think you must know why the news that Allerdale intended to marry you moved me quite so much, ma'am."

Georgianna inserted a pin into the end of the bandage and raised her eyes to his. Alexander gazed into their deep blue depths and saw a quiet determination and a hint of vulnerability.

"My father is going to invite you to visit us at Avondale. I hope you will accept. I would like to know you better, sir," she said softly.

Alexander reached for her hand and raised it to his lips. "Thank you for tending my wound, fair maiden. I shall certainly accept his invitation."

Of the Brigham party, only the duke did not set out for Broughton Hall. Alexander offered to stay behind and keep him company, but got his nose snapped off for his trouble.

"Do not fuss, Somerton! I shall be quite happy with a light supper, a good claret, and an early night."

Sir Gerard greeted them with typical bonhomie.

"We shall be an odd number for dinner, but I am sure that none of you will care a button for that. Invited my future son-in-law, Mr Tucker. I couldn't be more pleased with Hannah's choice," he said, as if she had had a host of admirers to choose from. "I'm not sure what I shall do without her, but at least I'll have the comfort of knowing she is happily settled."

Mr Tucker, a robust, ruddy-faced gentleman, with an amiable countenance, seemed a little embarrassed by these words of approbation, but grinned and said, "You've no need to worry on that score, sir, I will do everything in my power to make Hannah happy."

"I adore weddings," Lady Brigham said. "I do hope we shall be invited."

"We have not set the date as yet," Sir Gerard said, "but you'll be amongst the first to know, you may be sure."

Lord Westbury, although inclined to think Sir Gerard a trifle vulgar, could not help but be impressed by Broughton Hall. It was a fortified manor house boasting an intact fourteenth-century pele tower. The main house was slightly later in date, but the great hall housed a fine example of an Eliza-bethan carved overmantle, impressive oak panelling, and some exquisite examples of French furniture at its finest.

"Very impressive," he said. "Tell me, Sir Gerard, are the fireplaces and windows in the tower original?"

"They certainly are," Sir Gerard said. "The floors too. Would you like me to give you a quick tour? We have half an hour before dinner."

"Thank you," Lord Westbury said. "I would like that very much."

"I never thought I would see my brother hobnobbing with someone of Sir Gerard's stamp," Lady Colyford murmured to Georgianna.

"Have you two never been friends?"

Lady Colyford sighed. "He adored me when he was a child, but we had very little to do with each other once I married. Your grandfather never forgave me my indiscretion and saw fit to inform your father when he was old enough to understand."

"I do wonder, Aunt, if you have been quite fair to Papa. He may not be as proud as you think. Not only has he not insisted I marry Allerdale, but he says he will not force me to marry anyone whom I do not favour."

"I am glad to hear it. But the fact remains that when I came to Avondale and applied to him for assistance, I did not receive it."

"That was wrong of Papa," Georgianna acknowledged. "But Mama is not at all pleasant when she is displeased. I am not surprised Papa spends so little time at home."

"I believe your grandfather arranged the match," she said. "I expect Westbury had very little choice in the matter; when your grandfather issued an order, he expected to be obeyed." She sighed. "Perhaps I have been guilty of tarring Westbury with the same brush. I am pleased that you are becoming better acquainted with him, at all events. I do not think your mama will be quite so mean-spirited towards you once she realises you have him as an ally."

Georgianna saw Miss Hughes beckoning her and went to her and Mr Tucker.

"I wanted to thank you, Lady Georgianna, for coming to Hannah's rescue the other evening," he said, a twinkle in his eyes.

"It was my pleasure, sir. It could have happened to anyone, I am sure."

Mr Tucker gave a deep, throaty chuckle.

"If something can happen, you may be sure it is Hannah it will happen to, whether it's tearing her dress on a nail or falling in a muddy puddle."

"Finlay, I would rather you didn't parade all my accidents in front of our guests."

"But I haven't, my dear, I have hardly begun."

Georgianna smiled. "I am afraid it will have to wait, Mr Tucker, I believe we are about to go in to dinner."

"We will not stand on ceremony this evening," Sir Gerard said. "You may sit where you wish."

"I'm glad to hear it, Sir Gerard," Lord Westbury said. "I'd like to talk to you a little more about the history of this house. I must say, I thought James the first had insisted that all pele towers be pulled down."

"He did," Sir Gerard confirmed, "but my family has always kept its head down and gone its own way whether we were under the influence of the English or the Scots."

"There's a firm friendship in the making there, I think," Alexander said to Georgianna as he held a chair out for her.

"I have my own reasons for hoping you may be right," Georgianna said with a small smile.

Alexander adopted a severe tone. "If you mean to tell me I have a rival in your affections—"

Georgianna laughed. "Do not be so ridiculous; it is my aunt Sir Gerard hankers after."

"I can quite see that they would suit, but I cannot imagine Lady Colyford would abandon her friends," Alexander said.

"She will not have to," Georgianna said in a low voice. "They have already abandoned her."

Alexander raised a brow. "Do I detect the hand of Miss Felsham at play?"

Georgianna looked surprised. "How did you know?"

"She is a very quiet, observant, and wise lady."

He proceeded to describe to her his encounter with Miss Ravenchurch in the moonlight. So well did he describe the ridiculous figure he had cut, that Georgianna found herself in tucks of laughter. When she recovered her composure, her conscience smote her.

"I should not have laughed."

"In the darkest moments there is humour," Alexander said softly. "Laughter has saved me from despair many times. Besides, you were laughing at me, not Miss Ravenchurch."

Sir Gerard was no stranger to laughter, and at that moment, he gave full rein to an unrestrained guffaw.

"Ghosts? Hester! Do not tell me you believe in 'em?"

Lord Westbury raised a brow at this familiarity but said nothing.

"I did not say I believe in them," she said. "I merely enquired if there had been any reports of them in this house. It is very old after all. The house I grew up in was also old and there was rumoured to be a lady dressed all in grey who roamed the gallery."

Lord Westbury raised his head, an arrested look in his eyes.

"So there was. I had forgotten it. I remember you borrowed your governess's gown, Hester, and tried to frighten me out of my wits."

"Tried?" she said, with a wry smile.

Lord Westbury held up his hands. "I admit I ran screaming, but I could not have been more than nine, after all."

"And you certainly wreaked your revenge. You put a slug in my reticule."

"Did I?"

"Yes, but I forgave you. I am not at all squeamish."

"Then it was not much of a revenge, was it?"

"Unfortunately," she continued, "my governess was extremely squeamish. She asked me if I had a handkerchief about me when she had a fit of the sneezes. I retrieved the one I had in my reticule and handed it to her. She opened it and the slug fell in her lap. She thought I had done it on purpose and complained bitterly to Mama. I was in deep disgrace for a week."

"You should have told them it was me," Lord Westbury said, a little embarrassed.

"Why? I had deserved it. Besides, I could have supported any amount of disapproval after seeing the look of abject horror on Miss Granger's face. I never liked her."

Sir Gerard looked at her indulgently. "I am not surprised she did not bleat on you, Westbury. Two of the things I most admire in Hester, are her spirit and her loyalty to her friends."

He shook his head and assumed a forlorn demeanour.

"It has been far too long since I have had you under my roof, Hester. You know it is the dearest wish of my heart to have you fixed here permanently."

"Eh?" spluttered Lord Westbury. "I'll take leave to inform you, Sir Gerard, that jest was in poor taste—"

Sir Gerard chuckled and reached for his glass. "I meant as my wife, of course."

"Oh, I see. Well, that puts a different complexion—"

"Perhaps I will be one of these days," Hester said.

Sir Gerard choked on his wine. He wiped his streaming eyes with his napkin.

"Do you mean it, Hester?"

That lady suddenly clutched her hands to her breast and said in tragic tones, "Miss Felsham has gone and taken Miss Ravenchurch with her, Gerard. My friends have deserted me! What am I to do? I find myself friendless and all alone."

"And are we not your fr—?"

The feel of her lord's hand squeezing her knee silenced Lady Brigham.

"Hester," Lord Westbury said. "You are not alone. You may come to Avondale and live there as long as you wish. I am very sorry that I did not insist on it before."

"No, dash it!" Sir Gerard protested. "I have spent years trying to persuade Hester to be my wife, Westbury, do not pull the rug from under my feet now!"

He took Lady Colyford's hand and pressed a fervent kiss upon it.

"Hester! Put me out of my misery! Say you will marry me."

"Very well, Gerard," she said, her eyes suspiciously bright, although whether from amusement or some deeper emotion was not entirely clear, "I will marry you."

Sir Gerard looked down the table at his daughter, a look of triumph in his eyes.

"I'm afraid you will have to wait a little longer, Hannah. I intend to marry Hester as soon as possible, before she comes to her senses."

CHAPTER 21

It was a little over a month later when Lord Westbury and Georgianna arrived at Avondale. They had stayed on at Brigham to witness the wedding and attend the breakfast afterwards, which was an extremely jolly and joyous affair. Father and daughter were now far better acquainted than they had been before and both were pleased with the other.

Lord Westbury found Georgianna to be all that he could wish for in a daughter. Her dignity, intelligence, and composure were matched by a burgeoning humour and an understated kindness. When they had returned to Lake Cottage to collect the remainder of her things, they had gone no more than a few yards from the end of the drive, when she had asked him to stop the carriage, rummaged in one of her trunks, and withdrew an old wooden doll.

"I must give Peggy to Martha Tweddle," she had said. "I have no more need of her."

When this deed was done, he had asked her about the doll and been quite horrified to discover that until very recently Georgianna had only had an inanimate object to confide in. He had patted her hand a little awkwardly, and said, "You may talk to me anytime you wish, my dear. Not that I understand a great deal about females; you are all a bit of a mystery to me."

Georgianna had said, "I have some real friends now, Papa. Marianne, whom I shared a room with at the seminary, is my particular friend, and I cannot understand why I have not heard from her. I wrote to her before I left Avondale, and I have been expecting to hear that she has married the Earl of Cranbourne for some time."

"Then let us hope that you will find a letter awaiting you when we go home."

For her part, Georgianna found her papa to be very good company. He was knowledgeable and patiently answered any number of questions she asked him on a variety of subjects, from their ancestors to politics. She had particularly asked him to explain to her the war that had recently been waged in Portugal, Spain, and France, wishing to understand something of what Lord Somerton had experienced.

He had taken the duke home some weeks ago and she found that her thoughts often turned to him. He had accepted her father's invitation to visit and should be arriving at Avondale not many days hence. She felt her stomach flutter a little at the thought and smiled, finding this correlation between emotion and physical response quite fascinating.

As Avondale at last came into view, Georgianna examined her feelings closely. This time she felt no great anxiety about returning to her home, but neither did she feel any particular affection towards the house or its environs. It would certainly be no great wrench to leave it.

As they descended from the carriage in front of the house, Rupert came tearing out of the front door at full tilt. His eyes widened as he saw his father. As he attempted to come to an abrupt halt, he lost his balance and fell, his whole body sliding on the gravel until he ended up at Lord Westbury's feet.

A strident voice followed him through the open door, causing Lord Westbury to wince. "Master Rupert! Master Rupert! You naughty child!"

Stokes hurried out, a forbidding look upon her face. She gasped as she saw Lord Westbury and dipped into a curtsy.

Rupert sat up and touched his hand to his red, grazed cheek.

"Good day, Papa," he said warily.

"Good day, Rupert," Lord Westbury said calmly. "Tell me, does your cheek hurt?"

"Yes, sir," he said, climbing to his feet.

"Good. Let that be a lesson to you. You should not run away from your nurse. My father used to whip me if I behaved badly."

The boy's bottom lip trembled. "Will you do that to me, sir?"

"Not on this occasion," Lord Westbury said sternly. "But I shall be very tempted to do so the next time I hear you have been misbehaving. Now, get up to the schoolroom and do not run."

Rupert walked in a stately fashion back towards the house. Stokes turned to follow him.

"Wait a moment, er…"

"Stokes, sir," she said.

"Ah, yes. I believe you are temporarily taking charge of my son whilst Miss Tremlow recuperates from her broken ankle."

"She's gone, milord. She left as soon as she could get about with a stick."

"One can hardly blame her," he said. "But it seems that you have no greater control over my son than she did."

"I'm doing my best, sir, but I am trained to be a lady's maid, not a nurse."

"I am aware," he said. "You were, in fact, my daughter's maid, were you not?"

Stokes sent an uneasy glance in Georgianna's direction.

"Yes, milord."

"It seems you were not very satisfactory in that role, either."

"I only followed Lady Westbury's orders, sir."

"Quite. But it was rather Lady Georgianna's orders you should have followed. She is no longer a child, after all."

"Papa," Georgianna said, laying a hand on his arm.

He glanced down at her. "No doubt you are about to tell me not to turn her off. Do not waste your breath."

"Oh, sir!" Stokes cried.

"I shall not do so immediately, Stokes. It is time Rupert had a tutor rather than a nurse. It will take some weeks to find one; that should give you ample opportunity to look about you for a new position."

Stokes turned and fled into the house on a sob,

brushing past Adams who had come out to greet them.

"Welcome home, Lord Westbury, Lady Georgianna."

"Thank you, Adams. Is Lady Westbury at home?"

"Yes, sir, she is in her sitting room."

"Excellent," Lord Westbury said. "There are a number of matters I must discuss with her."

"Shall I bring you some refreshment, sir?"

"No, Adams. I believe it will be better if we are not disturbed. However, I am sure Lady Georgianna would benefit from something."

As Lord Westbury made his way to the staircase, Adams turned to Georgianna and lifted an eyebrow.

"I think you may well find, Adams," she said softly, "that a number of things are about to change for the better. Now, I shall take some tea in Mrs Adams' sitting room, if you please."

The butler allowed himself a small smile. "I think *you* have changed, Lady Georgianna, also for the better."

"I believe I am more myself than I have ever been, Adams."

Mrs Adams broke into a broad smile as she came into her sitting room. "Lady Georgianna! I do not think I have ever seen you look so well!"

"Thank you, Mrs Adams. I am very well."

"I hope you will forgive me for my presumption, my lady, but might it have something to do with the gentleman who is arriving tomorrow?"

"Tomorrow?" Lady Georgianna said. "I thought he was not due for a few days yet."

The housekeeper gave a satisfied smile. "It seems

as he grew a little impatient, Lady Georgianna. We received a letter only this morning saying as how he had some business in the area and would be arriving a little earlier than expected."

The colour that flooded Georgianna's cheeks spoke volumes.

"Ah, it is a visit to be welcomed, I see. I never thought Lord Wedmore would do; he was far too staid for you. Is Lord Somerton *the one*, my lady?"

"I believe so," Georgianna said softly. "I was not perfectly sure, but the journey home has given me ample time to reflect on all I know of him, of us. He is a gentleman, he is strong yet gentle, he is kind but also formidable, he is serious and yet also humorous…" Georgianna suddenly laughed. "I sound so missish."

"Not at all, my lady," Mrs Adams said, her eyes brimming with tears. "You sound like a young lady very much in love and I couldn't be happier."

"Yes, well, let us not get ahead of ourselves, Mrs Adams," Georgianna said. "My reflections over the last few weeks might have persuaded *me* of our suitability, but we do not know, after all, what is in Lord Somerton's mind. Now, Rupert has several small grazes upon his cheek, have you perhaps an ointment made from yarrow in the stillroom?"

Mrs Adams looked very impressed. "Indeed, I do, my lady."

Georgianna made her way to the schoolroom and found Rupert upon his rocking horse, wielding an imaginary whip. "Faster, Star, faster!"

"Star?" Georgianna said as she entered the room. "That is an unusual name for a horse but I find I rather like it."

Rupert dropped his arm and allowed his furious rocking to slow. "I am very interested in the stars, Georgie," he said, using the name he had called her before he could pronounce her full name. "But none of my nurses have known anything about them."

"Is that so?" Georgianna said, sitting down and placing the ointment jar on the table. "I must admit, I know nothing of them myself. It is a sad deficiency in my education, but ladies, you see, are not thought to be interested in such things."

Rupert frowned as he assimilated this information. "Are you interested, Georgie?"

"I would very much like to know about the stars, Rupert. Perhaps the tutor our father is going to find for you will teach you about them, and then you can teach me."

Rupert dismounted from the rocking horse. "Papa is going to find me a man teacher?"

"Oh yes," Georgianna said. "I think it is time, don't you?"

Rupert smiled, revealing an engaging gap where he had lost one of his front teeth.

"If he can teach me about the stars, I will try to be obedient."

"Try?"

"I will be obedient," he said more firmly.

"Come here, little devil," Georgianna said softly. "I have some ointment to soothe your face."

Rupert scowled. "Stokes cleaned my knee and it hurt."

Georgianna smiled. "I may not know much about the stars, little brother, but I know something of herbal remedies. Trust me."

Rupert considered her words for a moment and then came and sat beside her. "I do trust you, Georgie," he said.

Georgianna smiled. "And so you should, you little terror."

She gently smeared the ointment over his face. "Better?"

"Yes," he said.

He then surprised her by throwing his arms about her and bursting into tears. "Do not go away again, Georgie. Everything is so dull and horrid when you are not here."

Georgianna gently stroked his back. "I may well go away again one day, Rupert."

Rupert reared back from her and furiously wiped at his eyes.

"No! Everything will be horrid again if you go away."

"Not necessarily," she said gently. "Not only are you going to benefit from a tutor who will teach you about the stars, but Papa is going to be at home more often."

"But he will whip me," Rupert said truculently.

"Only if you persist in being naughty," Georgianna pointed out. "And when I told him you had not been allowed to ride the pony he purchased for you, he was most put out."

"Do you mean… can you mean that he is going to let my ride my pony?" Rupert said, his eyes shining with hope.

"Not only is he going to let you, Rupert, he is going to insist upon it."

The boy started to gallop about the room.

Stokes, having recovered her composure, came in. "Master Rupert!"

Georgianna rose. "I do not believe you have yet apologised to Stokes, Rupert."

A resentful frown clouded his brow. Seeing that Stokes' gaze was not directed at her, Georgianna pretended to have reins in her hand and simulated the motion of riding a horse.

Rupert grinned and said, "I am sorry that I ran away from you, Stokes."

"Well, you don't look very sorry—"

"Stokes," Georgianna said firmly. "Take Rupert down to the stables and request that our head groom, Stanley, gives him his first riding lesson."

"On whose authority, ma'am?"

"I think you will find that my father and I are as one on this matter, Stokes. But if you wish that I tell him that you disobeyed me, I shall certainly do so."

Sensing that the balance of power within the house had changed, Stokes inclined her head and said, "Very well, ma'am."

Rupert gave a whoop of pure joy and ran towards the door.

"Remember the whip, Rupert," Georgianna said dryly.

Her brother immediately slowed his pace to a fast walk.

A footman jumped out of the way as Rupert rushed past him.

"Marcus?" Lady Georgianna said.

"You have a visitor, milady," he said. "Lady Cranbourne is waiting for you in the drawing room."

Apparently, the rules pertaining to schoolboys did

not extend to young ladies, for Georgianna picked up her skirts and ran. When she was only a few steps behind Stokes on the stairs, she slowed and assumed a more dignified demeanour.

She stood in the doorway of the drawing room for a moment, but when Marianne's candid brown gaze met her own, she rushed forward and embraced her friend. Marianne laughed as she was nearly bowled over by the fierceness of Georgianna's reception. They clung to each other for a moment, and then both started speaking at once.

"Why did you not write?"

"You never returned my letter!"

They broke apart as Adams came into the room.

"I hope I do not presume too much, Lady Georgianna, but I thought you and your friend might enjoy a glass of ratafia."

Georgianna's eyes widened in surprise as she said, "Thank you, Adams."

When he had left the room, Marianne smiled. "What an excellent butler."

"What makes you say that?" Georgianna asked.

Marianne picked up a glass and raised it before her. "A good butler always knows when there is cause for celebration. If I was very conceited, I might assume my visit alone had prompted him to bring us something other than lemonade or tea, but I am not, and I am inclined to believe you have some interesting news."

Georgianna also raised her glass. "I hope you have found happiness with Lord Cranbourne, Marianne."

"Oh, I have," she said softly.

They took a sip of their drinks and then sat down together on a small sofa.

"Now," Georgianna said. "Tell me everything that has happened since I left Cranbourne."

When Marianne described how she had climbed down a muddy bank to rescue a fox cub that did not need rescuing after all, before being rescued and promptly proposed to by Lord Cranbourne, Georgianna smiled.

"How very like you to be proposed to when you were covered in mud."

She laughed outright when she was told how Sir Robert Pinkington had whisked Lady Brancaster off to the cathedral to marry her, aided by Miss Bragg.

"And Charlotte?"

"She was married to Sir Horace only last week. Her wedding was delayed a little because her guardian wished to be married first."

"I am very pleased. Charlotte and Sir Horace will deal admirably together. They are as amiable as each other and never a cross word will pass between them. I am not at all surprised that Lord Seymore put his own desires before Charlotte's, however," Georgianna said. "Has he not always done so? Who is the poor female who had the dubious pleasure of becoming his wife?"

"Miss Hayes. We were mistaken in him, Georgianna. He followed Charlotte to Priddleton to ensure that she was happy with her great aunt, and when he discovered she was, remained there to get to know her better. It was just that he had not known what to do with her before, and she seemed much happier at the seminary than in his house."

Georgianna thought of her father and conceded

that the scenario Marianne had drawn was entirely possible.

"Apparently, he had met Miss Hayes some years before, when she made her come out, only she became engaged to another man. But that is a long story and must wait for another time," Marianne said. "Anthony, I mean Cranbourne, is at present occupying himself looking over your father's stable, but I am sure he will join us before long. We are on our way home after a brief visit to London."

"At this season?"

"I know," Marianne said. "It was horribly hot and dusty, but Cranbourne insisted he wished to purchase an amber necklace for me, as well as a host of other things which I assured him I had no need of. I pestered him into bringing me here as I wished to see for myself what had become of you."

"Amber is a lovely colour," Georgianna said, a little wistfully.

"Yes," Marianne acknowledged. "The fox cub I attempted to rescue had amber eyes."

"Lord Somerton's eyes are golden, but they deepen to amber when he is moved," Georgianna said softly.

Marianne pounced and within a very few minutes had drawn every last detail of Georgianna's adventures from her.

She looked upon her friend fondly and said, "Georgianna! You talk of all these exciting events as if you were reciting a shopping list. But you cannot hide your feelings for Lord Somerton from me; your eyes change when you speak of him."

"How so?" Georgianna asked.

"They soften and glow," Marianne informed her. "Are you going to marry him?"

Georgianna flushed. "Yes, I think so, if he asks me."

Marianne laughed and grasped Georgianna's hands. "I remember distinctly when you told me that you did not think you would enjoy being in love because the feelings it aroused in its victims were confusing and contradictory, or something along those lines. Is that how you are feeling now?"

Georgianna shook her head. "No, it is not that at all. I know my own feelings."

"Then what is it?" Marianne asked.

Georgianna said with some difficulty, "I do not know what happens in the marriage bed, Marianne, but I do know that my mother has always found it extremely unpleasant."

Marianne smiled reassuringly at her friend. "Has Lord Somerton ever kissed your bare hand or whispered in your ear?"

"Yes."

"And did your hand tingle when he kissed it? Did his breath on your ear or neck make you shiver?"

"Yes."

"Do you wish that he would kiss you?"

"I have nearly let him twice," Georgianna whispered.

Footsteps sounded in the hall and Marianne squeezed her friend's hand and quickly said, "Next time, let him. You need not worry, Georgianna; if he provokes such responses in you, it is a sure indication that you will enjoy the experience."

They both rose as Lord Cranbourne was shown into the room. He bowed and smiled.

"Lady Georgianna, I am pleased to see you safe and well. Marianne would not rest until she had discovered for herself that it was so."

"Thank you for bringing her to me. Our letters somehow got lost."

"Our postal system is not all it could be," he acknowledged. "I have just met your brother, ma'am, sitting astride a pony as proud as a peacock, but he cannot understand why he must be led and cannot go galloping across the park on his mount."

Georgianna laughed. "It is his first time upon horseback!"

"Then he is certainly intrepid!" Lord Cranbourne said. "I am sorry to break up this happy reunion, but we still have some way to go. Please come and see us very soon, Lady Georgianna."

CHAPTER 22

After Marianne and Lord Cranbourne left, Georgianna went to her room. Kate was still busily unpacking her trunks.

"There you are, milady," she said. "There's some hot water in the stand if you would like a wash."

"A wash and a change of dress," Georgianna said. "And tidy my hair if you will, Kate."

Georgianna did not wait to be summoned this time but went to her mother's sitting room of her own accord. They had parted acrimoniously, and she wished to establish some sort of accord before Lord Somerton arrived. When she knocked lightly on the door, her mother's maid answered. She frowned when she saw Georgianna.

"Lady Westbury is indisposed," she said. "She cannot see anyone at the moment."

"I am sorry that she is not feeling well," Georgianna said coolly, "but I *will* see my mother."

When the maid remained in the doorway, Georgianna raised an eyebrow. "Are you going to step aside, or do I need to move you?"

The maid's mouth gaped open, but as Georgianna stepped forwards, she dropped her eyes and scurried past her. Georgianna entered the room and closed the door softly behind her.

The curtains were drawn, and the room was lit only by an oil lamp and the glow of the fire. Lady Westbury lay on a day bed, a vinaigrette clutched in her hand. She raised it to her nose as Georgianna approached.

"Have you come to gloat?" she said bitterly. "Do you rejoice in seeing me laid so low?"

Georgianna sat down and said gently, "No, to both questions, Mama. I came because we parted on such bad terms, and I hoped we could perhaps start afresh."

Lady Westbury's laugh had a distinctly hysterical edge to it. "Start afresh? You have turned your father against me. He has never before spoken to me in the way he did today. He has seen fit to instruct me how to deal with you and Rupert. He has ridden roughshod over my opinions and even hinted that I have failed in my duty to you both. And this from a man who has been quite happy to leave all the responsibility for our children's upbringing to me!"

"I did not turn Papa against you, Mama, at least not intentionally. And it is true that he has left Rupert and me to your care. I can quite see that you must have felt very alone. But I think Papa intends to spend much more time at home in the future."

Lady Westbury turned her face towards the fire. "I do not want him here."

Georgianna sighed. "Mama, Rupert needs him and although you will not admit it, I think you do too."

Lady Westbury pushed herself upright and laughed scornfully.

"How dare you tell me what I need? Do you think because you have caught the heir to a duke in your trap that you are suddenly superior to me?"

Georgianna rose. "I do not feel myself superior to anyone, Mama."

Lady Westbury's eyes glittered in the dim light.

"I always knew you for a liar, Georgianna. All that nonsense you spouted about wishing to feel some affection and respect for your husband is a prime example. I must admit I underrated your ambition. No wonder Lord Wedmore was unpalatable to you; you had far grander hopes."

Realising that it would futile to try and persuade her mother to the contrary, Georgianna said softly, "I do not think you know anything about me, Mama. I shall leave you now."

Georgianna hoped her mother would regain her composure before Lord Somerton arrived. She realised, however, that she no longer had any power to wound her and she felt only pity for her.

Georgianna and Lord Westbury watched Rupert being led around the stable yard the following afternoon.

"Give me the reins, Stanley" he demanded, not for the first time. "I am not a baby."

"He is full of pluck, I will give him that," Lord Westbury said.

He nodded as the groom lifted a questioning brow. Stanley showed him how to hold the reins, instructed him to gently squeeze his legs against the pony's sides, and strolled beside Rupert as he walked the horse around the yard unaided.

"Well done, Rupert," Georgianna said.

"He is a natural," Lord Westbury said, a hint of pride in his voice.

Rupert had not haunted the stables for the last year without observing how the stable hands rode a horse. He maintained an angelic demeanour as he once more walked the pony around the yard, but as soon as Stanley relaxed and took a step backwards, he kicked his heels against his mount's sides. The obedient pony moved into a trot and Rupert discovered that riding was not as easy as it looked. He tightened his grip on the reins and pulled, shouting, "Stop, Star! Stop."

Alexander rode into the yard and casually leaned over and took the reins from Rupert, leading him back to the groom. Lord Westbury's heir may have been a little frightened, but he was not overly impressed with this high-handed treatment.

"I did not need any help," he grumbled.

"Is that so?" Alexander said, swinging himself out of the saddle.

He intercepted a look from Lord Westbury, shook his head slightly, and winked.

"And I don't suppose you need any help dismounting either?" he said, lifting Rupert down.

Georgianna hid a smile as Rupert had to take

several steps back to be able to look up into Alexander's face. He clasped his hands behind his back and puffed out his chest.

"I will be an earl one day," he informed him gravely. "And I do not like strangers carrying me."

"Really?" Alexander said. "I will be a duke one day, which outranks you, little breeches." He bent down until his head was only inches from Rupert's. "And I was a major in the army. Do you know what I used to do to any men who showed me disrespect or did not follow my orders?"

Rupert shook his head.

"I used to punish them."

"How?" Rupert asked warily.

"That would depend on the severity of the offence. You, little breeches, have only been guilty of poor manners and so your punishment will be relatively light."

As Rupert took another step backwards, he scooped him up, tucked him under one arm, and began to tickle him mercilessly. The boy was soon squirming and laughing until tears ran down his face. He eventually cried, "Stop or I will be sick."

"Are you sorry for being a bad-mannered, ungrateful little scamp?" Alexander said.

"Yes," Rupert gasped. "I'm sorry. Please put me down."

"Very well."

"Make your bow to Lord Somerton, Rupert," his father said.

He did so and said, "Thank you for your help, Lord Somerton."

Alexander smiled. "That is better. If I see an

improvement in your manners over the next few days, I might even take you up before me on my stallion. Would you like that?"

The little boy's eyes grew round. "Do you mean it, sir?"

"I never say anything I do not mean, Rupert."

As the boy returned to the house, Alexander made his bow.

"I hope you do not mind me arriving a day or two early, sir?"

Although his question was directed at Lord Westbury, his eyes did not leave Georgianna.

"Of course not, Somerton. Come into my study and have a glass of wine."

When Alexander did not answer, he looked from his daughter to his guest as they stood gazing at each other, smiled, and gave a discreet cough.

"Or perhaps you would like to stretch your legs after your ride. Georgianna, might I suggest you show Lord Somerton the lake?"

A slow smile spread across Georgianna's face. No great welling of joy overcame her, but she was aware of a warm content feeling, as if she had found something important that she had lost.

"Certainly, Papa."

She accepted the arm Alexander offered to her and they strolled out of the yard and into the garden. Lord Westbury's voice drifted after them.

"I am not paying you all to stand about gawping. You can wipe those silly grins off your faces now and get back to work!"

They walked in silence for a time, each happy just to be in the presence of the other. As they came to the large ornamental lake, Georgianna said, "It cannot compare with the lake at Buttermere. Nothing man does to recreate nature ever quite matches it, does it?"

"No," Alexander said, taking her hands and gazing into her eyes. "I could not stay away any longer, Georgianna. I know that you have not always been happy here and wished to shield you from any unpleasantness."

"You need not have worried," she said. "My father and I understand each other much better now."

He looked at her searchingly. "And your mother?"

"My mother is an extremely unhappy lady," she admitted. "But she no longer has the power to hurt me."

"And why is that?" he said softly, stepping so close to her that his coat brushed her dress.

"Because it is not her love that I wish for any longer," Georgianna whispered. "It is yours."

Her lips parted and her heart fluttered as she watched his eyes turn to the hot amber she had dreamed of so often over the last few weeks. As his lips lowered slowly towards her own, she tilted up her head the sooner to meet them. Her eyelids felt heavy and dipped over her eyes as his firm, warm lips grazed hers. She shivered.

"I was beyond rage when I discovered that Allerdale had kissed you," Alexander murmured.

Georgianna reached up her hands and cupped them about his face. "He may have been the first man to kiss me," she said softly. "But you are the first man I have kissed."

She pressed her lips against his and did not protest when he pulled her tightly against him. As the kiss deepened, the world faded away until there was only his embrace and the desire that flared between them. Hot sweet sensations flooded her, and she abandoned herself to the glorious feelings.

When Alexander lifted his head, she gave a little mew of disappointment.

"I understand your wish to know me better," he said, his breathing ragged. "But trust your heart, Georgianna, trust me. I would be honoured if you would agree to be my wife, the mother to my children, and the light in my life."

"My heart and my head are as one on this," Georgianna said firmly, entwining her fingers around his. "Your actions prove your character, Alexander Knight. There is nothing that would please me more than to be your wife."

Other books by Jenny Hambly

Belle – Bachelor Brides 0

Rosalind – Bachelor Brides 1

Sophie – Bachelor Brides 2

Katherine – Bachelor Brides 3

Bachelor Brides Collection

Marianne - Miss Wolfraston's Ladies Book 1

Miss Hayes - Miss Wolfraston's Ladies Book2

What next? I think Lord Allerdale's story needs to be told, don't you?

ABOUT THE AUTHOR

I love history and the Regency period in particular. I grew up on a diet of Jane Austen, Charlotte and Emily Bronte, and Georgette Heyer. Later, I put my love of reading to good use and gained a 1st class honours degree in literature.

I have been a teacher and tennis coach. I now write traditional Regency romance novels. I like to think my characters, though flawed, are likeable, strong, and true to the period. Writing has always been my dream and I am fortunate enough to have been able to realise that dream.

I live by the sea in Plymouth, England, with my partner, Dave. I like reading, sailing, wine, getting up early to watch the sunrise in summer, and long quiet evenings by the wood burner in our cabin on the cliffs in Cornwall in winter.

ACKNOWLEDGMENTS

Thank you Melanie Underwood for catching the things that fell through my net!

Thank you Dave; if I wasn't so very much in love myself, I doubt I could write about it!

Thank you to my loyal readers; without your encouragement I would never have come this far!

Printed in Great Britain
by Amazon